Les Dieux ont Soif

THE GODS ARE A-THIRST

BY ANATOLE FRANCE

The authorised translation from the French
by Alfred Allinson: with an Introduction
by André Maurois and Illustrations
by Jean Oberlé

London: The Nonesuch Press, 1942

THE INTRODUCTION BY

ANDRÉ MAUROIS

DURING THE YEARS that followed the death of Anatole France it was the "right thing" amongst the younger men no longer to admit that he had been a great writer. That post-war period was violent and crude. Minds that had lost their bearings demanded sweeping assertions, fearing error less than doubt. Culture went against the grain, compassion bored, and irony exasperated. For that generation the art of Anatole France could have no appeal. But we foresee another generation of young men who will "discover" with delight the *Histoire Contemporaine* and *Les Dieux ont Soif*. Formal perfection is the surest guarantee of permanence. What is written in a style combining ingenuity with purity of diction and depicts emotions that are eternal is proof against time's ravages. Better still if the emotions thus depicted are those by which the author himself has been moved. The encounter between a writer of genius and a theme bound up with the tastes and spiritual conflicts of his adolescent years rarely fails to bring forth a work of the first rank. By such a predisposed affinity Anatole France was destined to write the best of his novels on the theme of the French Revolution.

It was a period he had at his finger-tips. His father, François Noel Thibault, a bookseller on the Quai Malplaquais, had spent his life collecting books, posters, prints, autographs and pamphlets concerning the Revolution. In 1862, shortly after leaving the Collège Stanislas, his son had set to work in the family bookshop cataloguing the Comte de La Bédoyère's collection. Thus Anatole France had come to be on intimate terms with Robespierre, Marat and their

clan down to its humblest members. He had handled their correspondence, sorted out their bric-à-brac, docketed their papers. In
the setting of the Revolution he was thoroughly at home. Paris
born, and bred of a family of common folk, he had roamed old streets
that had not changed a whit since the days of the Convention. Did
he set out to depict a Paris springtime, the golden glow, the light
mist tinged with blue that hovers on the Seine, or the red brick
houses striped with courses of white stone in the Place Dauphine,
he had but to delve into his childhood memories. He had been born
into that humble social class which, fifty years before, had produced
Citizen Trubert and Citizen Gamelin. Thus it came quite easy to
him to imagine just how such men had felt, and how they had
talked.

Did he share their sentiments? That question has given rise to
endless controversy. According to his political tendencies and personal bias each reader tries to bring the book into line with his own
views. Let us try to analyze it as a chemist analyzes a solution, without prejudice. Évariste Gamelin is a monster. If, to safeguard the
Revolution, he has to guillotine his friends, he will cause the wisest
and most charming heads to fall, without compunction. But this
monster is a patriot. He is brave and risks his own neck as he sacri-
fices those of others. He is disinterested and genuinely believes that
the sole object of his cruel acts is to promote the welfare of mankind.
A sentimentalist, he melts into tears of loving-kindness at the pros-
pect of the joys in store for poor humanity, once the Revolution has
purged the State of scoundrels. Unfortunately these scoundrels per-
sist in their evil practices, stern measures still are called for, and
torrents of "tainted blood" must still be shed. What is wrong with
Évariste Gamelin? Why should his very real virtues bring forth
only bloodshed and betrayal? Because he is convinced of being in
possession of the Truth. To make men equal and contented, this
fanatic is quite prepared to kill them all.

There is no shadow of doubt as to the horror the bloodthirstiness
of such a man as Gamelin inspires in Anatole France. No one has
depicted with more severity the Revolutionary Tribunal, its scorn
for the rights of those arraigned before it, the infamy of the accusers,
the baseness and subservience of the judges. France does not believe
that the Terror was a necessity or that it led to happy results.
Gamelin's old mother takes a much saner view of it than does her

son. "I am no aristocrat. I have seen the great in the full tide of their power, and I can bear witness that they abused their privileges. . . . But never tell me the Revolution is going to establish equality, because men will never be equal; it is an impossibility, and, let them turn the country upside down to their heart's content, there will still be great and small, fat and lean in it." In the days of Thermidor the people of Paris were weary of Revolution; they considered it had lasted too long. Anatole France brings out this weariness. "Believe me, friend, the Revolution is a bore; it lasts over long. Five years of enthusiasm, five years of fraternal embraces, of massacres, of fine speeches, of *Marseillaises*, of tocsins, of 'hang up the aristocrats,' of heads promenaded on pikes, of women mounted astride of cannon, of trees of Liberty crowned with the red cap, of white-robed maidens and old men drawn about the streets in flower-wreathed cars; of imprisonments and guillotinings, of proclamations, and short commons, of cockades and plumes, swords and *carmagnoles*—it grows tedious! And then folk are beginning to lose the hang of it all."

Of the various characters in the novel the one that seems most nearly to express the author's view is Brotteaux, the ex-aristocrat. His philosophy is that of the "Garden of Epicurus" and regards pleasure as the goal of life. Brotteaux is devoted to Reason, but not fanatically so. He might well have said in the words of his creator: "The more I ponder over human life, the more I am convinced that Irony and Pity should be called to witness and to judgment on it. The former smiles and makes life amiable; the latter weeps and gives it sanctity. The irony I have in mind is not a cruel one. It does not scoff at love or beauty. It is gentle and good-natured. It tempers anger with a smile and teaches us to laugh at fools and rascals whom otherwise we might be weak enough to hate." Brotteaux does not hate even Évariste who has him put to death so stupidly. At the scaffold's foot, in a scene that recalls *Les Misérables*, a friar asks the old Epicurean for his prayers. In short, Anatole France regards Brotteaux as a sort of saint. But a voluptuary saint, who even in the tumbrel taking him to the guillotine lets his eyes linger with admiration and regret on a girl's white bosom.

Does the fact that France depicts so tellingly the blood-lust of the terrorists and the philosophic resignation of their victims oblige us to infer he is against the Revolution? Are there good grounds for such a view, or would not such an attitude on his part be wholly incompatible with what we know of his political career? Was he not to be seen, towards the close of his life, on the platforms of revolutionary parties? To these questions there is only one answer possible, Walt Whitman's remark: "Do I contradict myself? Very well, then, I contradict myself." In the course of his long life Anatole France was a conservative and a revolutionary turn by turn—and simultaneously at whiles.

He was, like all of us, and more than most, a blend of very disparate elements. Born on a humble social level, he had a natural affection of those of his class, and instinctively, we may presume, shared in the vague hostility of that class towards the "top dog", the tax-gatherer, the catchpoll. Educated in an institution staffed by priests, he owed to them his style, akin to that of Renan, in which a realistic homeliness strikes an entertaining contrast with ecclesiastic unction. But, like the young seminarist whom he portrays under the name of Firmin Piédangel, he derived from his schooling not only a love of classical beauty but feelings of revolt and a turn for bantering scepticism. One has the impression that richer or more happily placed schoolmates must have wounded his feelings during that period; and such wounds never are completely healed.

Later on, a first marriage into the *bourgeoisie*, coupled with success, made of him a conservative. The Parisian salons had given a cordial welcome to one who was so good a talker and whose taste and culture were so highly spoken of. And soon the rebellious tendencies of his youth seemed left behind for good and all. A singular concatenation of circumstances was needed to throw France back into the ranks of the left-wing parties. At Madame Arman de Cáillavet's parties he met the great ones of the day, and found them highly ridiculous. Then came the Dreyfus Case and the salon in the Avenue Hoche was on the side of Dreyfus. France who, as we see in *Les Dieux ont Soif*, had a horror of party prejudice masquerading in the robes of justice, came in the course of that famous "affaire" to be the ally of men who hitherto had moved outside his range—the socialist leader Jaurès, for example. Contact with them revived some of the sentiments of his earlier days. To appreciate the point of view of poor folk, more than art and intelligence is needed; it is a matter also of temperament and upbringing. If France in his declining years was drawn so readily into the socialist camp, it was because in his youth the inequalities of fortune had galled him. All his life long he had kept in touch with the rank and file, welcoming every chance of talking to a fishwife of the Paris Market, a carpenter, a cooper of Bordeaux. Always he had endorsed Crainquebille's political outlook.

Crainquebille has no malice in him. The men who figured on Revolutionary Tribunals were not poor folk like him but men of the stamp of Renaudin, insensitive and callous, would-be *bourgeois* who had failed to "make good", talentless writers, inexpert lovers who sought the thrills and pleasure they could not achieve in normal love-life, in sadistic cruelty. Like Évariste Gamelin's mother, Anatole France certainly believed that it was necessary in 1789 to put an end to the gross abuses then prevalent in France; but, like her again, he held that it was needless to pour out floods of blood and persecute innocent people to that end. At the time when he wrote *Les Dieux ont Soif* he was neither for nor against the Revolution; he was all for Crainquebille.

In any case why, in a novel, should he be expected to take sides? A great artist does not sit in judgment. "When I write about horse-thieves," Chekov said, "some people expect me to declare that stealing horses is a crime; but that's none of my business, I leave that to the courts." If *Les Dieux ont Soif* achieves a great and permanent beauty it is because Anatole France is not trying in it to press home a "lesson", but to depict men's lives as they were in those stormy times. He puts into the mouths of Brotteaux the Epicurean, Longuemare the priest, Blaise the merchant, and the grim fanatic Gamelin, the remarks that they would actually have made. Each man, searching his conscience, honestly believes his conduct justified. Wherein all alike are self-deceived—except, possibly, Brotteaux, whose sanity of outlook is preserved by scepticism.

Nevertheless, in the midst of the national upheaval, private life went on much as usual. On the very shambles of the Revolution men still found time to dally with young women when the glimpse of a white bosom between the widely parted neckerchief caught their fancy. Athenaïs, the little sixteen-year-old prostitute of the Rue Fromenteau, plies her trade as best she can during the Terror. Tears add savour to a kiss. When Elodie welcomes Gamelin still reeking of his murders, she feels her senses tingling with mingled sensuality and horror. "She loved him with all her flesh, and the more terrible, cruel, atrocious she thought him, the more she saw him reeking with the blood of his victims, the more consuming was her hunger and thirst for him." For Anatole France, who admired Racine and sprinkled his prose with alexandrines culled from *Phèdre* and *Bajazet*, had, like his classic predecessor, the gift of turning to account the splendid dissonances great artists can evoke by juxtaposing love and death.

The novel closes with Robespierre's execution and that of Gamelin. The wheel has come full circle; those who heap insults on them as they pass by in the tumbrel are the same people who had heaped insults on their victims. The vendors of revolutionary prints re-set their shop-windows with displays of "Robespierre's Foul Conspiracy". All great social upheavals are followed by such revulsions of opinion. Some months after Cromwell's death the populace of London gave a triumphal welcome to Charles Stuart, whose father the same populace had hooted to the scaffold. The revolution brought off by Lenin and Trotzky found fruition, after Lenin's death, with Trotzky's exile. The truth is that mankind comprises a relatively stable aggregate of virtues and shortcomings. Those who try to uplift it above itself, or to abase it below its natural level, may be sure of seeing it one day swing back abruptly and with terrifying violence to the norm. "There are elements," France said, "in human nature that revolutions cannot change."

Beside this dictum we may set a remark of Valéry's. "A revolution does within two days the work of two years; thereafter it undoes within two months the work of two centuries." The philosopher, the historian and the poet know intuitively that, sooner or later, every revolution is doomed to end in a reaction. A man of the calibre of Brotteaux can predict with absolute certainty, at the height of the Terror, the restoration of the Bourbons. But such disenchanted wisdom is powerless to control the headstrong aspirations of the mob. Valéry and France notwithstanding, the unfortunates of the earth will always choose to think that one of these days a revolution will sweep away the evil-doers and, by the same token, bridge the gulf between men and a bliss beyond compare; and always such hopes will lead to orgies of indiscriminate bloodshed. When the gods are a-thirst for blood-offerings, vainly will Irony and Pity plead the victims' cause.

Les Dieux ont Soif

Chapter 1

ÉVARISTE GAMELIN, painter, pupil of
David, member of the Section du Pont-Neuf, formerly Section Henri
IV, had betaken himself at an early hour in the morning to the old
church of the Barnabites, which for three years, since 21st May
1790, had served as meeting-place for the General Assembly of the
Section. The church stood in a narrow, gloomy square, not far from
the gates of the Palais de Justice. On the façade, which consisted of
two of the Classical orders superimposed and was decorated with
inverted brackets and flaming urns, blackened by the weather and
disfigured by the hand of man, the religious emblems had been battered to pieces, while above the doorway had been inscribed in black
letters the Republican catchword of "Liberty, Equality, Fraternity
or Death." Évariste Gamelin made his way into the nave; the same
vaults which had heard the surpliced clerks of the Congregation of
St. Paul sing the divine offices, now looked down on red-capped patriots assembled to elect the Municipal magistrates and deliberate
on the affairs of the Section. The Saints had been dragged from their
niches and replaced by the busts of Brutus, Jean-Jacques and Le
Peltier. The altar had been stripped bare and was surmounted by
the Table of the Rights of Man.

It was here in the nave that twice a week, from five in the evening
to eleven, were held the public assemblies. The pulpit, decorated
with the colours of the Nation, served as tribune for the speakers
who harangued the meeting. Opposite, on the Epistle side, rose a
platform of rough planks, for the accommodation of the women and
children, who attended these gatherings in considerable numbers.

On this particular morning, facing a desk planted underneath the
pulpit, sat in red cap and *carmagnole* complete the joiner from the
Place Thionville, the *citoyen* Dupont senior, one of the twelve forming the Committee of Surveillance. On the desk stood a bottle and

3

glasses, an ink-horn, and a folio containing the text of the petition urging the Convention to expel from its bosom the twenty-two members deemed unworthy.

Évariste Gamelin took the pen and signed.

"I was sure," said the carpenter and magistrate, "I was sure you would come and give in your name, *citoyen* Gamelin. You are the real thing. But the Section is lukewarm; it is lacking in virtue. I have proposed to the Committee of Surveillance to deliver no certificate of citizenship to any one who has failed to sign the petition."

"I am ready to sign with my blood," said Gamelin, "for the proscription of these Federalists, these traitors. They have desired the death of Marat: let them perish."

"What ruins us," replied Dupont senior, "is indifferentism. In a Section which contains nine hundred citizens with the right to vote there are not fifty attend the assembly. Yesterday we were eight and twenty."

"Well then," said Gamelin, "citizens must be obliged to come under penalty of a fine."

"Oh, ho!" exclaimed the joiner frowning, "but if they all came, the patriots would be in a minority. . . . *Citoyen* Gamelin, will you drink a glass of wine to the health of all good *sansculottes?* . . ."

On the wall of the church, on the Gospel side, could be read the words, accompanied by a black hand, the forefinger pointing to the passage leading to the cloisters: *Comité civil, Comité de surveillance, Comité de bienfaisance.* A few yards further on, you came to the door of the erstwhile sacristy, over which was inscribed: *Comité militaire.*

Gamelin pushed this door open and found the Secretary of the Committee within; he was writing at a large table loaded with books, papers, steel ingots, cartridges and samples of saltpetre-bearing soils.

"Greeting, *citoyen* Trubert. How are you?"

"I? . . . I am perfectly well."

The Secretary of the Military Committee, Fortuné Trubert, invariably made this same reply to all who troubled about his health, less by way of informing them of his welfare than to cut short any discussion on the subject. At twenty-eight, he had a parched skin, thin hair, hectic cheeks and bent shoulders. He was an optician on the Quai des Orfèvres, and owned a very old house which he had given up in '91 to a superannuated clerk in order to devote his energies to the discharge of his municipal duties. His mother, a charming woman, whose memory a few old men of the neighbourhood still cherished fondly, had died at twenty; she had left him her fine eyes, full of gentleness and passion, her pallor and timidity. From his father, optician and mathematical instrument maker to the King, carried off by the same complaint before his thirtieth year, he inherited an upright character and an industrious temperament.

Without stopping his writing:

"And you, *citoyen*," he asked, "how are you?"

"Very well. Anything new?"

"Nothing, nothing. You can see,—we are all quiet here."

"And the situation?"

"The situation is just the same."

The situation was appalling. The finest army of the Republic blockaded in Mayence; Valenciennes besieged; Fontenay taken by the Vendéens; Lyons rebellious; the Cévennes in insurrection, the frontier open to the Spaniards; two-thirds of the Departments invaded or revolted; Paris helpless before the Austrian cannon, without money, without bread!

Fortuné Trubert wrote on calmly. The Sections being instructed by resolution of the Commune to carry out the levy of twelve thousand men for La Vendée, he was drawing up directions relating to the enrolment and arming of the contingent which the "Pont-Neuf," erstwhile "Henri IV," was to supply. All the muskets in store were to be handed over to the men requisitioned for the front; the National Guard of the Section would be armed with fowling-pieces and pikes.

"I have brought you here," said Gamelin, "the schedule of the church-bells to be sent to the Luxembourg to be converted into cannon."

Évariste Gamelin, albeit he had not a penny, was inscribed among the active members of the Section; the law accorded this privilege only to such citizens as were rich enough to pay a contribution equivalent in amount to three days' work, and demanded a ten days' contribution to qualify an elector for office. But the Section du Pont-Neuf, enamoured of equality and jealous of its independence, regarded as qualified both for the vote and for office every citizen who had paid out of his own pocket for his National Guard's uniform.

5

This was Gamelin's case, who was an *active* citizen of his Section and member of the Military Committee.

Fortuné Trubert laid down his pen:

"*Citoyen* Évariste," he said, "I beg you to go to the Convention and ask them to send us orders to dig up the floor of cellars, to wash the soil and flag-stones and collect the saltpetre. It is not everything to have guns, we must have gunpowder too."

A little hunchback, a pen behind his ear and a bundle of papers in his hand, entered the erstwhile sacristy. It was the *citoyen* Beauvisage, of the Committee of Surveillance.

"*Citoyens*," he announced, "we have bad news: Custine has evacuated Landau."

"Custine is a traitor!" cried Gamelin.

"He shall be guillotined," said Beauvisage.

Trubert, in his rather breathless voice, expressed himself with his habitual calmness:

"The Convention has not instituted a Committee of Public Safety for fun. It will enquire into Custine's conduct. Incompetent or traitor, he will be superseded by a General resolved to win the victory, and *ça ira!*"

He turned over a heap of papers, scrutinizing them with his tired eyes:

"That our soldiers may do their duty with a quiet mind and stout heart, they must be assured that the lot of those they leave behind at home is safeguarded. If you are of the same opinion, *citoyen* Gamelin, you will join me in demanding, at the next assembly, that the Committee of Benevolence concert measures with the Military Committee to succour the families that are in indigence and have a relative at the front."

He smiled and hummed to himself: "*Ça ira! ça ira! . . .*"

Working twelve and fourteen hours a day at his table of unpainted deal for the defence of the fatherland in peril, this humble Secretary of the Sectional Committee could see no disproportion between the immensity of the task and the meagreness of his means for performing it, so filled was he with a sense of the unity in a common effort between himself and all other patriots, so intimately did he feel himself one with the Nation at large, so merged was his individual life in the life of a great People. He was of the sort who combine enthusiasm with long-suffering, who, after each check, set about organizing the victory that is impossible, but is bound to come. And verily they *must* win the day. These men of no account, who had destroyed Royalty and upset the old order of things, this Trubert, a penniless optician, this Évariste Gamelin, an unknown dauber, could expect no mercy from their enemies. They had no choice save between victory and death. Hence both their fervour and their serenity.

Chapter 2

Q UITTING the Barnabites, Évariste
Gamelin set off in the direction of the Place Dauphine, now renamed
the Place de Thionville in honour of a city that had shown itself
impregnable.

Situated in the busiest quarter of Paris, the Place had long lost
the fine stateliness it had worn a hundred years ago; the mansions
forming its three sides, built in the days of Henri IV in one uniform
style, of red brick with white stone dressings, to lodge splendour-
loving magistrates, had had their imposing roofs of slate removed
to make way for two or three wretched storeys of lath and plaster
or had even been demolished altogether and replaced by shabby
whitewashed houses, and now displayed only a series of irregular,
poverty-stricken, squalid fronts, pierced with countless narrow,
unevenly spaced windows enlivened with flowers in pots, birdcages,
and rags hanging out to dry. These were occupied by a swarm of
artisans, jewellers, metal-workers, clockmakers, opticians, printers,
laundresses, sempstresses, milliners, and a few grey-beard lawyers
who had not been swept away in the storm of revolution along with
the King's courts.

It was morning and springtime. Golden sunbeams, intoxicating
as new wine, played on the walls and flashed gaily in at garret case-
ments. Every sash of every window was thrown open, showing the
housewives' frowsy heads peeping out. The Clerk of the Revolutionary Tribunal, who had just left his house on his way to Court,
distributed amicable taps on the cheeks of the children playing under
the trees. From the Pont-Neuf came the crier's voice denouncing
the treason of the infamous Dumouriez.

Évariste Gamelin lived in a house on the side towards the Quai
de l'Horloge, a house that dated from Henri IV and would still have
preserved a not unhandsome appearance but for a mean tiled attic

that had been added on to heighten the building under the last but one of the *tyrants*. To adapt the lodging of some erstwhile dignitary of the *Parlement* to the exigencies of the bourgeois and artisan households that formed its present denizens, endless partitions and false floors had been run up. This was why the *citoyen* Remacle, *concierge* and jobbing tailor, perched in a sort of 'tween-decks, as low ceilinged as it was confined in area. Here he could be seen through the glass door sitting cross-legged on his work-bench, his bowed back within an inch of the floor above, stitching away at a National Guard's uniform, while the *citoyenne* Remacle, whose cooking stove boasted no chimney but the well of the staircase, poisoned the other tenants with the fumes of her stew-pots and frying-pans, and their little girl Joséphine, her face smudged with treacle and looking as pretty as an angel, played on the threshold with Mouton, the joiner's dog. The *citoyenne*, whose heart was as capacious as her ample bosom and broad back, was reputed to bestow her favours on her neighbour the *citoyen* Dupont senior, who was one of the twelve constituting the Committee of Surveillance. At any rate her husband had his strong suspicions, and from morning to night the house resounded with the racket of the alternate squabbles and reconciliations of the pair. The upper floors were occupied by the *citoyen* Chaperon, gold and silver-smith, who had his shop on the Quai de l'Horloge, by a health officer, an attorney, a goldbeater, and several employés at the Palais de Justice.

Évariste Gamelin climbed the old-fashioned staircase as far as the fourth and last storey, where he had his studio together with a bedroom for his mother. At this point ended the wooden stairs laid with tiles that took the place of the grand stairway of the more important floors. A ladder clamped to the wall led to a cock-loft, from which at that moment emerged a stout elderly man with a handsome, florid, rosy-cheeked face, climbing painfully down with an enormous package clasped in his arms, yet humming gaily to himself: *J'ai perdu mon serviteur*.

Breaking off his song, he wished a polite good-day to Gamelin, who returned him a fraternal greeting and helped him down with his parcel, for which the old man thanked him.

"There," said he, shouldering his burden again, "you have a batch of dancing-dolls which I am going to deliver straight away to a toy-merchant in the Rue de la Loi. There is a whole tribe of them inside;

9

I am their creator; they have received of me a perishable body, exempt from joys and sufferings. I have not given them the gift of thought, for I am a benevolent God."

It was the *citoyen* Maurice Brotteaux, once farmer of taxes and *ci-devant* noble; his father, having made a fortune in these transactions, had bought himself an office conferring a title on the possessor. In the good old times Maurice Brotteaux had called himself Monsieur des Ilettes and used to give at his mansion in the Rue de la Chaise elegant suppers which the fair Madame de Rochemaure, wife of a King's *procureur*, enlivened with her bright glances—a finished gentlewoman whose loyal fidelity was never impugned so long as the Revolution left Maurice Brotteaux des Ilettes in possession of his offices and emoluments, his hotel, his estates and his noble name. The Revolution swept them all away. He made his living by painting portraits under the archways of doors, making pancakes and fritters on the Quai de la Mégisserie, composing speeches for the representatives of the people and giving dancing lessons to the young *citoyennes*. At the present time, in his garret into which you climbed by a ladder and where a man could not stand upright, Maurice Brotteaux, the proud owner of a glue-pot, a ball of twine, a box of water-colours and sundry clippings of paper, manufactured dancing-dolls which he sold to wholesale toy-dealers, who resold them to the pedlars who hawked them up and down the Champs Élysées at the end of a pole,—glittering magnets to draw the little ones' eyes. Amidst the calamities of the State and the disaster that overwhelmed himself, he preserved an unruffled spirit, reading for the refreshment of his mind in his Lucretius, which he carried with him wherever he went in the gaping pocket of his plum-coloured surtout.

Évariste Gamelin pushed open the door of his lodging. It offered no resistance, for his poverty spared him any trouble about lock and key; when his mother from force of habit shot the bolt, he would tell her: "Why, what's the good? Folks don't steal spiders'-webs,—nor my pictures, neither." In his workroom were piled, under a thick layer of dust or with faces turned to the wall, the canvases of his student years,—when, as the fashion of the day was, he limned scenes of gallantry, depicting with a sleek, timorous brush emptied quivers and birds put to flight, risky pastimes and reveries of bliss,

high-kilted goose-girls and shepherdesses with rose-wreathed bos-
oms.

But it was not a genre that suited his temperament. His cold
treatment of such like scenes proved the painter's incurable purity
of heart. Amateurs were right: Gamelin had no gifts as an erotic
artist. Nowadays, though he was still short of thirty, these subjects
struck him as dating from an immemorial antiquity. He saw in them
the degradation wrought by Monarchy, the shameful effects of the
corruption of Courts. He blamed himself for having practised so
contemptible a style and prostituted his genius to the vile arts of
slavery. Now, citizen of a free people, he occupied his hand with bold
charcoal sketches of Liberties, Rights of Man, French Constitutions, Republican Virtues, the People as Hercules felling the Hydra
of Tyranny, throwing into each and all his compositions all the fire
of his patriotism. Alas! he could not make a living by it. The times
were hard for artists. No doubt the fault did not lie with the Convention, which was hurling its armies against the kings gathered on
every frontier, which, proud, unmoved, determined in the face of
the coalesced powers of Europe, false and ruthless to itself, was
rending its own bosom with its own hands, which was setting up
terror as the order of the day, establishing for the punishment of
plotters a pitiless tribunal to whose devouring maw it was soon to
deliver up its own members; but which through it all, with calm and
thoughtful brow, the patroness of science and friend of all things
beautiful, was reforming the calendar, instituting technical schools,
decreeing competitions in painting and sculpture, founding prizes to
encourage artists, organizing annual exhibitions, opening the Mu-
seum of the Louvre, and, on the model of Athens and Rome, endowing with a stately sublimity the celebration of National festivals
and public obsequies. But French Art, once so widely appreciated
in England, and Germany, in Russia, in Poland, now found every
outlet to foreign lands closed. Amateurs of painting, dilettanti of
the fine arts, great noblemen and financiers, were ruined, had emigrated or were in hiding. The men the Revolution had enriched,
peasants who had bought up National properties, speculators, army-
contractors, gamesters of the Palais-Royal, durst not at present
show their wealth, and did not care a fig for pictures, either. It
needed Regnault's fame or the youthful Gérard's cleverness to sell a

11

canvas. Greuze, Fragonard, Houin were reduced to indigence. Prud'hon could barely earn bread for his wife and children by drawing subjects which Copia reproduced in stippled engravings. The patriot painters Hennequin, Wicar, Topino-Lebrun were starving. Gamelin, without means to meet the expenses of a picture, to hire a model or buy colours, abandoned his vast canvas of *The Tyrant pursued in the Infernal Regions by the Furies*, after barely sketching in the main outlines. It blocked up half the studio with its half-finished threatening shapes, greater than life-size, and its vast brood of green snakes, each darting forth two sharp, forked tongues. In the foreground, to the left, could be discerned Charon in his boat, a haggard, wild-looking figure,—a powerful and well conceived design, but of the schools, schooly. There was far more of genius and less of artificiality in a canvas of smaller dimensions, also unfinished, that hung in the best lighted corner of the studio. It was an Orestes whom his sister Electra was raising in her arms on his bed of pain. The maiden was putting back with a moving tenderness the matted hair that hung over her brother's eyes. The head of the hero was tragic and fine, and you could see a likeness in it to the painter's own countenance.

Gamelin cast many a mournful look at this composition; sometimes his fingers itched with the craving to be at work on it, and his arms would be stretched longingly towards the boldly sketched figure of Electra, to fall back again helpless to his sides. The artist was burning with enthusiasm, his soul aspired to great achievements. But he had to exhaust his energy on pot-boilers which he executed indifferently, because he was bound to please the taste of the vulgar and also because he had no skill to impress trivial things with the seal of genius. He drew little allegorical compositions which his comrade Desmahis engraved cleverly enough in black or in colours and which were bought at a low figure by a print-dealer in the Rue Honoré, the *citoyen* Blaise. But the trade was going from bad to worse, declared Blaise, who for some time now had declined to purchase anything.

This time, however, made inventive by necessity, Gamelin had conceived a new and happy thought, as *he* at any rate believed,—an idea that was to make the printseller's fortune, and the engraver's and his own to boot. This was a "patriotic" pack of cards, where for

12

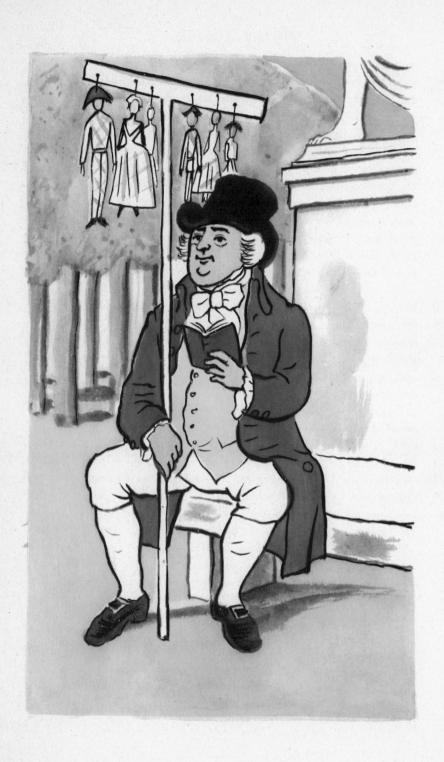

the kings and queens and knaves of the old style he meant to sub-
stitute figures of Genius, of Liberty, of Equality and the like. He
had already sketched out all his designs, had finished several and was
eager to pass on to Desmahis such as were in a state to be engraved.
The one he deemed the most successful represented a soldier dressed
in the three-cornered hat, blue coat with red facings, yellow breeches
and black gaiters of the Volunteer, seated on a big drum, his feet on
a pile of cannon-balls and his musket between his knees. It was the
citizen of hearts replacing the *ci-devant* knave of hearts. For six
months and more Gamelin had been drawing soldiers with never-
failing gusto. He had sold some of these while the fit of martial
enthusiasm lasted, while others hung on the walls of the room, and
five or six, water-colours, colour-washes and chalks in two tints, lay
about on the table and chairs. In the days of July, '92, when in
every open space rose platforms for enrolling recruits, when all the
taverns were gay with green leaves and resounded to the shouts of
"Vive la Nation! freedom or death!" Gamelin could not cross the
Pont-Neuf or pass the Hôtel de Ville without his heart beating high
at sight of the beflagged marquee in which magistrates in tricolour
scarves were inscribing the names of volunteers to the sound of the
Marseillaise. But for him to join the Republic's armies would have
meant leaving his mother to starve.

Heralded by a grievous sound of puffing and panting the old
citoyenne, Gamelin's widowed mother, entered the studio, hot, red
and out of breath, the National cockade hanging half unpinned in
her cap and on the point of falling out. She deposited her basket on
a chair and still standing, the better to get her breath, began to
groan over the high price of victuals.

A shopkeeper's wife till the death of her husband, a cutler in the
Rue de Grenelle-Saint-Germain, at the sign of the Ville de Châ-
tellerault, now reduced to poverty, the *citoyenne* Gamelin lived in
seclusion, keeping house for her son the painter. He was the elder of
her two children. As for her daughter Julie, at one time employed
at a fashionable milliner's in the Rue Honoré, the best thing was
not to know what had become of her, for it was ill saying the truth,
that she had emigrated with an aristocrat.

"Lord God!" sighed the *citoyenne*, showing her son a loaf baked
of heavy dun-coloured dough, "bread is too dear for anything; the

more reason it should be made of pure wheat! At market neither eggs nor green-stuff nor cheese to be had. By dint of eating chestnuts, we're like to grow into chestnuts."

After a long pause, she began again:

"Why, I've seen women in the streets who had nothing to feed their little ones with. The distress is sore among poor folks. And it will go on the same till things are put back on a proper footing."

"Mother," broke in Gamelin with a frown, "the scarcity we suffer from is due to the unprincipled buyers and speculators who starve the people and connive with our foes over the border to render the Republic odious to the citizens and to destroy liberty. This comes of the Brissotins' plots and the traitorous dealings of your Pétions and Rolands. It is well if the federalists in arms do not march on Paris and massacre the patriot remnant whom famine is too slow in killing! There is no time to lose; we must tax the price of flour and guillotine every man who speculates in the food of the people, foments insurrection or palters with the foreigner. The Convention has set up an extraordinary tribunal to try conspirators. Patriots form the court; but will its members have energy enough to defend the fatherland against our foes? There is hope in Robespierre; he is virtuous. There is hope above all in Marat. He loves the people, discerns its true interests and promotes them. He was ever the first to unmask traitors, to baffle plots. He is incorruptible and fearless. He, and he alone, can save the imperilled Republic."

The *citoyenne* Gamelin shook her head, paying no heed to the cockade that fell out of her cap at the gesture.

"Have done, Évariste; your Marat is a man like another and no better than the rest. You are young and your head is full of fancies. What you say today of Marat, you said before of Mirabeau, of La Fayette, of Pétion, of Brissot."

"Never!" cried Gamelin, who was genuinely oblivious.

After clearing one end of the deal table of the papers and books, brushes and chalks that littered it, the *citoyenne* laid out on it the earthenware soup-bowl, two tin porringers, two iron forks, the loaf of brown bread and a jug of thin wine.

Mother and son ate the soup in silence and finished their meal with a small scrap of bacon. The *citoyenne*, putting her titbit on her bread, used the point of her pocket knife to convey the pieces one by

14

one slowly and solemnly to her toothless jaws and masticated with a proper reverence the victuals that had cost so dear.

She had left the best part on the dish for her son, who sat lost in a brown study.

"Eat Évariste," she repeated at regular intervals, "eat,"—and on her lips the word had all the solemnity of a religious commandment.

She began again with her lamentations on the dearness of provisions, and again Gamelin demanded taxation as the only remedy for these evils.

But she shrilled:

"There is no money left in the country. The *émigrés* have carried it all off with them. There is no confidence left either. Everything is desperate."

"Hush, mother, hush!" protested Gamelin. "What matter our privations, our hardships of a moment? The Revolution will win for all time the happiness of the human race."

The good dame sopped her bread in her wine; her mood grew more cheerful and she smiled as her thoughts returned to her young days, when she used to dance on the green in honour of the King's birthday. She well remembered too the day when Joseph Gamelin, cutler by trade, had asked her hand in marriage. And she told over, detail by detail, how things had gone,—how her mother had bidden her: "Go dress. We are going to the Place de Grève, to Monsieur Bienassis' shop, to see Damiens drawn and quartered," and what difficulty they had to force their way through the press of eager spectators. Presently, in Monsieur Bienassis' shop, she had seen Joseph Gamelin, wearing his fine rose-pink coat and had known in an instant what he would be at. All the time she sat at the window to see the regicide torn with red-hot pincers, drenched with molten lead, dragged at the tail of four horses and thrown into the flames, Joseph Gamelin had stood behind her chair and had never once left off complimenting her on her complexion, her hair and her figure.

She drained the last drop in her cup and continued her reminiscences of other days:

"I brought you into the world, Évariste, sooner than I had expected, by reason of a fright I had when I was big. It was on the Pont-Neuf, where I came near being knocked down by a crowd of sightseers hurrying to Monsieur de Lally's execution. You were so little at your birth the surgeon thought you would not live. But I felt sure God would be gracious to me and preserve your life. I reared you to the best of my powers, grudging neither pains nor expense. It is fair to say, my Évariste, that you showed me you were grateful and that, from childhood up, you tried your best to recompense me for what I had done. You were naturally affectionate and tender-hearted. Your sister was not bad at heart; but she was selfish and of unbridled temper. Your compassion was greater than ever was hers for the unfortunate. When the little ragamuffins of the neighbourhood robbed birds' nests in the trees, you always fought hard to rescue the nestlings from their hands and restore them to the mother, and many a time you did not give in till after you had been kicked and cuffed cruelly. At seven years of age, instead of wrangling with bad boys, you would pace soberly along the street saying over your catechism; and all the poor people you came across you insisted on bringing home with you to relieve their needs, till I was forced to whip you to break you of the habit. You could not see a living creature suffer without tears. When you had done growing, you turned out a very handsome lad. To my great surprise, you appeared not to know it,—how different from most pretty boys, who are full of conceit and vain of their good looks!"

His old mother spoke the truth. Évariste at twenty had had a grave and charming cast of countenance, a beauty at once austere and feminine, the countenance of a Minerva. Now his sombre eyes and pale cheeks revealed a melancholy and passionate soul. But his gaze, when it fell on his mother, recovered for a brief moment its childish softness.

She went on:

"You might have profited by your advantages to run after the girls, but you preferred to stay with me in the shop, and I had sometimes to tell you not to hang on always to my apron-strings, but to go and amuse yourself with your young companions. To my dying day I shall always testify that you have been a good son, Évariste. After your father's death, you bravely took me and provided for me; though your work barely pays you, you have never let me want for anything, and if we are at this moment destitute and miserable, I cannot blame you for it. The fault lies with the Revolution."

He raised his hand to protest; but she only shrugged and continued:

16

"I am no aristocrat. I have seen the great in the full tide of their power, and I can bear witness that they abused their privileges. I have seen your father cudgelled by the Duc de Canaleilles' lackeys because he did not make way quick enough for their master. I could never abide *the Austrian*—she was too haughty and too extravagant. As for the King, I thought him good-hearted, and it needed his trial and condemnation to alter my opinion. In fact, I do not regret the old régime,—though I have had some agreeable times under it. But never tell me the Revolution is going to establish equality, because men will never be equal; it is an impossibility, and, let them turn the country upside down to their heart's content, there will still be great and small, fat and lean in it."

As she talked, she was busy putting away the plates and dishes. The painter had left off listening. He was thinking out a design,—for a sansculotte, in red cap and *carmagnole*, who was to supersede the discredited knave of spades in his pack of cards.

There was a sound of scratching on the door, and a girl appeared, —a country wench, as broad as she was long, red-haired and bandy-legged, a wen hiding the left eye, the right so pale a blue it looked white, with monstrous thick lips and teeth protruding beyond them.

She asked Gamelin if he was Gamelin the painter and if he could do her a portrait of her betrothed, Ferrand (Jules), a volunteer serving with the Army of the Ardennes.

Gamelin replied that he would be glad to execute the portrait on the gallant warrior's return.

But the girl insisted gently but firmly that it must be done at once.

The painter protested, smiling in spite of himself as he pointed out that he could do nothing without the original.

The poor creature was dumfounded; she had not foreseen the difficulty. Her head drooping over the left shoulder, her hands clasped in front of her, she stood still and silent as if overwhelmed by her disappointment. Touched and diverted by so much simplicity, and by way of distracting the poor, love-sick creature's grief, the painter handed her one of the soldiers he had drawn in water-colours and asked her if he was like that, her sweetheart in the Ardennes.

She bent her doleful look on the sketch, and little by little her eye brightened, sparkled, flashed, and her moon face beamed out in a radiant smile.

17

"It is his very likeness," she cried at last. "It is the very spit of Ferrand (Jules), it is Ferrand (Jules) to the life."

Before it occurred to the artist to take the sheet of paper out of her hands, she folded it carefully with her coarse red fingers into a tiny square, slipped it over her heart between her stays and her shift, handed the painter an assignat for five livres, and wishing the company a very good day, hobbled light-heartedly to the door and so out of the room.

Chapter 3

ON THE afternoon of the same day Évariste
set out to see the *citoyen* Jean Blaise, printseller, as well as dealer in
ornamental boxes, fancy goods and games of all sorts, in the Rue
Honoré, opposite the Oratoire and near the office of the Messageries,
at the sign of the *Amour peintre*. The shop was on the ground floor
of a house sixty years old, and opened on the street by a vaulted arch
the keystone of which bore a grotesque head with horns. The semi-
circle beneath the arch was occupied by an oil-painting representing
"the Sicilian or Cupid the Painter," after a composition by Boucher,
which Jean Blaise's father had put up in 1770 and which sun and
rain had been doing their best to obliterate ever since. On either side
of the door a similar arched opening, with a nymph's head on the
keystone arch glazed with the largest panes to be got, exhibited for
the benefit of the public the prints in vogue at the time and the latest
novelties in coloured engravings. To-day's display included a series
of scenes of gallantry by Boilly, treated in his graceful, rather stiff
way, *Leçons d'amour conjugal*, *Douces résistances* and the like, which
scandalized the Jacobins and which the rigid moralists denounced to
the Society of Arts, Debucourt's *Promenade publique*, with a dandy
in canary-coloured breeches lounging on three chairs, a group of
horses by the young Carle Vernet, pictures of air balloons, the *Bain
de Virginie* and figures after the antique.

Amid the stream of citizens that flowed past the shop it was the
raggedest figures that loitered longest before the two fascinating
windows. Easily amused, delighting in pictures and bent on getting
their share, if only through the eyes, of the good things of this world,
they stood in open-mouthed admiration, whereas the aristocrats
merely glanced in, frowned and passed on.

The instant he came within sight of the house, Évariste fixed his
eyes on one of the row of windows above the shop, the one on the

left hand, where there was a red carnation in a flower-pot behind a balcony of twisted ironwork. It was the window of Élodie's chamber, Jean Blaise's daughter. The print-dealer lived with his only child on the first floor of the house.

Évariste, after halting a moment as if to get his breath in front of the *Amour peintre*, turned the hasp of the shop-door. He found the *citoyenne* Élodie within, she had just sold a couple of engravings by Fragonard *fils* and Naigeon, carefully selected from a number of others, and before locking up the assignats received in payment in the strong-box, was holding them one after the other between her fine eyes and the light, to scrutinize the delicate lines and intricate curves of engraving and the watermark. She was naturally suspicious, for as much forged paper was in circulation as true, which was a great hindrance to commerce. As in former days, in the case of such as copied the King's signature, forgers of the national currency were punished by death; yet plates for printing assignats were to be found in every cellar, the Swiss smuggled in counterfeits by the million, whole packets were put in circulation in the inns, the English landed bales of them every day on our coasts, to ruin the Republic's credit and bring good patriots to destitution. Élodie was in terror of accepting bad paper, and still more in terror of passing it and being treated as an accomplice of Pitt, though she had a firm belief in her own good luck and felt pretty sure of coming off best in any emergency.

Évariste looked at her with the sombre gaze that speaks more movingly of love than the most smiling face. She returned his gaze with a mocking curl of the lips and an arch gleam in the dark eyes,— an expression she wore because she knew he loved her and liked to know it and because such a look provokes a lover, makes him complain of ill-usage, brings him to the speaking point, if he has not spoken already, which was Évariste's case.

Before depositing the assignats in the strong-box, she produced from her work-basket a white scarf, which she had begun to embroider, and set to work on it. At once industrious and a coquette, she knew instinctively how to ply her needle so as to fascinate an admirer and make a pretty thing for her wearing at one and the same time; she had quite different ways of working according to the person watching her,—a nonchalant way for those she would lull into a gentle languor, a capricious way for those she was fain to see in a more or less despairing mood. For Évariste, she bent with an air of painstaking absorption over her scarf, for she wanted to stir a sentiment of serious affection in his heart.

Élodie was neither very young nor very pretty. She might have been deemed plain at the first glance. She was a brunette, with an olive complexion under the broad white kerchief knotted carelessly about her head, from which the dark lustrous ringlets escaped, her eyes of fire gleamed as if they would burn their orbits. Her round face with its prominent cheek-bones, laughing lips and rather broad nose, that gave it a wild-wood, voluptuous expression, reminded the painter of the faun of the Borghese, a cast of which he had seen and been struck with admiration for its freakish charm. A faint down of moustache accentuated the curve of the full lips. A bosom that seemed big with love was confined by a crossed kerchief in the fashion of the year. Her supple waist, her active limbs, her whole vigorous body expressed in every movement a wild, delicious freedom. Every glance, every breath, every quiver of the warm flesh called for love and promised passion. There, behind the tradesman's counter, she seemed rather a dancing nymph, a bacchante of the opera, stripped of her lynx skin and thyrsus, imprisoned, and travestied by a magician's spell under the modest trappings of a housewife by Chardin.

"My father is not at home," she told the painter; "wait a little, he will not be long."

In the small brown hands the needle travelled swiftly over the fine lawn.

"Is the pattern to your taste, Monsieur Gamelin?"

It was not in Gamelin's nature to pretend. And love, exaggerating his confidence, encouraged him to speak quite frankly.

"You embroider cleverly, *citoyenne*; but, if I am to say what I think, the pattern you have traced is not simple enough or bold enough, and smacks of the affected taste that in France governed too long the ornamentation of dress and furniture and woodwork; all those rosettes and wreaths recall the pretty, finikin style that was in favour under the tyrant. There is a new birth of taste. Alas! we have much leeway to make up. In the days of the infamous Louis XV the art of decoration had something Chinese about it. They made pot-bellied cabinets with drawer handles grotesque in their contortions, good for nothing but to be thrown on the fire to warm good patriots. Simplicity alone is beautiful. We must hark back to the antique. David designs beds and chairs from the Etruscan vases and the wall-paintings of Herculaneum."

"Yes, I have seen those beds and chairs," said Élodie, "they are lovely. Soon we shall want no other sort. I am like you, I adore the antique."

"Well, then, *citoyenne*," returned Évariste, "if you had limited your pattern to a Greek border, with ivy leaves, serpents or crossed arrows, it would have been worthy of a Spartan maiden . . . and of you. But you can still keep this design by simplifying it, reducing it to the plain lines of beauty."

She asked her preceptor what should be picked out.

He bent over the work, and the girl's ringlets swept lightly over his cheek. Their hands met and their breaths mingled. For an instant Évariste tasted an ecstatic bliss, but to feel Élodie's lips so close to his own filled him with fear, and dreading to alarm her modesty, he drew back quickly.

The *citoyenne* Blaise was in love with Évariste Gamelin; she thought his great ardent eyes superb no less than the fine oval of his pale face, and his abundant black locks, parted above the brow and falling in showers about his shoulders; his gravity of demeanour, his cold reserve, his severe manner and uncompromising speech which never condescended to flattery, were equally to her liking. She was in love, and therefore believed him possessed of supreme artistic genius that would one day blossom forth in incomparable masterpieces and make his name world-famous,—and she loved him the better for the belief. The *citoyenne* Blaise was no prude on the score of masculine purity and her scruples were not offended because a man should satisfy his passions and follow his own tastes and caprices; she loved Évariste, who was virtuous; she did not love him because he was virtuous, albeit she appreciated the advantage of his being so that she had no cause for jealousy or suspicion or any fear of rivals in his affections.

Nevertheless, for the time being, she deemed his reserve a little overdone. If Racine's "Aricie," who loved "Hippolyte," admired the youthful hero's untameable virtue, it was with the hope of winning a victory over it, and she would quickly have bewailed a sternness of moral fibre that had refused to be softened for her sake. At the first opportunity she more than half declared her passion to con-

22

strain him to speak out himself. Like her prototype the tender-hearted "Aricie," the *citoyenne* Blaise was much inclined to think that in love the woman is bound to make the advances. "The fondest hearts," she told herself, "are the most fearful; they need help and encouragement. Besides, they are so simple a woman can go half way and even further without their even knowing it, if only she lets them fancy the credit is theirs of the bold attack and the glorious victory." What made her more confident of success was the fact that she knew for a certainty (and indeed there was no doubt about it) that Évariste, before ever the Revolution had made him a hero, had loved a mistress like any ordinary mortal, a very unheroic crea-ture, no other than the *concierge* at the Academy of Painting. Élodie, who was a girl of some experience, quite realised that there are differ-ent sorts of love. The sentiment Évariste inspired in her heart was profound enough for her to dream of making him the partner of her life. She was very ready to marry him, but hardly expected her father would approve the union of his only daughter with a poor and unknown artist. Gamelin had nothing, while the printseller turned over large sums of money. The *Amour peintre* brought him in large profits, the share market larger still, and he was in partnership with an army contractor who supplied the cavalry of the Republic with rushes in place of hay and mildewed oats. In a word, the cutler's son of the Rue Saint-Dominique was a very insignificant personage beside the publisher of engravings, a man known throughout Europe, related to the Blaizots, Basans and Didots, and an hon-oured guest at the houses of the *citoyens* Saint-Pierre and Florian. Not that, as an obedient daughter should, she held her father's con-sent to be an indispensable preliminary to her settlement in life. The latter, early left a widower, and a man of a self-indulgent, vola-tile temper, as enterprising with women as he was in business, had never paid much heed to her and had left her to develop at her own sweet will, untrammelled whether by parental advice or parental affection, more careful to ignore than to safeguard the girl's be-haviour, whose passionate temperament he appreciated as a con-noisseur of the sex and in whom he recognized charms far and away more seductive than a pretty face. Too generous-hearted to be cir-cumspect, too clever to come to harm, cautious even in her caprices, passion had never made her forget the social proprieties. Her father was infinitely grateful for this prudent behaviour, and as she had inherited from him a good head for business and a taste for money-making, he never troubled himself as to the mysterious reasons that deterred a girl so eminently marriageable from entering that estate and kept her at home, where she was as good as a housekeeper and four clerks to him. At twenty-seven she felt old enough and experienced enough to manage her own concerns and had no need to ask the advice or consult the wishes of a father still a young man, and one of so easy-going and careless a temper. But for her to marry Gamelin, Monsieur Blaise must needs contrive a future for a son-in-law with such poor prospects, give him an interest in the business, guarantee him regular work as he did to several artists already — in fact, one way or another, provide him with a livelihood; and such a favour was out of the question, she considered, whether for the one to offer or the other to accept, so small was the bond of sympathy between the two men.

The difficulty troubled the girl's tender heart and wise brain. She saw nothing to alarm her in a secret union with her lover and in taking the author of nature for sole witness of their mutual troth. Her creed found nothing blameworthy in such a union, which the independence of her mode of life made possible and which Évariste's honourable and virtuous character gave her good hopes of forming without apprehension as to the result. But Gamelin was hard put to it to live and provide his old mother with the barest necessaries, and it did not seem as though in so straitened an existence room could well be found for an amour even when reduced to the simplicity of nature. Moreover, Évariste had not yet spoken and declared his intentions, though certainly the *citoyenne* Blaise hoped to bring him to this before long.

She broke off her meditations, and the needle stopped at the same moment.

"*Citoyen* Évariste," she said, "I shall not care for the scarf, unless you like it too. Draw me a pattern, please. Meanwhile, I will copy Penelope and unravel what I have done in your absence."

He answered in a tone of sombre enthusiasm:

"I promise you I will, *citoyenne*. I will draw you the brand of the tyrannicide Harmodius,—a sword in a wreath,"—and pulling out his pencil, he sketched in a design of swords and flowers in the sober, unadorned style he admired. And as he drew, he expounded his views of art:

24

"A regenerated People," he declared, "must repudiate all the legacies of servitude, bad taste, bad outline, bad drawing. Watteau, Boucher, Fragonard worked for tyrants and for slaves. Their works show no feeling for good style or purity of line, no love of nature or truth. Masks, dolls, fripperies, monkey-tricks,—nothing else! Posterity will despise their frivolous productions. In a hundred years all Watteau's pictures will be banished to the garrets and falling to pieces from neglect; in 1893 struggling painters will be daubing their studies over Boucher's canvases. David has opened the way; he approaches the Antique, but he has not yet reached true simplicity, true grandeur, bare and unadorned. Our artists have many secrets still to learn from the friezes of Herculaneum, the Roman bas-reliefs, the Etruscan vases."

He dilated at length on antique beauty, then came back to Fragonard, whom he abused with inexhaustible venom:

"Do you know him, *citoyenne?*"

Élodie nodded.

"You likewise know good old Greuze, who is ridiculous enough, to be sure, with his scarlet coat and his sword. But he looks like a wise man of Greece beside Fragonard. I met him, a while ago, the miserable old man, trotting by under the arcades of the Palais-Égalité, powdered, genteel, sprightly, spruce, hideous. At sight of him, I longed that, failing Apollo, some sturdy friend of the arts might hang him up to a tree and flay him alive like Marsyas as an everlasting warning to bad painters."

Élodie gave him a long look out of her dancing, wanton eyes.

"You know how to hate, Monsieur Gamelin, are we to conclude you know also how to lo . . . ?"

"Is that you, Gamelin?" broke in a tenor voice; it was the *citoyen* Blaise just come back to his shop. He advanced, boots creaking, charms rattling, coat-skirts flying, an enormous black cocked hat on his head, the corners of which touched his shoulders.

Élodie, picking up her work-basket, retreated to her chamber.

"Well, Gamelin!" enquired the *citoyen* Blaise, "have you brought me anything new?"

"May be," declared the painter,—and proceeded to expound his ideas.

"Our playing cards present a grievous and startling contrast with our present ways of thinking. The names of knave and king offend the ears of a patriot. I have designed and executed a reformed, Revolutionary pack in which for kings, queens and knaves are substituted Liberties, Equalities, Fraternities; the aces in a border of fasces, are called Laws. . . . You call Liberty of clubs, Equality of spades, Fraternity of diamonds, Law of hearts. I venture to think my cards are drawn with some spirit; I propose to have them engraved on copper by Desmahis, and to take out letters of patent."

So saying and extracting from his portfolio some finished designs in water-colour, the artist handed them to the printseller.

The *citoyen* Blaise declined to take them, and turning away:

"My lad," he sneered, "take 'em to the Convention; they will perhaps accord you a vote of thanks. But never think to make a *sol* by your new invention which is not new at all. You're a day behind the fair. Your Revolutionary pack of cards is the third I've had brought me. Your comrade Dugourc offered me last week a picquet set with four Geniuses of the People, four Liberties, four Equalities. Another was suggested, with Sages and Heroes, Cato, Rousseau, Hannibal,—I don't know what all! . . . And these cards had the advantage over yours, my friend, in being coarsely drawn and cut on wood blocks—with a penknife. How little you know the world to dream that players will use cards designed in the taste of David and engraved à la Bartolozzi! And then again, what a strange mistake to think it needs all this to-do to suit the old packs to the new ideas. Out of their own heads, the good *sansculottes* can find a corrective for what offends them, saying, instead of 'king'—'The Tyrant!' or just 'The fat pig!' They go on using the same old filthy cards and never buy new ones. The great market for playing-cards is the gaming-hells of the Palais-Égalité; well, I advise you to go there and offer the croupiers and punters there your Liberties, your Equalities, your . . . what d'ye call 'em? . . . Laws of hearts . . . and come back and tell me what sort of a reception they gave you!"

The *citoyen* Blaise sat down on the counter, filliped away sundry grains of snuff from his nankeen breeches and looking at Gamelin with an air of gentle pity:

"Let me give you a bit of advice, *citoyen;* if you want to make your living, drop your patriotic packs of cards, leave your Revolutionary symbols alone, have done with your Hercules, your hydras, your Furies pursuing guilt, your Geniuses of Liberty, and paint me

26

pretty girls. The people's ardour for regeneration grows lukewarm with time, but men will always love women. Paint me women, all pink and white, with little feet and tiny hands. And get this into your thick skull that nobody cares a fig about the Revolution or wants to hear another word about it."

But Évariste drew himself up in indignant protest:

"What! not hear another word of the Revolution! . . . But, why surely, the restoration of liberty, the victories of our armies, the chastisement of tyrants are events that will startle the most remote posterity. How could we not be struck by such portents? . . . What! the sect of the *sansculotte* Jesus has lasted well-nigh eighteen centuries, and the religion of Liberty is to be abolished after barely four years of existence!"

But Jean Blaise resumed in a tone of superiority:

"You walk in a dream; *I* see life as it is. Believe me, friend, the Revolution is a bore; it lasts over long. Five years of enthusiasm, five years of fraternal embraces, of massacres, of fine speeches, of *Marseillaises*, of tocsins, of 'hang up the aristocrats,' of heads promenaded on pikes, of women mounted astride of cannon, of trees of Liberty crowned with the red cap, of white-robed maidens and old men drawn about the streets in flower-wreathed cars; of imprisonments and guillotinings, of proclamations, and short commons, of cockades and plumes, swords and *carmagnoles*—it grows tedious! And then folk are beginning to lose the hang of it all. We have gone through too much, we have seen too many of the great men and noble patriots whom you have led in triumph to the Capitol only to hurl them afterwards from the Tarpeian rock,—Necker, Mirabeau, La Fayette, Bailly, Pétion, Manuel, and how many others! How can we be sure you are not preparing the same fate for your new heroes? . . . Men have lost all count."

"Their names, *citoyen* Blaise; name them, these heroes we are making ready to sacrifice!" cried Gamelin in a tone that recalled the print-dealer to a sense of prudence.

"I am a Republican and a patriot," he replied, clapping his hand on his heart. "I am as good a Republican as you, as ardent a patriot as you, *citoyen* Gamelin. I do not suspect your zeal nor accuse you of any backsliding. But remember that my zeal and my devotion to the State are attested by numerous acts. Here you have my principles. I give my confidence to every individual competent to

27

serve the Nation. Before the men whom the general voice elects to the perilous honour of the Legislative office, such as Marat, such as Robespierre, I bow my head; I am ready to support them to the measure of my poor ability and offer them the humble co-operation of a good citizen. The Committees can bear witness to my ardour and self-sacrifice. In conjunction with true patriots, I have furnished oats and fodder to our gallant cavalry, boots for our soldiers. This very day I am despatching from Vernon a convoy of sixty oxen to the Army of the South through a country infested with brigands and patrolled by the emissaries of Pitt and Condé. I do not talk; I act."

Gamelin calmly put back his sketches in his portfolio, the strings of which he tied and then slipped it under his arm.

"It is a strange contradiction," he said through his clenched teeth, "to see men help our soldiers to carry through the world the liberty they betray in their own homes by sowing discontent and alarm in the soul of its defenders. . . . Greeting and farewell, *citoyen* Blaise."

Before turning down the alley that runs alongside the Oratoire, Gamelin, his heart big with love and anger, wheeled round for a last look at the red carnations blossoming on a certain window-sill.

He did not despair; the fatherland would yet be saved. Against Jean Blaise's unpatriotic speeches he set his faith in the Revolution. Still he was bound to recognize that the tradesman had some show of reason when he asserted that the people of Paris had lost its old interest in public events. Alas! it was but too manifest that to the enthusiasm of the early days had little by little succeeded a widespread indifference, that never again would be seen the mighty crowds, unanimous in their ardour, of '89, never again the millions, one in heart and soul, that in '90 thronged round the altar of the *fédérés*. Well, good citizens must show double zeal and courage, must rouse the people from its apathy, bidding it choose between liberty and death.

Such were Gamelin's thoughts, and the memory of Élodie was a spur to his confidence.

Coming to the Quais, he saw the sun setting in the distant west behind lowering clouds that were like mountains of blowing lava; the roofs of the city were bathed in a golden light; the windows flashed back a thousand dazzling reflections. And Gamelin pictured the Titans forging out of the molten fragments of by-gone worlds Diké, the city of brass.

Not having a morsel of bread for his mother or himself, he was dreaming of a place at the limitless board that should have all the world for guests and welcome regenerated humanity to the feast. Meantime, he tried to persuade himself that the fatherland, as a good mother should, would feed her faithful child. Shutting his mind against the gibes of the printseller, he forced himself to believe that his notion of a Revolutionary pack of cards was a novel one and a good one, and that with these happily conceived sketches of his he held a fortune in the portfolio under his arm. "Desmahis," he told himself, "shall engrave them. We will publish for ourselves the new patriotic toy and we are sure to sell ten thousand packs in a month, at twenty *sols* apiece."

In his impatience to realize the project, he strode off at once for the Quai de la Ferraille, where Desmahis lived over a glazier's shop.

The entrance was through the shop. The glazier's wife informed Gamelin that the *citoyen* Desmahis was not in, a fact that in no wise surprised the painter, who knew his friend was of a vagabond and dissipated humour and who marvelled that a man could engrave so much and so well as he did while showing so little perseverance. Gamelin made up his mind to wait a while for his return and the woman offered him a chair. She was in a black mood and began to grumble at the badness of trade, though she had always been told that the Revolution, by breaking windows, was making the glaziers' fortunes.

Night was falling; so abandoning his idea of waiting for his comrade, Gamelin took his leave of his hostess of the moment. As he was crossing the Pont-Neuf, he saw a detachment of National Guards debouch from the Quai des Morfondus. They were mounted and carried torches. They were driving back the crowd, and amid a mighty clatter of sabres escorting a cart driving slowly on its way to the guillotine with a man whose name no one knew, a *ci-devant* noble, the first prisoner condemned by the newly constituted Revolutionary Tribunal. He could be seen by glimpses between the guardsmen's hats, sitting with hands tied behind his back, his head bared and swaying from side to side, his face to the cart's tail. The headsman stood beside him lolling against the rail. The passers-by had stopped to look and were telling each other it was likely one of the fellows who starved the people, and staring with eyes of indifference. Gamelin, coming closer, caught sight of Desmahis among the spectators; he was struggling to push a way through the press and cut across the line of march. He called out to him and clapped a hand on his shoulder,—and Desmahis turned his head. He was a young man with a handsome face and a stalwart person. In former days, at the Academy, they used to say he had the head of Bacchus on the torso of Hercules. His friends nicknamed him "Barbaroux" because of his likeness to that representative of the people.

"Come here," Gamelin said to him, "I have something of importance to say to you, Desmahis."

"Leave me alone," the latter answered peevishly, muttering some half-heard explanation, looking out as he spoke for a chance of darting across:

"I was following a divine creature, in a straw hat, a milliner's wench, with her flaxen hair down her back; that cursed cart has blocked my way. . . . She has gone on ahead, she is at the other end of the bridge by now!"

Gamelin endeavoured to hold him back by his coat skirts, swearing his business was urgent.

But Desmahis had already slipped away between horses, guards, swords and torches, and was in hot pursuit of the milliner's girl.

Chapter 4

I

T WAS ten o'clock in the forenoon. The April
sun bathed the tender leafage of the trees in light. A storm had
cleared the air during the night and it was deliciously fresh and
sweet. At long intervals a horseman passing along the Allée des Veuves
broke the silence and solitude. On the outskirts of the shady avenue,
over against a rustic cottage known as *La Belle Lilloise*, Évariste sat
on a wooden bench waiting for Élodie. Since the day their fingers had
met over the embroidery and their breaths had mingled, he had never
been back to the *Amour peintre*. For a whole week his proud stoicism
and his timidity, which grew more extreme every day, had kept him
away from Élodie. He had written her a letter conceived in a key of
gravity, at once sombre and ardent, in which, explaining the grievance
he had against the *citoyen* Blaise, but saying no word of his love and
concealing his chagrin, he announced his intention of never returning
to her father's shop, and was now showing greater steadfastness in
keeping this resolution than a woman in love was quite likely to
approve.

A born fighter whose bent was to defend her property under all
circumstances, Élodie instantly turned her mind to the task of winning back her lover. At first she thought of going to see him at the
studio in the Place de Thionville. But knowing his touchy temper
and judging from his letter that he was sick and sore, she feared he
might come to regard daughter and father with the same angry displeasure and make a point of never seeing her again; so she deemed
it wiser to invite him to a sentimental, romantic rendezvous which
he could not well decline, where she would have ample time to cajole
and charm him and where solitude would be her ally to fascinate his
senses and overcome his scruples.

At this period, in all the English gardens and all the fashionable
promenades, rustic cottages were to be found, built by clever archi-

tects, whose aim it was to flatter the taste of the city folk for a country life. The *Belle Lilloise* was occupied as a house of light refreshment; its exterior bore a look of poverty that was part of the *mise en scène* and it stood on the fragments, artistically imitated, of a fallen tower, so as to unite with the charm of rusticity the melancholy appeal of a ruined castle. Moreover, as though a peasant's cot and a shattered donjon were not enough to stir the sensibilities of his customers, the owner had raised a tomb beneath a weeping-willow,— a column surmounted by a funeral urn and bearing the inscription: "Cléonice to her faithful Azor." Rustic cots, ruined keeps, imitation tombs,—on the eve of being swept away, the aristocracy had erected in its ancestral parks these symbols of poverty, of decadence and of death. And now the patriot citizen found his delight in drinking, dancing, making love in sham hovels, under the broken vaults, a sham in their very ruin, of sham cloisters and surrounded by a sham graveyard; for was not he too, like his betters, a lover of nature, a disciple of Jean-Jacques? was not his heart stuffed as full as theirs with sensibility and the philosophy of humanity?

Reaching the rendezvous before the appointed time, Évariste waited, measuring the minutes by the beating of his heart as by the pendulum of a clock. A patrol passed, guarding a convoy of prisoners. Ten minutes after a woman dressed all in pink, carrying a bouquet as the fashion was, escorted by a gentleman in a three-cornered hat, red coat, striped waistcoat and breeches, slipped into the cottage, both so very like the gallants and dames of the ancien régime one was bound to think with the *citoyen* Blaise that mankind possesses characteristics Revolutions cannot change.

A few minutes later, coming from Rueil or Saint-Cloud, an old woman carrying a cylindrical box, painted in brilliant colours, arrived and sat down beside Gamelin, on his bench. She put down her box in front of her, and he saw that the lid had a turning needle fixed on it; the poor woman's trade was to hold a lottery in the public gardens for the children to try their luck at. She also dealt in "ladies' pleasures," an old-fashioned sweetmeat which she sold under a new name; whether because the time-honoured title of "forget-me-nots" called up inappropriate ideas of unhappiness and retribution or that folks had just got tired of it in course of time, "forget-me-nots" were now yclept "ladies' pleasures."

The old dame wiped the sweat from her forehead with a corner of her apron and broke out into railings against heaven, upbraiding God for injustice when he made life so hard for his creatures. Her husband kept a tavern on the river-bank at Saint-Cloud, while she came in every day to the Champs Élysées, sounding her rattle and crying: *"Ladies' pleasures,* come buy, come buy!" And with all this toil the old couple could not scrape enough together to end their days in comfort.

Seeing the young man beside her disposed to commiserate with her, she expounded at great length the origin of her misfortunes. It was all the Republic; by robbing the rich, it was taking the bread out of poor people's mouths. And there was no hoping for a better state of affairs. Things would only go from bad to worse,—she knew that from many tokens. At Nanterre a woman had had a baby born with a serpent's head; the lightning had struck the church at Rueil and melted the cross on the steeple; a were-wolf had been seen in the woods of Chaville. Masked men were poisoning the springs and throwing plague powders in the air to cause diseases. . . .

Évariste saw Élodie spring from a carriage and run forward. The girl's eyes flashed in the clear shadow cast by her straw hat; her lips, as red as the carnations she held in her hand, were wreathed in smiles. A scarf of black silk, crossed over the bosom, was knotted behind the back. Her yellow gown displayed the quick movements of the knees and showed a pair of low-heeled shoes below the hem. The hips were almost entirely unconfined; the Revolution had enfranchised the waists of its *citoyennes.* For all that, the skirts, still puffed out below the loins, marked the curves by exaggerating them and veiled the reality beneath an artificial amplitude of outline.

He tried to speak but could not find his voice, and was chagrined at his failure, which Élodie preferred to the most eloquent greeting. She noticed also and looked upon it as a good omen, that he had tied his cravat with more than usual pains.

She gave him her hand.

"I wanted to see you," she began, "and talk to you. I did not answer your letter; I did not like it and I did not think it worthy of you. It would have been more to my taste if it had been more outspoken. It would be to malign your character and common sense to suppose you do not mean to return to the *Amour peintre* because you

33

had a trifling altercation there about politics with a man many years your senior. Rest assured you have no cause to fear my father will receive you ill whenever you come to see us again. You do not know him; he had forgotten both what he said to you and what you said in reply. I do not say there is any great bond of sympathy between you two; but he bears no malice; I tell you frankly he pays no great heed to you . . . nor to me. He thinks only of his own affairs and his own pleasures."

She stepped towards the shrubberies surrounding the *Belle Lilloise*, and he followed her with something of repugnance, knowing it to be the trysting-place of mercenary lovers and amours of a day. She selected the table furthest out of sight.

"How many things I have to tell you, Évariste. Friendship has its rights; you do not forbid me to exercise them? I have much to say about you . . . and something about myself, if you will let me."

The landlord having brought a carafe of lemonade, she filled their glasses herself with the air of a careful housewife; then she began to tell him about her childhood, described her mother's beauty, which she loved to dilate upon both as a tribute to the latter's memory and as the source of her own good looks, and boasted of her grandparents' sturdy vigour, for she was proud of her bourgeois blood. She related how at sixteen she had lost this mother she adored and had entered on a life without anyone to love or rely upon. She painted herself as she was, a vehement, passionate nature, full of sensibility and courage, and concluded:

"Oh, Évariste, my girlhood was so sad and lonely I cannot but know what a prize is a heart like yours, and I will not surrender, I give you fair warning, of my own free will and without an effort to retain it, a sympathy on which I trusted I might count and which I held dear."

Évariste gazed at her tenderly.

"Can it be, Élodie, that I am not indifferent to you? Can I really think . . . ?"

He broke off, fearing to say too much and thereby betray so trusting a friendliness.

She gave him a little confiding hand that half-peeped out of the long narrow sleeve with its lace frillings. Her bosom rose and fell in long-drawn sighs.

"Credit me, Évariste, with all the sentiments you would have me feel for you, and you will not be mistaken in the dispositions of my heart."

"Élodie, Élodie, you say that? will you still say it when you know . . ."—he hesitated.

She dropped her eyes; and he finished the sentence in a whisper: ". . . when you know I love you?"

As she heard the declaration, she blushed,—with pleasure. Yet, while her eyes still spoke of a tender ecstasy, a quizzical smile flickered in spite of herself about one corner of her lips. She was thinking:

"And he imagines he proposed first! . . . and he is afraid perhaps of offending me! . . ."

Then she said to him fondly:

"So you had never seen, dear heart, that I loved you?"

They seemed to themselves to be alone, the only two beings in the universe. In his exaltation, Évariste raised his eyes to the firmament flashing with blue and gold:

"See, the sky is looking down at us! It is benign; it is adorable, as you are, beloved; it has your brightness, your gentleness, your smile."

He felt himself one with all nature, it formed part and parcel of his joy and triumph. To his eyes, it was to celebrate his betrothal that the chestnut blossoms lit their flaming candles, the poplars burned aloft like giant torches.

He exulted in his strength and stature. She, with her softer as well as finer nature, more pliable and more malleable, rejoiced in her very weakness and, his subjection once secured, instantly bowed to his ascendancy; now she had brought him under her slavery, she acknowledged him for the master, the hero, the god, burned to obey, to admire, to offer her homage. In the shade of the shrubbery he gave her a long, ardent kiss, which she received with head thrown back and, clasped in Évariste's arms, felt all her flesh melt like wax.

They went on talking a long time of themselves, forgetful of the universe. Évariste abounded mainly in vague, high thoughts, which filled Élodie with ecstasy. She spoke sweetly of things of practical utility and personal interest. Then, presently, when she felt she could stay no longer, she rose with a decided air, gave her lover the three red carnations from the flower in her balcony and sprang lightly into the cabriolet in which she had driven there. It was a hired carriage, painted yellow, hung on very high wheels, and certainly had

35

nothing out of the common about it, or the coachman either. But Gamelin was not in the habit of hiring carriages and his friends were hardly more used to such an indulgence. To see the great wheels whirling her away gave him a strange pang and a painful presentiment assailed him; by a sort of hallucination of the mind, the hack horse seemed to be carrying Élodie away from him beyond the bounds of the actual world and present time towards a city of wealth and pleasure, towards abodes of luxury and enjoyment, which he would never be able to enter.

The carriage disappeared. Évariste recovered his calm by degrees; but a dull anguish remained and he felt that the hours of tender abandonment he had just lived would never be his again.

He returned by the Champs Élysées, where women in light summer dresses were sitting on wooden chairs, talking or sewing, while their children played under the trees. A woman selling "ladies' pleasures,"—*her* box was shaped like a drum—reminded him of the one he had spoken to in the Allée des Veuves, and it seemed as if a whole epoch of his life had elapsed between the two encounters. He crossed the Place de la Révolution. In the Tuileries gardens he caught the distant roar of a host of men, a sound of many voices shouting in accord, so familiar in those great days of popular enthusiasm which the enemies of the Revolution declared would never dawn again. He quickened his pace as the noise grew louder and louder, reached the Rue Honoré and found it thronged with a crowd of men and women yelling: "Vive la République! Vive la Liberté!" The walls of the gardens, the windows, the balconies, the very roofs were black with lookers-on waving hats and handkerchiefs. Preceded by a sapper, who cleared a way for the procession, surrounded by Municipal Officers, National Guards, gunners, gendarmes, hussars, advanced slowly, high above the backs of the citizens, a man of a bilious complexion, a wreath of oak leaves about his brow, his body wrapped in an old green surtout with an ermine collar. The women threw him flowers, while he cast about him the piercing glance of his jaundiced eyes, as though in this enthusiastic multitude he was still searching out enemies of the people to denounce, traitors to punish. As he went by, Gamelin bent his head and joining his voice to a hundred thousand others, shouted his:

"Vive Marat!"

The triumphant hero entered the Hall of the Convention like Fate personified. While the crowd slowly dispersed Gamelin sat on a stone post in the Rue Honoré and pressed his hand over his heart to check its wild beating. What he had seen filled him with high emotion and burning enthusiasm.

He loved and worshipped Marat, who, sick and fevered, his veins on fire, eaten up by ulcers, was wearing out the last remnants of his strength in the service of the Republic, and in his own poor house, closed to no man, welcomed him with open arms, conversed eagerly with him of public affairs, questioned him sometimes on the machinations of evil-doers. He rejoiced that the enemies of *The Just*, conspiring for his ruin, had prepared his triumph; he blessed the Revolutionary Tribunal, which acquitting the Friend of the People had given back to the convention the most zealous and most immaculate of its legislators. Again his eyes could see the head racked with fever, garlanded with the civic crown, the features instinct with virtuous pride and pitiless love, the worn, ravaged, powerful face, the close-pressed lips, the broad chest, the strong man dying by inches who, raised aloft in the living chariot of his triumph, seemed to exhort his fellow-citizens: "Be ye like me,—patriots to the death!"

The street was empty, darkening with the shadows of approaching night; the lamplighter went by with his cresset, and Gamelin muttered to himself:

"Yes, to the death!"

Chapter 5

BY NINE in the morning Évariste reached the gardens of the Luxembourg, to find Élodie already there seated on a bench waiting for him.

It was a month ago they had exchanged their vows, and since then they had seen each other every day, either at the *Amour peintre* or at the studio in the Place de Thionville. Their meetings had been very tender, but at the same time characterized by a certain reserve that checked their expansiveness,—a reserve due to the staid and virtuous temper of the lover, a deist and a good citizen, who, while ready to make his beloved mistress his own before the law or with God alone for witness according as circumstances demanded, would do nothing save publicly and in the light of day. Élodie knew the resolution to be right and honourable; but, despairing of a marriage that seemed impossible from every point of view and loath to outrage the prejudices of society, she contemplated in her inmost heart a liaison that could be kept a secret till the lapse of time gave it sanction. She hoped one day to overcome the scruples of a lover she could have wished less scrupulous, and meantime, unwilling to postpone some necessary confidences as to the past, she had asked him to meet her for a lover's talk in a lonely corner of the gardens near the Carthusian Priory.

She threw him a tender look, took his hand frankly, invited him to share the bench and speaking slowly and thoughtfully:

"I esteem you too well, Évariste, to hide anything from you. I believe myself worthy of you; I should not be so were I not to tell you everything. Hear me and be my judge. I have no act to reproach myself with that is degrading or base, or even merely selfish. I have only been weak and credulous. . . . Do not forget, dear Évariste, the difficult circumstances in which I found myself. You know how it was with me; I had lost my mother, my father, still a young man, thought only of his own amusement and neglected me. I had a feeling heart, nature has dowered me with a loving temper and a generous soul; it was true she had not denied me a firm will and a sound judgment, but in those days what ruled my conduct was passion, not reason. Alas! it would be the same again to-day, if the two were not in harmony; I should be driven to give myself to you, beloved, heart and soul, and for ever!"

She expressed herself in firm, well-balanced phrases. She had well thought over what she would say, having long ago made up her mind to this confession for several reasons—because she was naturally candid, because she found pleasure in following Rousseau's example, and because, as she told herself reasonably enough:

"One day Évariste must fathom a secret which is known to others as well as myself. A frank avowal is best. It is unforced and therefore to my credit, and only tells him what some time or other he would discover to my shame."

Soft-hearted as she was and amenable to nature's promptings, she did not feel herself to be very much to blame, and this made her confession the easier; besides which, she had no intention of telling more than was absolutely requisite.

"Ah!" she sighed, "why did I not know you, Évariste, in the days when I was alone and forsaken?"

Gamelin had taken her request quite literally when Élodie asked him to be her judge. Primed at once by nature and the education of books for the exercise of domestic justice, he sat ready to receive Élodie's admissions.

As she still hesitated, he motioned to her to proceed. Then she began speaking very simply:

"A young man, who with many defects of character combined some good qualities, and only showed the latter, found me to his taste and courted me with a perseverance that was surprising in such a case; he was in the flower of his youth, full of charm and the idol of a bevy of charming women who made no attempt to hide their adoration. It was not his good looks nor even his brilliance that appealed to me. . . . He touched my heart by the tokens of true love he gave me, and I do think he loved me truly. He was tender, impassioned. I asked no pledge save of his heart, and alas! his heart was fickle. . . . I blame no one but myself; it is my confession I am making, not his. I lay nothing to his charge, for indeed he is become a stranger to me. Ah! believe me, Évariste, I swear it, he is no more to me than if he had never existed."

She had finished, but Gamelin vouchsafed no answer. He unfolded his arms, a steadfast, sombre look settling in his eyes. His mistress and his sister Julie were running together in his thoughts. Julie too had hearkened to a lover; but, unlike, altogether unlike, he thought, the unhappy Élodie, *she* had let him have his will and carry her off, not misled by the promptings of a tender heart, but to enjoy, far from her home and friends, the sweets of luxury and pleasure. He was a stern moralist; he had condemned his sister and he was half inclined to condemn his mistress.

Élodie resumed in a very pleading voice:

"I was full of Jean-Jacques' philosophy; I believed men were naturally honest and honourable. My misfortune was to have encountered a lover who was not formed in the school of nature and natural morality, and whom social prejudice, ambition, self-love, a false point of honour had made selfish and treacherous."

The words produced the effect she had calculated on. Gamelin's eyes softened. He asked:

"Who was your seducer? Is he a man I know?"

"You do not know him."

"Tell me his name."

She had foreseen the question and was firmly resolved not to answer it.

She gave her reasons:

"Spare me, I beseech you. For your peace of mind as for my own, I have already said too much."

Then, as he still pressed her:

"In the sacred name of our love, I refuse to tell you anything to give you a definite notion of this stranger: I will not give your jealousy a shape to feed on. I will not bring a harassing shadow between you and me. I have not forgotten the man's name, but I will never let you know it."

Gamelin insisted on knowing the name of the seducer,—that was the word he employed all through, for he felt no doubt Élodie had been seduced, cajoled, trifled with. He could not so much as conceive any other possibility,—that she had obeyed an overmastering desire, an irresistible craving, listened to the tempter's voice in the shape of her own flesh and blood; he could not find it credible that the fair victim, a creature of hot passion and a fond heart, had offered herself a willing sacrifice; to satisfy his ideal, she must needs have been overborne by force or fraud, constrained by sheer violence, caught in snares spread about her steps on every side. He questioned her in guarded terms, but with a close, searching, embarrassing persistency. He asked her how the liaison began, if it was long or short, tranquil or troubled, under what circumstances it was broken off. And his enquiries came back again and again to the means the fellow had used to cajole her, as if these must surely have been extraordinary and unheard of. But all his cross-examination was in vain. She kept her own counsel with a gentle, deprecatory obstinacy, her lips tightly pressed together and tears welling in her eyes.

Presently, however, Évariste having asked where the man was now, she told him:

"He has left the Kingdom — France, I mean," she corrected herself in an instant.

"An *émigré!*" ejaculated Gamelin.

She looked at him, speechless, at once reassured and disheartened to see him create in his own mind a truth in accordance with his political passions and of his own motion give his jealousy a Jacobin complexion.

In actual fact Élodie's lover was a little lawyer's clerk, a very pretty lad, half Adonis, half gutter-snipe, whom she had adored and the thought of whom, though three years had gone by since, still thrilled her nerves. Rich old women were his particular game, and he deserted Élodie for a woman of the world of a certain age who could and did recompense his merits. Having, after the abolition of offices, attained a post in the Mairie of Paris, he was now a *sansculotte* dragoon and the hanger-on of a *ci-devant* Countess.

"A noble! an *émigré!*" muttered Gamelin, whom she took good care not to undeceive, never having been desirous he should know the whole truth. "And he deserted you like a dastard?"

She nodded in answer. He clasped her to his heart:

"Dear victim of the vile corruption of monarchies, my love shall avenge his villainy! Heaven grant, I may meet the scoundrel! I shall not fail to know him!"

She turned away, at one and the same time saddened and smiling,—and disappointed. She would fain have had him wiser in the lore of love, with more of the natural man about him, more perhaps even of the brute. She felt he forgave so readily only because his imagination was cold and the secret she had revealed awoke in him none of the mental pictures that torture sensuous natures,—in a word, that he saw her seduction solely under a moral and social aspect.

They had risen, and while they walked up and down the shady avenues of the gardens, he informed her that he only esteemed her the more because she had suffered wrong. Élodie entertained no such high claims; however, take him as he was, she loved him, and admired the brilliant artistic genius she divined in him.

As they left the Luxembourg, they came upon crowds thronging the Rue de l'Égalité and the whole neighbourhood of the Théâtre de la Nation. There was nothing to surprise them in this; for several days great excitement had prevailed in the most patriotic Sections; denunciations were rife against the Orleans faction and the Brissotin plotters, who were conspiring, it was said, to bring about the ruin of Paris and the massacre of good Republicans. Gamelin himself a short time back had signed a petition from the Commune demanding the expulsion of the Twenty-one.

Just before passing under the arcade, joining the theatre to the neighbouring house, they had to find their way through a group of citizens *en carmagnole* who were listening to a harangue from a young soldier mounted on the top of the gallery. He looked as beautiful as the Eros of Praxiteles in his helmet of panther skin. This fascinating warrior was charging the People's Friend with indolence:

"Marat, you are asleep," he was crying, "and the Federalists are forging fetters to bind us."

Hardly had Élodie cast eyes on the orator before she turned rapidly to Évariste and begged him to get her away. The crowd, she declared, frightened her and she was afraid of fainting in the crush.

They parted in the Place de la Nation, swearing an oath of eternal fidelity.

That same morning early the *citoyen* Brotteaux had made the *citoyenne* Gamelin the magnificent present of a capon. It would have been an act of indiscretion for him to mention how he had come by it; as a fact, he had it of a *Dame de la Halle* at the Pointe Eustache for whom he sometimes acted as amanuensis, and as everybody knows, these "Ladies of the Market" cherished Royalist sympathies and were in correspondence with the *émigrés*. The *citoyenne* Gamelin had received the gift with heartfelt gratitude. Such dainties were scarce ever seen then; victuals grew dearer every day. The people feared a famine; the aristocrats, they said, wished it, and the "corner" makers were at work to bring it about.

The *citoyen* Brotteaux, being invited to eat his share of the capon at the midday dinner, appeared in due course and congratulated his hostess on the rich aroma of cooking that assailed his nostrils. Indeed a noble smell of rich, savoury broth filled the painter's studio.

"You are very obliging, sir," replied the good dame. "To prepare the digestion for your capon, I have made a vegetable soup with a slice of fat bacon and a big beef bone. There's nothing like a marrow-bone, sir, to give soup a flavour."

"The maxim does you honour, *citoyenne*," returned the old man. And you will be doing wisely to put back again to-morrow and the day after, all the week, in fact, to put back again, I say, this precious bone in the pot, which it will continue to flavour. The wise woman of Panzoust always did so; she used to make a soup of green cabbages with a rind of rusty bacon and an old *savorados*. That is what in her country, which is also mine, they call the medullary bone, the most tasty and most succulent of all bones."

"This lady you speak of, sir," remarked the *citoyenne* Gamelin, "was she not rather a saving soul, to make the same bone serve so many times over?"

"Oh! she lived in a small way," explained Brotteaux, "she was poor, albeit a prophetess."

At that moment, Évariste Gamelin returned, agitated by the confession he had heard and determined to know who was Élodie's betrayer, to avenge at one and the same time the Republic's wrong and his own on the miscreant.

After the usual greetings had been exchanged, the *citoyen* Brotteaux resumed the thread of his discourse:

"It is seldom those who make a trade of foretelling the future grow rich. Their impostures are too soon found out and their trickery renders them odious. But indeed we should be bound to detest them much worse if they prophesied truly. A man's life would be intolerable if he knew what is to befall him. He would be aware of calamities to come and suffer their pains in advance, while he would get no joy of present blessings whose end he would foresee. Ignorance is a necessary condition of human happiness, and it must be owned that in most cases we fulfil it well. We know almost nothing about ourselves; absolutely nothing about our neighbours. Ignorance constitutes our peace of mind; self-deception our felicity."

The *citoyenne* Gamelin set the soup on the table, said the Benedicite and seated her son and her guest at the board. She stood up herself to eat, declining the chair the *citoyen* Brotteaux offered her beside him; she said she knew what good manners required of a woman.

Chapter 6

TEN o'clock in the forenoon. Not a breath of wind. It was the hottest July ever known. In the narrow Rue de Jérusalem a hundred or so citizens of the Section were waiting in queue at the baker's door, under the eye of four National Guards who stood at ease smoking their pipes.

The National Convention had decreed the *maximum*,—and instantly corn and flour had disappeared. Like the Israelites in the wilderness, the Parisians had to rise before daybreak if they wished to eat. The crowd was lined up, men, women and children tightly packed together, under a sky of molten lead. The heat beat down on the rotting foulness of the kennels and exaggerated the stench of unwashed, sweating humanity. All were pushing, abusing their neighbours, exchanging looks fraught with every sort of emotion one human being can feel for another,—dislike, disgust, interest, attraction, indifference. Painful experience had taught them there was not bread enough for everybody; so the late comers were always trying to push forward, while those who lost ground complained bitterly and indignantly and vainly claimed their rights. Women shoved and elbowed savagely to keep their place or squeeze into a better. When the press grew too intolerable, cries rose of "Stop pushing there!" while each and all protested they could not help it—it was someone else pushing them.

To obviate these daily scenes of disorder, the officials appointed by the Section had conceived the notion of fastening a rope to the shop-door which each applicant held in his proper order; but hands at such close quarters *would* come in contact on the rope and a struggle would result. Whoever lost hold could never recover it, while the disappointed and the mischievously inclined sometimes cut the cord. In the end the plan had to be abandoned.

On this occasion there was the usual suffocation and confusion.

45

While some swore they were dying, others indulged in jokes or loose remarks; all abused the aristocrats and Federalists, authors of all the misery. When a dog ran by, wags hailed the beast as Pitt. More than once a loud slap showed that some *citoyenne* in the line had resented with a vigorous hand the insolence of a lewd admirer, while, pressed close against her neighbour, a young servant girl, with eyes half shut and mouth half open, stood sighing in a sort of trance. At any word, or gesture, or attitude of a sort to provoke the sportive humour of the coarse-minded populace, a knot of young libertines would strike up the *Ça-ira* in chorus, regardless of the protests of an old Jacobin, highly indignant to see a dirty meaning attached to a refrain expressive of the Republican faith in a future of justice and happiness.

His ladder under his arm, a billsticker appeared to post up on a blank wall facing the baker's a proclamation by the Commune apportioning the rations of butcher's-meat. Passers-by halted to read the notice, still sticky with paste. A cabbage vendor going by, basket on back, began calling out in her loud cracked voice:

"They'm all gone, the purty oxen! best rake up the guts!"

Suddenly such an appalling stench of putrefaction rose from a sewer near by that several people were turned sick; a woman was taken ill and handed over in a fainting condition to a couple of National Guards, who carried her off to a pump a few yards away. All held their noses, and fell to growling and grumbling, exchanging conjectures each more ghastly and alarming than the last. What was it? a dead animal buried thereabouts, or perhaps a poison, put in for mischief's sake, or more likely a victim of the September massacres, some noble or priest, left to rot in a cellar.

"They buried them in cellars, eh?"

"They got rid of 'em anywhere and anyhow."

"It will be one of the Châtelet prisoners. On the 2nd I saw three hundred in a heap on the Port au Change."

The Parisians dreaded the vengeance of these aristocrats who were like to poison them with their dead bodies.

Évariste Gamelin joined the line; he was resolved to spare his old mother the fatigues of the long wait. His neighbour, the *citoyen* Brotteaux, went with him, calm and smiling, his Lucretius in the baggy pocket of his plum-coloured coat.

The good old fellow enjoyed the scene, calling it a bit of low life worthy the brush of a modern Teniers.

"These street-porters and goodwives," he declared, "are more amusing than the Greeks and Romans our painters are so fond of nowadays. For my part, I have always admired the Flemish style."

One fact he was too sensible and tactful to mention — that he had himself owned a gallery of Dutch masters rivalled only by Monsieur de Choiseul's in the number and excellence of the examples.

"Nothing is beautiful save the Antique," returned the painter, "and what is inspired by it. Still, I grant you these low-life scenes by Teniers, Jan Steen or Ostade are better stuff than the frills and furbelows of Watteau, Boucher, or Van Loo; humanity is shown in an ugly light, but it is not degraded as it is by a Baudouin or a Fragonard."

A hawker went by bawling:

"Bulletin of the Revolutionary Tribunal! . . . list of the condemned!"

"One Revolutionary Tribunal is not enough," said Gamelin, "there should be one in every town . . . in every town, do I say?—nay, in every village, in every hamlet. Fathers of families, citizens, one and all, should constitute themselves judges. At a time when the enemy's cannon is at her gates and the assassin's dagger at her throat, the Nation must hold mercy to be parricide. What! Lyons, Marseilles, Bordeaux in insurrection, Corsica in revolt, La Vendée on fire, Mayence and Valenciennes in the hands of the Coalition, treason in the country, town and camp, treason sitting on the very benches of the National Convention, treason assisting, map in hand, at the council board of our Commanders in the field! . . . The fatherland is in danger — and the guillotine must save her!"

"I have no objection on principle to make to the guillotine," replied Brotteaux. "Nature, my only mistress and my only instructress, certainly offers me no suggestion to the effect that a man's life is of any value; on the contrary, she teaches in all kinds of ways that it is of none. The sole end and object of living beings seems to be to serve as food for other beings destined to the same end. Murder is of natural right; therefore, the penalty of death is lawful, on condition it is exercised from no motives either of virtue or of justice, but by necessity or to gain some profit thereby. However, I must have perverse instincts, for I sicken to see blood flow, and this defect of character all my philosophy has failed so far to correct."

"Republicans," answered Évariste, "are humane and full of feeling. It is only despots who hold the death penalty to be a necessary

47

attribute of authority. The sovereign people will do away with it one day. Robespierre fought against it, and all good patriots were with him; the law abolishing it cannot be too soon promulgated. But it will not have to be applied till the last foe of the Republic has perished beneath the sword of law and order."

Gamelin and Brotteaux had by this time a number of late comers behind them, and amongst these several women of the Section, including a stalwart, handsome *tricoteuse*, in head-kerchief and sabots, wearing a sword in a shoulder belt, a pretty girl with a mop of golden hair and a very tumbled neckerchief, and a young mother, pale and thin, giving the breast to a sickly infant. The child, which could get no milk, was screaming, but its voice was weak and stifled by its sobs. Pitifully small, with a pallid, unhealthy skin and inflamed eyes, the mother gazed at it with mingled anxiety and grief.

"He is very young," observed Gamelin, turning to look at the unhappy infant groaning just at his back, half stifled amid the crowd of new arrivals.

"He is six months, poor love! . . . His father is with the army; he is one of the men who drove back the Austrians at Condé. His name is Dumonteil (Michel), a draper's assistant by trade. He enlisted at a booth they had established in front of the Hôtel de Ville. Poor lad, he was all for defending his country and seeing the world. . . . He writes telling me to be patient. But pray, how am I to feed Paul (he's called Paul, you know) when I can't feed myself?"

"Oh, dear!" exclaimed the pretty girl with the flaxen hair, "we've got another hour before us yet, and to-night we shall have to repeat the same ceremony over again at the grocer's. You risk your life to get three eggs and a quarter of a pound of butter."

"Butter!" sighed the *citoyenne* Dumonteil, "why, it's three months since I've see a scrap!"

And a chorus of female voices rose, bewailing the scarcity and dearness of provisions, cursing the *émigrés* and devoting to the guillotine the Commissaries of Sections who were ready to give good-for-nothing minxes, in return for unmentionable services, fat hens and four-pound loaves. Alarming stories passed round of cattle drowned in the Seine, sacks of flour emptied in the sewers, loaves of bread thrown into the latrines. . . . It was all those Royalists, and Rolandists, and Brissotins, who were starving the people, bent on exterminating every living thing in Paris!

All of a sudden, the pretty, fair-haired girl with the rumpled neck-erchief broke into shrieks as if her petticoats were afire. She was shaking these violently and turning out her pockets, vociferating that somebody had stolen her purse.

At news of the petty theft, a flood of indignation swept over this crowd of poor folks, the same who had sacked the mansions of the Faubourg Saint-Germain and invaded the Tuileries without appro-priating the smallest thing, artisans and housewives, who would have burned down the Palace of Versailles with a light heart, but would have thought it a dire disgrace if they had stolen the value of a pin. The young rakes greeted the pretty girl's loss with some ribald jokes, that were immediately drowned under a burst of public indignation. There was some talk of instant execution—hanging the thief to the nearest lamp-post, and an investigation was begun, where everyone spoke at once and nobody would listen to a word of reason. The tall *tricoteuse*, pointing her finger at an old man, strongly suspected of being an unfrocked monk, swore it was the "Capuchin" yonder who was the cut-purse. The crowd believed her without fur-ther evidence and raised a shout of "Death! death!"

The old man so unexpectedly exposed to the public vengeance was standing very quietly and soberly just in front of the *citoyen* Brot-teaux. He had all the look, there was no denying it, of a *ci-devant* cleric. His aspect was venerable, though the face was changed and drawn by the terrors the poor man had suffered from the violence of the crowd and the recollection of the September days that were still vivid in his imagination. The fear depicted on his features stirred the suspicion of the populace, which is always ready to believe that only the guilty dread its judgments, as if the haste and recklessness with which it pronounces them were not enough to terrify even the most innocent.

Brotteaux had made it a standing rule never to go against the popular feeling of the moment, above all when it was manifestly illogical and cruel, "because in that case," he would say, "the voice of the people was the voice of God." But Brotteaux proved himself untrue to his principles; he asseverated that the old man, whether he was a Capuchin or not, could not have robbed the *citoyenne*, hav-ing never gone near her for one moment.

The crowd drew its own conclusion,—the individual who spoke up for the thief was of course his accomplice, and stern measures were

49

proposed to deal with the two malefactors, and when Gamelin offered to guarantee Brotteaux's honesty, the wisest heads suggested sending *him* along with the two others to the Sectional headquarters.

But the pretty girl gave a cry of delight; she had found her purse again. The statement was received with a storm of hisses, and she was threatened with a public whipping, like a Nun.

"Sir," said the ex-monk, addressing Brotteaux, "I thank you for having spoken in my defence. My name is of no concern, but I had better tell you what it is; I am called Louis de Longuemare. I am in truth a Regular; but not a Capuchin, as those women would have it. There is the widest difference; I am a clerk regular of the Order of the Barnabites, which has given Doctors and Saints without number to the Church. It is only a half-truth to refer its origin to St. Charles Borromeo; we must account as the true founder the Apostle St. Paul, whose cipher it bears on its arms. I have been compelled to quit my cloister, now headquarters of the Section du Pont-Neuf, and adopt a secular habit.

"Nay, Father," said Brotteaux, scrutinizing Monsieur de Longuemare's frock, "your dress is token enough that you have not forsworn your profession; to look at it, one might think you had reformed your Order rather than forsaken it. It is your good heart makes you expose yourself in these austere habiliments to the insults of a godless populace."

"Yet I cannot very well," replied the ex-monk, "wear a blue coat, like a roisterer at a dance!"

"What I mention, Father, about your dress is by way of paying homage to your character and putting you on your guard against the risks you run."

"On the contrary, sir, it would be much better to inspirit me to confess my faith. For indeed, I am only too prone to fear danger. I have abandoned my habit, sir, which is a sort of apostasy; I would fain not have deserted, had it been possible, the House where God granted me for so many years the grace of a peaceable and retired life. I got leave to stay there, and I still continued to occupy my cell, while they turned the church and cloister into a sort of petty *hôtel de ville* they called the Section. I saw, sir, I saw them hack away the emblems of the Holy Verity; I saw the name of the Apostle Paul replaced by a convicted felon's cap. Sometimes I was actually present at the confabulations of the Section, where I heard amazing

errors propounded. At last I quitted this place of profanation and
went to live on the pension of a hundred pistoles allowed me by the
Assembly in a stable that stood empty, the horses having been requisitioned for the service of the armies. There I sing Mass for a few
of the faithful, who come to the office to bear witness to the eternity
of the Church of Jesus Christ."

"For my part, Father," replied the other, "if you care to know
my name, I am called Brotteaux, and I was a publican in former
days."

"Sir," returned the Père Longuemare, "I was aware by St.
Matthew's example that one may look for good counsel from a
publican."

"Father, you are too obliging."

"*Citoyen* Brotteaux," remarked Gamelin, "pray admire the virtues of the people, more hungry for justice than for bread; consider
how everyone here is ready to lose his place to chastise the thief.
These men and women, victims of such poverty and privation, are
of so stern a probity they cannot tolerate a dishonest act."

"It must indeed be owned," replied Brotteaux, "that in their
hearty desire to hang the pilferer, these folks were like to do a mischief to this good cleric, to his champion and to his champion's
champion. Their avarice itself and their selfish eagerness to safeguard their own welfare were motives enough; the thief in attacking
one of them threatened all; self-preservation urged them to punish
him. . . . At the same time, it is like enough the most part of these
workmen and goodwives are honest and keep their hands off other
folk's goods. From the cradle these sentiments have been instilled
in them by their father and mother, who have whipped them well
and soundly and inculcated the virtues through their backside."

Gamelin did not conceal the fact from his old neighbour that he
deemed such language unworthy of a philosopher.

"Virtue," said he, "is natural to mankind; God has planted the
seed of it in the heart of mortals."

Old Brotteaux was a sceptic and found in his atheism an abundant
source of self-satisfaction.

"I see this much, *citoyen* Gamelin, that, while a Revolutionary
for what is of this world, you are, where Heaven is concerned, of a
conservative, or even a reactionary temper. Robespierre and Marat
are the same as you. For me, I find it strange that Frenchmen who

51

will not put up with a mortal king any longer, insist on retaining an immortal tyrant, far more despotic and ferocious. For what is the Bastille, or even the *Chambre Ardente*[1] beside Hellfire? Humanity models its gods on its tyrants, and you, who reject the original, preserve the copy!"

"Oh! *citoyen!*" protested Gamelin, "are you not ashamed to hold such language? how can you confound the dark divinities born of ignorance and fear with the Author of Nature? Belief in a benevolent God is necessary for morality. The Supreme Being is the source of all the virtues, and a man cannot be a Republican if he does not believe in God. Robespierre knew this, who, as we all remember, had the bust of the philosopher Helvetius removed from the Hall of the Jacobins, because he had taught Frenchmen the lessons of slavery by preaching atheism. . . . I hope, at least, *citoyen* Brotteaux, that, as soon as the Republic has established the worship of Reason, you will not refuse your adhesion to so wise a religion!"

"I love reason, but I am no fanatic in my love," was Brotteaux's answer. "Reason is our guide and beacon-light; but when you have made a divinity of it, it will blind you and instigate you to crime," —and he proceeded to develop his thesis, standing both feet in the kennel, as he had once been used to perorate, seated in one of Baron d'Holbach's gilt armchairs, which, as he was fond of saying, formed the basis of natural philosophy.

"Jean Jacques Rousseau," he proceeded, "who was not without talents, particularly in music, was a scampish fellow who professed to derive his morality from Nature while all the time he got it from the dogmas of Calvin. Nature teaches us to devour each other and gives us the example of all the crimes and all the vices which the social state corrects or conceals. We should love virtue; but it is well to know that it is simply and solely a convenient expedient invented by men in order to live comfortably together. What we call morality is merely a desperate enterprise, a forlorn hope, on the part of our fellow creatures to reverse the order of the universe, which is strife and murder, the blind interplay of hostile forces. She destroys herself, and the more I think of things, the more convinced I am that the universe is mad. Theologians and philosophers, who make God the author of Nature and the architect of the universe, show Him

---

[1] *Chambre Ardente,*– under the ancien régime, a tribunal charged with the investigation of heinous crimes and having power to burn those found guilty.

to us as illogical and ill-conditioned. They declare Him benevolent, because they are afraid of Him, but they are forced to admit that His acts are atrocious. They attribute a malignity to him seldom to be found even in mankind. And that is how they get human beings to adore Him. For our miserable race would never lavish worship on just and benevolent deities from which they would have nothing to fear; they would not feel a barren gratitude for their benefits. Without purgatory and hell, your good God would be a mighty poor creature."

"Sir," said the Père Longuemare, "do not talk of Nature; you do not know what Nature is."

"Egad, I know it as well as you do, Father."

"You cannot know it, because you have not religion, and religion alone teaches us what Nature is, wherein it is good, and how it has been made evil. However, you must not expect me to answer you; God has vouchsafed me, to refute your errors, neither eloquence nor force of intellect. I should only be afraid, by my inadequate replies, of giving you occasion to blaspheme and further reasons for hardening your heart. I feel a strong desire to help you; yet the sole fruit of my importunate efforts would be to . . ."

The discussion was cut short by a tremendous shout coming from the head of the column to warn the whole regiment of famished citizens that the baker was opening his doors. The line began to push forward, but very, very slowly. A National Guard on duty admitted the purchasers one by one. The baker, his wife and boy presided over the sale, assisted by two Civil Commissaries. These, wearing a tricoloured riband round the left arm, saw that the customers belonged to the Section and were given their proper share in proportion to the number of mouths to be filled.

The *citoyen* Brotteaux made the quest of pleasure the one and only aim of life, holding that the reason and the senses, the sole judges when gods there were none, were unable to conceive any other. Accordingly, finding the painter's remarks somewhat overfull of fanaticism, and the monk's of simplicity, to please his taste, this wise man, bent on squaring his behaviour with his views and relieving the tedium of waiting, drew from the bulging pocket of his plum-coloured coat his Lucretius, now as always his chiefest solace and faithful comforter. The binding of red morocco was chafed by hard wear, and the *citoyen* Brotteaux had judiciously erased the coat of arms

that once embellished it,—three islets or, which his father the financier had bought for good money down. He opened the book at the
passage where the poet philosopher, who is for curing men of the
futile and mischievous passion of love, surprises a woman in the arms
of her serving-women in a state bound to offend all a lover's suscepti-
bilities. The *citoyen* Brotteaux read the lines, though not without
casting a surreptitious glance at the golden pate of the pretty girl in
front of him and enjoying a sniff of the heady perfume of the little
slut's hot skin. The poet Lucretius was a wise man, but he had only
one string to his bow; his disciple Brotteaux had several.

So he read on, taking two steps forward every quarter of an hour.
His ear, soothed by the grave and cadenced numbers of the Latin
Muse, was deaf to the women's scolding about the monstrous prices
of bread and sugar and coffee, candles and soap. In this calm and
unruffled mood he reached the threshold of the bakehouse. Behind
him, Évariste Gamelin could see over his head the gilt cornsheaf
surmounting the iron grating that filled the fan-light over the door.

When his turn came to enter the shop, he found the hampers and
lockers already emptied; the baker handed him the only scrap of
bread left, which did not weigh two pounds. Évariste paid his money
and the gate was slammed on his heels, for fear of a riot and the
people carrying the place by storm.

But there was no need to fear; these poor folks, trained to obedience
alike by their old-time oppressors and by their liberators of to-day,
slunk off with drooping heads and dragging feet.

As he reached the corner of the street, Gamelin caught sight of the
citoyenne Dumonteil, seated on a stone post, her nursling in her arms.
She sat there quite still; her face was colourless and her tearless eyes
seemed to see nothing. The infant was sucking her finger voraciously.
Gamelin stood a while in front of her, abashed and uncertain what
to do. She did not appear to see him.

He stammered something, then pulled out his pocket-knife, a
clasp-knife with a horn handle, cut his loaf in two and laid half on
the young mother's knee. She looked up at him in wonder; but he
had already turned the corner of the street.

On reaching home, Évariste found his mother sitting at the window darning stockings. With a light laugh he put his half of the
bread in her hand.

"You must forgive me, mother dear; I was tired out with standing about and exhausted by the heat, and out in the street there as I trudged home, mouthful by mouthful I have gobbled up half of our allowance. There's barely your share left,"—and as he spoke, he made a pretence of shaking the crumbs off his jacket.

Chapter 7

EMPLOYING a very old-fashioned locution, the *citoyenne* Gamelin had declared that by dint of eating chestnuts they would be turning into chestnuts. As a matter of fact, on that day, the 13th July, she and her son had made their midday dinner on a basin of chestnut porridge. As they were finishing this austere repast, a lady pushed open the door and the room was flooded in an instant with the splendour of her presence and the fragrance of her perfumes. Évariste recognised the *citoyenne* Rochemaure. Thinking she had mistaken the door and meant her visit for the *citoyen* Brotteaux, her friend of other days, he was already preparing to point her out the *ci-devant* aristocrat's garret or perhaps summon Brotteaux and so spare an elegant woman the task of scrambling up a mill-ladder; but she made it clear at once that the *citoyen* Évariste Gamelin and no other was the person she had come to see by announcing that she was happy to find him at home and was his servant to command.

They were not entirely strangers to each other, having met more than once in David's studio, in a box at the Assembly Hall, at the Jacobins, at Venua's restaurant. On these occasions she had been struck by his good looks and youth and interesting air.

Wearing a hat beribboned like a fairing and plumed like the headpiece of a Representative on mission, the *citoyenne* Rochemaure was wigged, painted, patched and scented. But her complexion was young and fresh behind all these disguises; these extravagant artificialities of fashion only betokened a frantic haste to enjoy life and the feverishness of these dreadful days when the morrow was so uncertain. Her corsage, with wide facings and enormous basques and all ablaze with huge steel buttons, was blood-red, and it was hard to tell, so aristocratic and so revolutionary at one and the same time was her array, whether it was the colours of the victims or of the

56

headsman that she sported. A young officer, a dragoon, accompanied her.

Dandling her long cane by its handle of mother-of-pearl, a tall, fine woman, of generous proportions and ample bosom, she made the circuit of the studio, and putting up to her grey eyes her double quizzing-glasses of gold, examined the painter's canvases with many smiles and exclamations of delight, admiring the handsome artist and flattering him in hopes of a return in kind.

"What," asked the *citoyenne*, "is that picture—it is so nobly conceived, so touching—of a gentle, beautiful woman standing by a young man lying sick?"

Gamelin told her it was meant to represent *Orestes tended by his sister Electra*, and that, had he been able to finish it, it might perhaps have been the least unsatisfactory of his works.

"The subject," he went on to say, "is taken from the *Orestes* of Euripides. I had read, in a translation of this tragedy made years ago, a scene that filled me with admiration,—the one where the young Electra, raising her brother on his bed of pain, wipes away the froth that gathers on his lips, puts aside the locks that blind his eyes and beseeches the brother she loves to hearken to what she will tell him while the Furies are at peace for the moment. . . . As I read and re-read this translation, I seemed to be aware of a kind of fog that shrouded the forms of Greek perfection, a fog I could not drive away. I pictured the original text to myself as more nervous and pitched in a different accent. Feeling a keen desire to get a precise idea of the thing, I went to Monsieur Gail, who was the Professor of Greek at the Collège de France (this was in '91), and begged him to expound the scene to me word by word. He did what I asked, and I then saw that the Ancients are much more simple and homely than people think. Thus, for instance, Electra says to Orestes: 'Dear brother, what joy it gave me to see thee sleep! Shall I help thee to rise?' And Orestes answers: 'Yes, help me, take me in thy arms, and wipe away the spume that still clings about my mouth and eyes. Put thy bosom against mine and part from my brow my tangled hair, for it blinds my eyes. . . .' My mind still full of this poetry, so young and vivid, ringing with these simple, strong phrases, I sketched the picture you see there, *citoyenne*."

The painter, who, as a rule, spoke so sparingly of his works, waxed eloquent on the subject of this one. At an encouraging gesture from the *citoyenne* Rochemaure, who lifted her quizzing-glasses in token of attention, he continued:

"Hennequin has depicted the madness of Orestes in masterly fashion. But Orestes appeals to us still more poignantly in his sorrow than when he is distraught. What a fate was his! It was filial piety, obedience to a sacred obligation, drove him to commit his dreadful deed,—a sin the gods cannot but pardon, but which men will never condone. To avenge outraged justice, he has repudiated Nature, has made himself a monster, has torn out his own heart. But his spirit remains unbroken under the weight of his horrible, yet innocent crime. . . . That is what I would fain have exhibited in my group of brother and sister." He stepped up to the canvas and looked at it not without satisfaction.

"Parts of the picture," he said, "are pretty nearly finished; the head and arm of Orestes, for instance."

"It is an admirable composition. . . . And Orestes reminds me of you, *citoyen* Gamelin."

"You think he is like me?" exclaimed the painter, with a grave smile.

She took the chair Gamelin offered her. The young dragoon stood beside her, his hand on the back of the chair on which she sat. Which showed plainly that the Revolution was an accomplished fact, for under the ancien régime, no man would ever, in company, have touched so much as with the tip of a finger, the seat occupied by a lady. In those days a gentleman was trained and broken in to the laws of politeness, sometimes pretty hard laws, and taught to understand that a scrupulous self-restraint in public places gives a peculiar zest to the sweet familiarity of the boudoir, and that to lose your respectful awe of a woman, you must first have that feeling.

Louise Masché de Rochemaure, daughter of a Lieutenant of the King's Hunt, widow of a Procureur and, for twenty years, the faithful mistress of the financier Brotteaux des Ilettes, had fallen in with the new ideas. She was to be seen, in July, 1790, digging the soil of the Champ de Mars. Her strong inclination to side with the powers that be had carried her readily enough along a political path that started with the Feuillants and led by way of the Girondins to end on the summit of *the Mountain*, while at the same time a spirit of compromise, a passion for conversion and a certain aptitude for intrigue still attached her to the aristocratic and anti-revolutionary

party. She was to be met everywhere,—at coffee houses and thea-
tres, fashionable restaurants, gaming-saloons, drawing-rooms, newspaper offices and ante-chambers of Committees. The Revolution
yielded her a hundred satisfactions—novelty and amusement, smiles
and pleasures, business ventures and profitable speculations. Combining political with amorous intrigue, playing the harp, drawing
landscapes, singing ballads, dancing Greek dances, giving supper
parties, entertaining pretty women, much as the Comtesse de Beau-
fort and the actress Mademoiselle Descoings, presiding all night long
over a *trente-et-un* or *biribi* table and an adept at *rouge et noir*, she
still found time to be charitable to her friends. Inquisitive and inter-
fering, giddy-pated and frivolous, she understood men but knew
nothing of the masses; as indifferent to the creed she professed as to
the opinions she felt bound to repudiate, understanding nothing
whatever of all that was happening in the country, she was enterprising, intrepid, and full of audacity from sheer ignorance of danger and an unbounded confidence in the efficacy of her charms.

The soldier who escorted her was in the heyday of youth. A brazen
helmet decorated with a panther skin and the crest set off with a
crimson cock's-comb shaded his fresh young face and displayed a
long and terrific mane that swept his back. His red jacket was cut
short and square, barely reaching to the waist, the better to show
off his elegant figure. In his girdle he carried an enormous sabre, the
hilt of which was a glittering eagle's beak. A pair of flapped breeches
of sky blue moulded the fine muscles of his legs and was braided in
rich arabesques of a darker blue on the thighs. He might have been
a dancer dressed for some warlike and dashing rôle, in *Achilles at
Scyros* or *Alexander's Wedding-Feast*, in a costume designed by a pupil of David with the one idea of accentuating every line of the shape.

Gamelin had a vague recollection of having seen him before. He
was, in fact, the same young soldier he had come upon a fortnight
previously haranguing the people from the arcades of the Théâtre de
la Nation.

The *citoyenne* Rochemaure introduced him by name:

"The *citoyen* Henry, Member of the Revolutionary Committee of
the Section of the Rights of Man."

She had him always at her heels,—a mirror of gallantry and a living and walking guarantee of patriotism.

The *citoyenne* complimented Gamelin on his talents and asked him if he would be willing to design a card for a protégée of hers, a fashionable milliner. He would, of course, choose an appropriate *motif*, —a woman trying on a scarf before a cheval glass, for instance, or a young workwoman carrying a bandbox on her arm.

She had heard several artists mentioned as competent to execute a little matter of the sort,—Fragonard *fils*, young Ducis, as well as a certain Prud'hon; but she would rather apply to the *citoyen* Évariste Gamelin. However, she made no definite proposal on this head and it was evident she had mentioned the commission merely by way of starting the conversation. In truth she had come for something quite different. She wanted the *citoyen* Gamelin to do her a favour; knowing he was a friend of the *citoyen* Marat, she had come to ask him to introduce her to the Friend of the People, with whom she desired an interview.

Gamelin replied that he was too insignificant an individual to present her to Marat, besides which, she had no need of anyone to be her sponsor; Marat, albeit overwhelmed with business, was not the inaccessible person he was said to be,—and, added Gamelin:

"He will receive you, *citoyenne*, if you are in distress; his great heart makes him compassionate to all who suffer. He will likewise receive you if you have any revelation to make concerning the public weal; he has vowed his days to the unmasking of traitors."

The *citoyenne* Rochemaure answered that she would be happy to greet in Marat an illustrious citizen, who had rendered great services to his country, who was capable of rendering greater still, and that she was anxious to bring the legislator in question into relation with friends of hers of good repute and good will, philanthropists favoured by fortune and competent to provide him with new means of satisfying his ardent affection for humanity.

"It is very desirable," she concluded, "to make the rich co-operate in securing public prosperity."

In actual fact, the *citoyenne* had promised the banker Morhardt to arrange a dinner where he and Marat should meet.

Morhardt, a Swiss like the Friend of the People, had entered into a combination with several deputies of the Convention, Julien (of Toulouse), Delaunay (of Angers) and the ex-Capuchin Chabot, to speculate in the shares of the *Compagnie des Indes*. The game was very simple,—to bring down the price of these shares to 650 livres by proposing motions pointing in the direction of confiscation, in

order to buy up the greatest possible number at this figure and then push them up to 4,000 or 5,000 livres by dint of proposals of a reassuring nature. But for Chabot, Julien, Delaunay, their little ways were too notorious, while suspicions were rife of Lacroix, Fabre d'Églantine, and even Danton. The arch-speculator, the Baron de Batz, was looking for new confederates in the Convention and had advised Morhardt to sound Marat.

This idea of the anti-revolutionary speculators was not so extravagant as might have been supposed at the first blush. It was always the way of these gentry to form alliance with those in power at the moment, and by virtue of his popularity, his pen, his character, Marat was a power to be reckoned with. The Girondists were near shipwreck; the Dantonists, battered by the hurricane, had lost their hold on the helm. Robespierre, the idol of the people, was a man jealous of his scrupulous honesty, full of suspicion, impossible to approach. The great thing was to get round Marat, to secure his good will against the day when he should be dictator—and everything pointed to this consummation,—his popularity, his ambition, his eagerness to recommend heroic measures. And it might be, after all, Marat would re-establish order, the finances, the prosperity of the country. More than once he had risen in revolt against the zealots who were for outbidding him in fanaticism; for some time past he had been denouncing the demagogues as vehemently as the moderates. After inciting the people to sack the "cornerers'" shops and hang them over their own counters, he was now exhorting the citizens to be calm and prudent. He was growing into an administrator.

In spite of certain rumours disseminated against him as against all the other chiefs of the Revolution, these pirates of the money-market did not believe he could be corrupted, but they did know him to be vain and credulous, and they hoped to win him over by flattery and still more by a condescending friendliness which they looked upon as the most seductive form of flattery from men like themselves. They counted, thanks to him, on blowing hot and cold on all the securities they might wish to buy and sell, and making him serve their interests while supposing himself to be acting solely for the public good.

Great as a go-between, albeit she was still of an age for amours on her own account, the *citoyenne* Rochemaure had made it her mission to bring together the legislator-journalist and the banker, and in her extravagant imagination she already saw the man of the underworld, the man whose hands were yet red with the blood of the September massacres, a partner in the game of the financiers whose agent she was; she pictured him drawn by his very warmth of feeling and unsophisticated candour into the whirlpool of speculation, a recruit to the côteries she loved of "corner" makers, contractors, foreign emissaries, gamblers, and women of gallantry.

She insisted on the *citoyen* Gamelin taking her to see the Friend of the People, who lived quite near, in the Rue des Cordeliers, near the church. After some little show of reluctance, the painter acceded to the *citoyenne's* wishes.

The dragoon Henry was invited to join them in the visit, but declined, declaring he meant to keep his liberty of action, even towards the *citoyen* Marat, who, he felt no doubt, had rendered services to the Republic, but was weakening nowadays; had he not, in his news sheet, counselled resignation as the proper thing for the people of Paris?

And the young man, in a sweet voice, broken by long-drawn sighs, deplored the fate of the Republic, betrayed by the men in whom she had put her trust,—Danton rejecting the notion of a tax on the rich, Robespierre opposing the permanence of the Sections, Marat, whose pusillanimous counsels were paralyzing the enthusiasm of the citizens.

"Ah!" he cried, "how feeble such men appear beside Leclerc and Jacques Roux! . . . Roux! Leclerc! *ye* are the true friends of the people!"

Gamelin did not hear these remarks, which would have angered him; he had gone into the next room to don his blue coat.

"You may well be proud of your son," observed the *citoyenne* Rochemaure, addressing the *citoyenne* Gamelin. "He is a great man; talent and character both make him so."

In answer, the widow Gamelin gave a good account of her son, yet without making much boast of him before a lady of high station, for she had been taught in her childhood that the first duty of the lowly is humility towards the great. She was of a complaining bent, having indeed only too good cause and finding in such jeremiads a salve for her griefs. She was garrulous in her revelations of all the hardships she had to bear to any whom she supposed in a position to relieve them, and Madame de Rochemaure seemed to belong to that class. She made the most, therefore, of this favourable opportunity and told a long and breathless story of their distresses,—how mother and son were both dying of slow starvation. Pictures could not be sold any more; the Revolution had killed business dead. Victuals were scarce and too dear for words. . . .

The good dame poured out her lamentations with all the loose-lipped volubility her halting tongue was capable of, so as to get them all finished by the time her son, whose pride would not brook such whining, should reappear. She was bent on attaining her object in the shortest possible time,—that of touching a lady whom she deemed rich and influential, and enlisting her sympathy in her boy's future. She felt sure that Évariste's good looks were an asset on her side to move the heart of a well-born lady. And so they were; the *citoyenne* Rochemaure proved tender-hearted and was melted to think of Évariste's and his mother's sufferings. She made plans to alleviate them; she had rich men amongst her friends and would get them to buy the artist's pictures.

"The truth is," she added, with a smile, "there is still money in France, but it keeps in hiding."

Better still, now Art was ruined, she would obtain Évariste a post in Morhardt's bank or with the Brothers Perregaux, or a place as clerk in the office of an army contractor.

Then she reflected that this was not what a man of his character needed; and, after a moment's thought, she nodded in sign that she had hit the nail on the head:

"There are still several jurymen left to be appointed on the Revolutionary Tribunal. Juryman, magistrate, that is the thing to suit your son. I have friendly relations with the Committee of Public Safety. I know Robespierre the elder personally; his brother frequently sups at my house. I will speak to them. I will get a word said to Montané, Dumas, Fouquier."

The *citoyenne* Gamelin, bursting with excitement and gratitude, put a finger to her lip; Évariste was coming back into the studio.

He escorted the *citoyenne* Rochemaure down the gloomy staircase, the steps of which, whether of wood or tiled, were coated with an ancient layer of dirt.

On the Pont-Neuf, where the sun, now near its setting, threw a lengthened shadow from the pedestal that had borne the Bronze Horse and was now gay with the National colours, a crowd of men and women of the people gathered in little groups were listening to some tale that was being told them. Consternation reigned and a heavy silence, broken at intervals by groans and fierce cries. Many were making off at a rapid pace in the direction of the Rue de Thionville, erstwhile Rue Dauphine; Gamelin joined one of these groups and heard the news—that Marat had just been assassinated.

Little by little the tidings were confirmed and particulars became known; he had been murdered in his bath by a woman who had come expressly from Caen to commit the crime.

Some thought she had escaped; but the majority declared she had been arrested.

There they stood like sheep without a shepherd, thinking sadly:

"Marat, the tender-hearted, the humane, Marat our benefactor, is no longer there to guide us, Marat who was never deceived, who saw through every subterfuge and never feared to reveal the truth! . . . What can we do, what is to become of us? We have lost our adviser, our champion, our friend." They knew very well whence the blow had come, and who had directed the woman's arm. They groaned aloud:

"Marat has been struck down by the same criminal hands that are bent on our extermination. His death is the signal for the slaughter of all good patriots."

Different reports were current, as to the circumstances of the tragic event and the last words of the victim; endless questions were asked concerning the assassin, all that anyone knew was that it was a young woman sent by those traitors, the Federalists. Baring teeth and nails, the *citoyennes* devoted the culprit to condign punishment; deeming the guillotine too merciful a death, they demanded this monster of iniquity should be scourged, broken on the wheel, torn limb from limb, and racked their brains to invent new tortures.

An armed body of National Guards was haling to the Section headquarters a man of determined mien. His clothes were in tatters, and streams of blood trickled down his white face. He had been overheard saying that Marat had earned his fate by his constant incitements to pillage and massacre, and it was only with great difficulty that the Guards had saved him from the fury of the populace. A hundred fingers pointed him out as the accomplice of the assassin, and threats of death followed him as he was led away.

Gamelin was stunned by the blow. A few hot tears blistered his burning eyes. With the grief he felt as a disciple mingled solicitude for the popular idol, and these combined feelings tore at his heart-strings. He thought to himself:

"After Le Peltier, after Bourdon, Marat! . . . I foresee the fate of the patriots; massacred on the Champ de Mars, at Nancy, at Paris, they will perish one and all." And he thought of Wimpfen, the traitor, who only a while before, at the head of sixty thousand Royalists, was marching on Paris, and who, had he not been stopped at Vernon by the gallant patriots, would have devoted the heroic city to fire and slaughter.

And how many perils still remained, how many criminal designs, how many treasonable plots, which only Marat's perspicacity and vigilance could unravel and foil! Now he was dead, who was there to denounce Custine loitering in idleness in the Camp of Cæsar and refusing to relieve Valenciennes, Biron tarrying inactive in the Lower Vendée letting Saumur be taken and Nantes blockaded, Dillon betraying the fatherland in the Argonne? . . .

Meantime, all about him, rose momentarily higher the sinister cry:

"Marat is dead; the aristocrats have killed him!"

As he was on his way, his heart bursting with grief and hate and love, to pay a last mark of respect to the martyr of liberty, an old country-woman, wearing the coif of the Limousin peasantry, accosted him to ask if the Monsieur Marat who had been murdered was not Monsieur le Curé Mara, of Saint-Pierre-de-Queyroix.

Chapter 8

IT WAS the even of the Festival, a calm, bright evening, and Élodie hanging on Évariste's arm, was strolling with him about the Champ de la Fédération. Workmen were hastily completing their task of erecting columns, statues, temples, a "mountain," an altar of the fatherland. Huge symbolic figures, Hercules (representing the people) brandishing his club, Nature suckling the Universe from her inexhaustible breasts, were rising at a moment's notice in the capital that, tortured by famine and fear, was listening for the dreaded sound of the Austrian cannon on the road from Meaux. La Vendée was making good its check before Nantes by a series of startling victories. A ring of fire and flame and hate was drawn about the great revolutionary city.

And meantime, she was preparing a superb welcome, like the sovereign of a vast empire, for the deputies of the primary Assemblies which had accepted the Constitution. Federalism was on its knees; the Republic, one and indivisible, would surely vanquish all its enemies.

Waving his arm towards the thronged expanse:

"There it was," cried Évariste, "that on the 17th July, '91, the infamous Bailly ordered the people to be shot down at the foot of the altar of the fatherland. Passavant, the grenadier, who witnessed the massacre, returned to his house, tore his coat from his back and cried: 'I have sworn to die with Liberty; Liberty is no more, and I fulfil my oath,'—and blew out his brains."

All this time artists and peaceful citizens were examining the preparations for the festival, their faces showing as joyless a joy in life as their lives were dull and joyless; to their minds the mightiest events shrank into insignificance and grew as insipid as they were themselves. Couple by couple they went, carrying in their arms or holding by the hand or letting them run on in front children as unpre-

66

possessing as their parents and promising to grow up no whit happier, who in due course would give birth to children of their own as poor in spirit and looks as they. Yet now and again a young girl would pass, tall and fair and desirable, rousing in young men a not ignoble passion to possess, and in the old regret for the bliss they had missed.

Near the *École Militaire* Évariste pointed out to his companion the Egyptian statues designed by David on Roman models of the age of Augustus, and they overheard a Parisian, an old man with powdered hair, ejaculate to himself:

"Egad! you might think yourself on the banks of the Nile!"

It was three days since Élodie had seen her lover, and serious events had befallen meantime at the *Amour peintre*. The *citoyen* Blaise had been denounced to the Committee of General Security for fraudulent dealings in the matter of supplies to the armies. Fortunately for himself, the print-dealer was well known in his Section; the Committee of Surveillance of the *Section des Piques* had stood guarantee of his patriotism with the general committee and had completely justified his conduct.

This alarming incident Élodie now recounted in trembling accents, concluding:

"We are quiet now, but the alarm was a hot one. A little more and my father would have been clapped in prison. If the danger had lasted a few hours more, I should have come to you, Évariste, to make interest for him among your influential friends."

Évariste vouchsafed no reply to this, but Élodie was very far from realizing all his silence portended.

They went on hand in hand along the banks of the river, discoursing of their mutual fondness in the phrases of Julie and Saint-Preux; the good Jean-Jacques gave them the colours to paint and prank their love withal.

The Municipality of Paris had wrought a miracle,—abundance reigned for a day in the famished city. A fair was installed on the Place des Invalides, beside the Seine, where hucksters in booths sold sausages, saveloys, chitterlings, hams decked with laurels, Nanterre cakes, gingerbreads, pancakes, four-pound loaves, lemonade and wine. There were stalls also for the sale of patriotic songs, cockades, tricolour ribands, purses, pinchbeck watch-chains and all sorts of cheap gewgaws. Stopping before the display of a petty jeweller,

Évariste selected a silver ring having a head of Marat in relief with a silk handkerchief wound about the brows, and put it on Élodie's finger.

The same Gamelin proceeded to the Rue de l'Arbre-Sec to call on the *citoyenne* Rochemaure, who had sent for him on pressing business. She received him in her bedchamber, reclining on a couch in a seductive dishabille.

While the *citoyenne's* attitude expressed a voluptuous languor, everything about her spoke of her accomplishments, her diversions, her talents,—a harp beside an open harpsichord, a guitar on a chair, an embroidering frame with a square of satin stretched on it, a half-finished miniature on a table among papers and books, a bookcase in dire disorder as if rifled by the hand of a fair reader as eager to know as to feel.

She gave him her hand to kiss, and addressed him:

"Greeting, sir juryman! . . . This very day Robespierre the elder gave me a letter in your favour to be handed to the President Herman, a very well-turned letter, pretty much to this effect:

"'I bring to your notice the *citoyen* Gamelin, commendable alike for his talents and for his patriotism. I have made it my duty to make known to you a patriot whose principles are good and his conduct steadfast in the right line of revolution. You will not let slip the opportunity of being useful to a Republican. . . .' This letter I carried there and then to the President Herman, who received me with an exquisite politeness and signed your appointment on the spot. This thing is done."

After a moment's pause:

"*Citoyenne*," said Gamelin, "though I have not a morsel of bread to give my mother, I swear on my honour I accept the duties of a juror only to serve the Republic and avenge her on her foes."

The *citoyenne* thought this but a cold way of expressing gratitude and considered the sentiment high-flown. The young man was no adept, she suspected, at graceful courtesies. But she was too great an admirer of youth not to excuse some little lack of polish. Gamelin was a handsome fellow, and that was merit enough in her eyes. "We will form him," she said to herself. So she invited him to her suppers to which she welcomed her friends every evening after the theatre.

"You will meet at my house men of wit and talent,—Elleviou,

Talma, the *citoyen* Vigée, who turns bouts-rimés with a marvellous aptitude. The *citoyen* François read us his 'Paméla' the other day, the piece rehearsing at the present moment at the Théâtre de la Nation. The style is elegant and chaste, as everything is that comes from the *citoyen* François' pen. The plot is touching; it brought tears to all our eyes. It is the young *citoyenne* Lange who is to take the part of 'Paméla.'"

"I believe it if you say so, *citoyenne*," answered Gamelin, "but the Théâtre de la Nation is scarcely National, and it is hard on the *citoyen* François that his works should be produced on the boards degraded by the contemptible verses of a Laya; the people has not forgotten the scandal of the *Ami des Lois*. . . ."

"Nay, *citoyen* Gamelin, say what you will of Laya; he is none of my friends."

It was not purely out of kindness that the *citoyenne* had employed her credit to get Gamelin appointed to a much envied post; after what she had done for him and what peradventure she might come to do for him in the future, she counted on binding him closely to her interests and in that way securing for herself a protector connected with a tribunal she might one day or another have to reckon with; for the fact is, she was in constant correspondence with the French provinces and foreign countries, and at that date such a circumstance was ground enough for suspicion.

"Do you often go to the theatre, *citoyen?*"

As she asked the question, Henry, the dragoon, entered the room, looking more charming than the youthful Bathyllus. A brace of enormous pistols was passed through his belt.

He kissed the fair *citoyenne's* hand. Turning to him:

"There stands the *citoyen* Évariste Gamelin," she said, "for whose sake I have spent the day at the Committee of General Security, and who is an ungrateful wretch. Scold him for me."

"Ah! *citoyenne*," cried the young soldier, "you have seen our Legislators at the Tuileries. What an afflicting sight! Is it seemly the Representatives of a free people should sit beneath the roof of a despot? The same lustres that once shone on the plots of Capet and the orgies of Antoinette now illumine the deliberations of our lawmakers. 'Tis enough to make Nature shudder."

"Pray, congratulate the *citoyen* Gamelin," was all her answer, "he is appointed juryman on the Revolutionary Tribunal."

"My compliments, *citoyen!*" said Henry. "I am rejoiced to see a man of your character invested with these functions. But, to speak truth, I have small confidence in this systematic justice, set up by the moderates of the Convention, in this complaisant Nemesis that is considerate to conspirators and merciful to traitors, that hardly dares strike a blow at the Federalists and fears to summon *the Austrian* to the bar. No, it is not the Revolutionary Tribunal will save the Republic. They are very culpable, the men who, in the desperate situation we are in, have arrested the flowing torrent of popular justice!"

"Henry," interrupted the *citoyenne* Rochemaure, "pass me that scent bottle, please. . . ."

On reaching home, Gamelin found his mother and old Brotteaux playing a game of piquet by the light of a smoky tallow-candle. At the moment the old woman was calling "sequence of kings" without the smallest scruple.

When she heard her son was appointed juryman, she kissed him in a transport of triumph, thinking what an honour it was for both of them and that henceforth they would have plenty to eat every day.

"I am proud and happy," she declared, "to be the mother of a juryman. Justice is a fine thing, and of all the most necessary; without justice the weak would be harassed every moment of their lives. And I think you will give right judgment, Évariste, my own boy; for from a child I have found you just and kind-hearted in all concerns. You could never endure wrong-doing and always tried what you could to hinder violence. You compassionated the unfortunate and that is the finest jewel in a juror's crown. . . . But tell me, Évariste, how are you dressed in your grand Tribunal?"

Gamelin informed her that the judges wore a hat with black plumes, but that the jury had no special costume, that they were dressed in their every-day attire.

"It would be better," returned the good woman, "if they wore wig and gown; it would inspire more respect. Though you are mostly dressed carelessly, you are a handsome man and you set off your clothes; but the majority of men need some fine feathers to make them look imposing; yes, the jury should have wigs and gowns."

The *citoyenne* had heard say that the duties of a juror of the Tribunal carried a salary; and she had no hesitation in asking the question whether the emoluments were enough to live respectably on, for a juryman, she opined, ought to cut a good figure in the world.

She was pleased to hear that each juror received an allowance of eighteen livres for every sitting and that the multiplicity of crimes against the security of the State obliged the court to sit very frequently.

Old Brotteaux gathered up the cards, rose from the table and addressing Gamelin:

"Citoyen," he said, "you are invested with an august and redoubtable office. I congratulate you on lending the light of your integrity to a tribunal more trustworthy and less fallible perhaps than any other, because it searches out good and evil, not in themselves and in their essence, but solely in relation to tangible interests and plain and obvious sentiments. You will have to determine betwixt hate and love, which is done spontaneously, not betwixt truth and falsehood, to discriminate which is impossible for the feeble mind of man. Giving judgment after the impulses of your heart, you will run no risk of mistake, inasmuch as the verdict will be good provided it satisfy the passions that are your sacred law. But, all the same, if I was your President, I should imitate Bridoie, I should appeal to the arbitrament of the dice. In matters of justice it is still the surest plan."

Chapter 9

ÉVARISTE GAMELIN was to enter on his duties on the 14th September, when the reorganization of the Tribunal was complete, according to which it was henceforth subdivided into four sections with fifteen jurors for each. The prisons were full to overflowing; the Public Prosecutor was working eighteen hours a day. Defeats in the field, revolts in the provinces, conspiracies, plots, betrayals, the Convention had one panacea for them all,—terror. The Gods were a-thirst.

The first act of the new juror was to pay a visit of ceremony to the President Herman, who charmed him by the amiability of his conversation and the courtesy of his bearing. A compatriot and friend of Robespierre's, whose sentiments he shared, he showed every sign of a feeling and virtuous temper. He was deeply attached to those humane sentiments, too long foreign to the heart of our judges, that redound to the everlasting glory of a Dupaty and a Beccaria. He looked with complacency on the greater mildness of modern manners as evidenced, in judicial matters, by the abolition of torture and of ignominious or cruel forms of punishment. He was rejoiced to see the death penalty, once so recklessly inflicted and employed till quite lately for the repression of the most trifling offences, applied less frequently and reserved for heinous crimes. For his own part, he agreed with Robespierre and would gladly have seen it abolished altogether, except only in cases touching the public safety. At the same time, he would have deemed it treason to the State not to adjudge the punishment of death for crimes against the National Sovereignty.

All his colleagues were of like mind; the old Monarchical idea of reasons of State still inspired the Revolutionary Tribunal. Eight centuries of absolute power had moulded the magisterial conscience, and it was by the principles of Divine Right that the Court even now tried and sentenced the enemies of Liberty.

72

The same day Évariste Gamelin sought an interview with the Public Prosecutor, the *citoyen* Fouquier, who received him in the Cabinet where he worked with his clerk of the court. He was a sturdily built man, with a rough voice, catlike eyes, bearing in his pockmarked face and leaden complexion marks of the mischief wrought by a sedentary and indoor life on a vigorous constitution adapted to the open air and violent exercise. Towering piles of papers shut him in like the walls of a tomb, and it was plain to see he was in his element amid all these dreadful documents that seemed like to bury him alive. His conversation was that of a hard-working magistrate, a man devoted to his task and whose mind never left the narrow groove of his official duties. His fiery breath reeked of the brandy he took to keep up his strength; but the liquor seemed never to fly to his brain, so clear-headed, albeit entirely commonplace, was every word he uttered.

He lived in a small suite of rooms in the Palais de Justice with his young wife, who had given him twin boys. His wife, an aunt Henriette and the maid-servant Pélagie made up the whole household. He was good and kind to these women. In a word, he was an excellent person in his family and professional relations, with a scarcity of ideas and a total lack of imagination.

Gamelin could not help being struck unpleasantly by the close resemblance in temper and ways of thought between the new magistrates and their predecessors under the old régime. In fact, they were of the old régime; Herman had held the office of Advocate General to the Council of Artois; Fouquier was a former Procureur at the Châtelet. They had preserved their character, whereas Gamelin believed in a revolutionary palingenesis.

Quitting the precincts of the court, he passed along the great gallery of the Palace and halted in front of the shops where articles of every sort and kind were exposed for sale in the most attractive fashion. Standing before the *citoyenne* Ténot's stall, he turned over sundry historical, political, and philosophical works:—"The Chains of Slavery," "An Essay on Despotism," "The Crimes of Queens." "Very good!" he thought, "here is Republican stuff!" and he asked the woman if she sold a great many of these books. She shook her head:

"The only things that sell are songs and romances,"— and pulling a duodecimo volume out of a drawer;

"Here," she told him, "here we have something good."

Évariste read the title: "La Religieuse en chemise," "The Nun in dishabille!"

Before the next shop he came upon Philippe Desmahis, who, with a tender, conquering-hero air, among the *citoyenne* Saint-Jorre's perfumes and powders and sachets, was assuring the fair trades-woman of his undying love, promising to paint her portrait and beg-ging her to vouchsafe him a moment's talk that evening in the Tuileries gardens. There was no resisting him; persuasion sat on his lips and beamed from his eye. The *citoyenne* Saint-Jorre was listen-ing without a word, her eyes on the ground, only too ready to believe him.

Wishing to familiarize himself with the awful duties imposed on him, the new juror resolved to mingle with the throng and look on at a case before the Tribunal as a member of the general public. He climbed the great stairs on which a vast crowd was seated as in an amphitheatre and pushed his way into the ancient Hall of the Parle-ment of Paris.

This was crammed to suffocation; some General or other was tak-ing his trial. For in those days, as old Brotteaux put it, "the Conven-tion, copying the example of His Britannic Majesty's Government, made a point of arraigning beaten Generals, in default of traitorous Generals, the latter taking good care not to stand their trial. Not that a beaten General," Brotteaux would add, "is necessarily crim-inal, for in the nature of things there must be one in every battle. But there's nothing like condemning a General to death for giving encouragement to others."

Several had already appeared before the Tribunal; they were all alike, these empty-headed, opinionated soldiers with the brains of a sparrow in an ox's skull. This particular commander was pretty nearly as ignorant of the sieges and battles of his own campaign as the magistrates who were questioning him; both sides, prosecution and defence, were lost in a fog of effectives, objectives, munitions and ammunitions, marches and counter-marches. But the mass of citizens listening to these obscure and never-ending details could see behind the half-witted soldier the bare and bleeding breast of the fatherland enduring a thousand deaths; and by look and voice urged

74

the jurymen, sitting quietly on their bench, to use their verdict as a club to fell the foes of the Republic.

Évariste was firmly convinced of one thing,—what they had to strike at in the pitiful creature was the two dread monsters that were battening on the fatherland, revolt and defeat. What a to-do to discover if this particular soldier was innocent or guilty! When La Vendée was recovering heart, when Toulon was surrendering to the enemy, when the Army of the Rhine was recoiling before the victors of Mayence, when the Army of the North, cowering in Cæsar's Camp, might be taken at a blow by the Imperialists, the English, the Dutch, now masters of Valenciennes, the one important thing was to teach the Generals of the Republic to conquer or to die. To see yonder feeble-witted muddle-pated veteran losing himself under cross-examination among his maps as he had done before in the plains of Northern France, Gamelin longed to yell "death! death!" with the rest, and fled from the Hall of Audience to escape the temptation.

At the meeting of the Section, the newly appointed juryman received the congratulations of the President Olivier, who made him swear on the old high altar of the Barnabites, now altar of the fatherland, to stifle in his heart, in the sacred name of humanity, every human weakness.

Gamelin, with uplifted right hand, invoked as witness of his oath the august shade of Marat, martyr of Liberty, whose bust had lately been set up against a pillar of the erstwhile church, facing that of Le Peltier.

There was some applause, interrupted by cries of protest. The meeting was a stormy one; at the entrance of the nave stood a group of members of the Section, armed with pikes and shouting clamorously:

"It is anti-Republican," declared the President, "to carry arms at a meeting of free citizens,"—and he ordered the muskets and pikes to be deposited there and then in the erstwhile sacristy.

A hunchback, with blazing eyes and lips drawn back so as to show the teeth, the *citoyen* Beauvisage, of the Committee of Vigilance, mounted to the pulpit, now become the speakers' tribune and surmounted by a red cap of Liberty.

"The Generals are betraying us," he vociferated, "and surrendering our armies to the enemy. The Imperialists are pushing forward their cavalry around Péronne and Saint-Quentin. Toulon has been given up to the English, who are landing fourteen thousand men there. The foes of the Republic are busy with plots in the very bosom of the Convention. In the capital conspiracies without number are afoot to deliver *the Austrian*. At this very moment while I speak there runs a rumour that the Capet brat has escaped from the Temple and is being borne in triumph to Saint-Cloud by those who would fain re-erect the tyrant's throne in his favour. The dearness of food, the depreciation of the assignats are the direct result of manœuvres carried out in our own homes, beneath our very eyes, by the agents of the foreigners. In the name of public safety I call upon the new juryman, our fellow-citizen, to show no pity to conspirators and traitors."

As he left the tribune, cries rose among the audience: "Down with the Revolutionary Tribunal! Down with the Moderates!"

A stout, rosy-faced man, the *citoyen* Dupont senior, a joiner living in the Place de Thionville, mounted the tribune, announcing that he wished to ask a question of the new juror. Then he demanded of Gamelin what attitude he meant to take up in the matter of the Brissotins and of the widow Capet.

Évariste was timid and unpractised in public speaking. But indignation gave him eloquence. He rose with a pale face and said in a voice of suppressed emotion:

"I am a magistrate. I am responsible to my conscience only. Any promise I might make you would be against my duty, which is to speak in the Court and hold my peace elsewhere. I have ceased to know you. It is mine to give judgment; I know neither friends nor enemies."

The meeting, made up like all meetings of divers elements and subject to sudden and incalculable moods, approved these sentiments. But the *citoyen* Dupont returned to the charge; he could not forgive Gamelin for having secured a post he had coveted himself.

"I understand," he said, "I even approve the juror's scruples. They say he is a patriot; it is for him to examine his conscience and see if it permits him to sit on a tribunal intended to destroy the enemies of the Republic and resolved to spare them. There are circumstances in which a good citizen is bound to repudiate all complicity. Is it not averred that more than one juror of this tribunal has let himself be corrupted by the gold of the accused, and that the President Montané falsified the procedure to save the head of the woman Corday?"

At these words the hall resounded with vehement applause. The vaults were still reverberating with the uproar when Fortuné Trubert mounted the tribune. He had grown thinner than ever in the last few months. His face was pale and the cheekbones seemed ready to pierce the reddened skin; his eyes had a glassy look under the inflamed lids.

"*Citoyens*," he began, in a weak, breathless voice that yet had a strangely penetrating quality, "we cannot suspect the Revolutionary Tribunal without at the same time suspecting the Convention and the Committee of Public Safety from which it derives its powers. The *citoyen* Beauvisage has alarmed us, showing us the President Montané tampering with the course of justice in favour of a culprit. Why did he not add, to relieve our fears, that on the denunciation of the Public Prosecutor, Montané has been dismissed his office and thrown into prison? . . . Is it impossible to watch over the public safety without casting suspicion on all and sundry? Is there no talent, no virtue left in the Convention? Robespierre, Couthon, Saint-Just, are not these honest men? It is a notable thing that the most violent language is held by individuals who have never been known to fight for the Republic. They could speak no otherwise if they wish to render her hateful. *Citoyens*, less talk, say I, and more work! It is with shot and shell and not with shouting that France will be saved. One-half of the cellars of the Section have not been dug up. Not a few citizens still hold considerable quantities of bronze. We would remind the rich that patriotic gifts are for them the most potent guarantees. I recommend to your generosity the wives and daughters of our soldiers who are covering themselves with glory on the frontiers and on the Loire. One of these, the hussar Pommier (Augustin), formerly a cellarman's lad in the Rue de Jérusalem, on the 10th of last month, before Condé, when watering the troop horses, was set upon by six Austrian cavalrymen; he killed two of them and brought in the others prisoners. I ask the Section to declare that Pommier (Augustin) has done his duty."

This speech was applauded and the Sectionaries dispersed with cries of "Vive la République!"

Left alone in the nave with Trubert, Gamelin pressed the latter's hand.

"Thank you. How are you?"

"I? Oh! Very well, very well!" replied Trubert, coughing and spitting blood into his handkerchief. "The Republic has many enemies without and within, and our own Section counts a not inconsiderable number of them. It is not with loud talk but with iron and laws that empires are founded . . . good night, Gamelin; I have letters to write."

And he disappeared, his handkerchief pressed to his lips, into the old-time sacristy.

· The widow Gamelin, her cockade now and henceforth fastened more carefully in her hood, had from one day to the next assumed a fine, consequential air, a Republican haughtiness and the dignified carriage suitable to the mother of a juror of the State.

The veneration for the law in which she had been brought up, the admiration with which the magistrate's gown and cassock had from a child inspired her, the holy terror she had always experienced at sight of those to whom God had delegated on earth His divine right of life and death, these feelings made her regard as an august and worshipful and holy being the son whom till yesterday she had thought of as little more than a child. To her simple mind the conviction of the continuity of justice through all the changes of the Revolution was as strong as was that of the legislators of the Convention regarding the continuity of the State under varying systems of government, and the Revolutionary Tribunal appeared to her every whit as majestic as any of the time-honoured jurisdictions she had been taught to revere.

The *citoyen* Brotteaux showed the young magistrate an interest mingled with surprise and a reluctant deference. His views were the same as the widow Gamelin's as to the continuity of justice under successive governments; but, in flat contradiction to that good lady's attitude, his scorn for the Revolutionary Tribunals was on a par with his contempt for the courts of the ancien régime. Not daring to express his opinions openly and unable to make up his mind to say nothing, he indulged in a string of paradoxes which Gamelin understood just well enough to suspect the anti-patriotism that underlay them.

78

"The august tribunal whereon you are soon to take your seat," he told him on one occasion, "was instituted by the French Senate for the security of the Republic; and it was for certain a magnanimous thought on the part of our legislators to set up a court to try our enemies. I appreciate its generosity, but I doubt its wisdom. It would have shown greater astuteness, it seems to me, if they had struck down in the dark the more irreconcilable of their adversaries and won over the rest by gifts and promises. A tribunal strikes slowly and effects less harm than it inspires fear; its first duty is to make an example. The mischief yours does is to unite together all whom it terrifies and make out of a mass of contradictory interests and passions a great party capable of common and effective action. You sow fear broadcast, and it is terror more than courage that produces heroes; I pray, *citoyen*, you may not one day see prodigies of terror arrayed against you!"

The engraver Desmahis, in love that week with a light o' love of the Palais-Égalité named Flora, a brown-locked giantess, had nevertheless found five minutes to congratulate his comrade and tell him that such an appointment was a great compliment to the fine arts.

Élodie herself, though without knowing it she detested everything revolutionary and who dreaded official functions as the most dangerous of rivals, the most likely to estrange her lover's affections, the tender Élodie was impressed by the glamour attaching to a magistrate called upon to pronounce judgment in matters of life and death. Besides which, Évariste's promotion as a juryman was followed by other fortunate results that filled her loving heart with satisfaction; the *citoyen* Jean Blaise made a point of calling at the studio in the Place de Thionville and embraced the young juror affectionately in a burst of manly sympathy.

Like all the anti-revolutionaries, he had a great respect for the authorities established by the Republic, and ever since he had been denounced for fraud in connection with his supplies for the army, the Revolutionary Tribunal had inspired him with a wholesome dread. He felt himself to be a person too much in the public eye and mixed up in too many transactions to enjoy perfect security; so the *citoyen* Gamelin struck him as a friend worth cultivating. When all was said, one was a good citizen and on the side of justice.

He gave the painter magistrate his hand, declaring himself his true friend and a true patriot, a well-wisher of the arts and of liberty. Gamelin forgot his injuries and pressed the hand so generously offered.

"*Citoyen* Évariste Gamelin," said Jean Blaise, "I appeal to you as a friend and as a man of talent. I am going to take you to-morrow for two days' jaunt in the country; you can do some drawing and we can enjoy a talk."

Several times every year the print-dealer was in the habit of making a two or three days' expedition of this sort in the company of artists who made drawings, according to his suggestions, of landscapes and ruins. He was quick to see what would please the public and these little journeys always resulted in some picturesque bits which were then finished at home and cleverly engraved; prints in red or colours were struck off from these, and brought in a good profit to the *citoyen* Blaise. From the same sketches he had over-doors and panels executed, which sold as well or better than the decorative works of Hubert Robert.

On this occasion he had invited the *citoyen* Gamelin to accompany him to sketch buildings after nature, so much had the juror's office increased the painter's importance in his eyes. Two other artists were of the party, the engraver Desmahis, who drew well, and an almost unknown man, Philippe Dubois, an excellent designer in the style of Robert. According to custom, the *citoyenne* Élodie with her friend the *citoyenne* Hasard accompanied the artists. Jean Blaise, an adept at combining pleasure with profit, had also extended an invitation to the *citoyenne* Thévenin, an actress at the Vaudeville, who was reputed to be on the best of terms with him.

Chapter 10

ON SATURDAY at seven in the morning the *citoyen* Blaise, in a black cocked-hat, scarlet waistcoat, doe-skin breeches, and boots with yellow tops, rapped with the handle of his riding-whip at the studio door. The *citoyenne* Gamelin was in the room in polite conversation with the *citoyen* Brotteaux, while Évariste stood before a bit of looking-glass knotting his high white cravat.

"A pleasant journey, Monsieur Blaise!" the *citoyenne* greeted him. "But, as you are going to paint landscapes, why don't you take Monsieur Brotteaux, who is a painter?"

"Well, well," said Jean Blaise, "will you come with us, *citoyen* Brotteaux?"

On being assured he would not be intruding, Brotteaux, a man of a sociable temper and fond of all amusements, accepted the invitation.

The *citoyenne* Élodie had climbed the four storeys to embrace the widow Gamelin, whom she called her good mother. She was in white from head to foot, and smelt of lavender.

An old two-horsed travelling *berline* stood waiting in the Place, with the hood down. Rose Thévenin occupied the back seat with Julienne Hasard. Élodie made the actress sit on the right, took the left-hand place herself and put the slim Julienne between the two of them. Brotteaux settled himself, back to the horses, facing the *citoyenne* Thévenin; Philippe Dubois, opposite the *citoyenne* Hasard; Évariste opposite Élodie. As for Philippe Desmahis, he planted his athletic figure on the box, on the coachman's left, and proceeded to amaze that worthy with a traveller's tale about a country in America where the trees bore chitterlings and saveloys by way of fruit.

The *citoyen* Blaise, who was a capital rider, took the road on horseback, going on in front to escape the dust from the *berline*.

As the wheels rattled merrily over the suburban roads the travellers

81

began to forget their cares, and at sight of the green fields and trees and sky, their minds turned to gay and pleasant thoughts. Élodie dreamed she was surely born to rear poultry with Évariste, a country justice, to help her, in some village on a river bank beside a wood. The roadside elms whirled by as they sped along. Outside the villages the peasants' mastiffs dashed out to intercept the carriage and barked at the horses, while a fat spaniel, lying in the roadway, struggled reluctantly to its feet; the fowls scattered and fled; the geese in a close-packed band waddled slowly out of the way. The children, with their fresh morning faces, watched the company go by. It was a hot day and a cloudless sky. The parched earth was thirsting for rain. They alighted just outside Villejuif. On their way through the little town, Desmahis went into a fruiterer's to buy cherries for the over-heated *citoyennes*. The shopkeeper was a pretty woman, and Desmahis showed no signs of reappearing. Philippe Dubois shouted to him, using the nickname his friends constantly gave him:

"Ho there! Barbaroux! . . . Barbaroux!"

At this hated name the passers-by pricked up their ears and faces appeared at every window. Then, when they saw a young and handsome man emerge from the shop, his jacket thrown open, his neckerchief flying loose over a muscular chest, and carrying over his shoulder a basket of cherries and his coat at the end of a stick, taking him for the proscribed girondist, a posse of *sansculottes* laid violent hands on him. Regardless of his indignant protests, they would have haled him to the townhall, had not old Brotteaux, Gamelin, and the three young women borne testimony that the *citoyen* was named Philippe Desmahis, a copper-plate engraver and a good Jacobin. Even then the suspect had to show his *carte de civisme*, which he had in his pocket by great good luck, for he was very heedless in such matters. At this price he escaped from the hands of these patriotic villagers without worse loss than one of his lace ruffles, which had been torn off; but this was a trifle after all. He even received the apologies of the National Guards who had hustled him the most savagely and who now spoke of carrying him in triumph to the Hôtel de Ville.

A free man again and with the *citoyennes* Élodie, Rose, and Julienne crowding round him, Desmahis looked at Philippe Dubois—he did not like the man and suspected him of having played him a practical joke—with a wry smile, and towering above him by a whole head:

"Dubois," he told him, "if you call me Barbaroux again, I shall

82

call you Brissot; he is a little fat man with a silly face, greasy hair, an oily skin and damp hands. They'll be perfectly sure you are the infamous Brissot, the people's enemy; and the good Republicans, filled with horror and loathing at sight of you, will hang you from the nearest lamp-post. You hear me?"

The *citoyen* Blaise, who had been watering his horse, announced that he had arranged the affair, though it was quite plain to everybody that it had been arranged without him.

The company got in again, and as they drove on, Desmahis informed the coachman that in this same plain of Longjumeau several inhabitants of the Moon had once come down, in shape and colour much like frogs, only very much bigger. Philippe Dubois and Gamelin talked about their art. Dubois, a pupil of Regnault, had been to Rome, where he had seen Raphael's tapestries, which he set above all the masterpieces of the world. He admired Correggio's colouring, Annibale Caracci's invention, Domenichino's drawing, but thought nothing comparable in point of style with the pictures of Pompeio Battoni. He had been in touch at Rome with Monsieur Ménageot and Madame Lebrun, who had both pronounced against the Revolution; so the less said of them the better. But he spoke highly of Angelica Kauffmann, who had a pure taste and a fine knowledge of the Antique.

Gamelin deplored that the apogee of French painting, belated as it was, for it only dated from Lesueur, Claude and Poussin and corresponded with the decadence of the Italian and Flemish schools, had been succeeded by so rapid and profound a decline. This he attributed to the degraded state of manners and to the Academy, which was the expression of that state. But the Academy had been happily abolished, and under the influence of new canons, David and his school were creating an art worthy of a free people. Among the young painters, Gamelin, without a trace of envy, gave the first place to Hennequin and Topino-Lebrun. Philippe Dubois preferred his own master Regnault to David, and founded his hopes for the future of painting on that rising artist Gérard.

Meantime Élodie complimented the *citoyenne* Thévenin on her red velvet toque and white gown. The actress repaid the compliment by congratulating her two companions on their toilettes and advising them how to do better still; the thing, she said, was to be more sparing in ornaments and trimmings.

"A woman can never be dressed too simply," was her dictum. "We see this on the stage, where the costume should allow every pose to be appreciated. That is its true beauty and it needs no other."

"You are right, my dear," replied Élodie. "Only there is nothing more expensive in dress than simplicity. It is not always out of bad taste we add frills and furbelows; sometimes it is to save our pockets."

They discussed eagerly the autumn fashions,—frocks entirely plain and short-waisted.

"So many women disfigure themselves through following the fashion!" declared Rose Thévenin. "In dressing every woman should study her own figure."

"There is nothing beautiful save draperies that follow the lines of the figure and fall in folds," put in Gamelin. "Everything that is cut out and sewn is hideous."

These sentiments, more appropriate in a treatise of Winckelmann's than in the mouth of a man talking to Parisiennes, met with the scorn they deserved, being entirely disregarded.

"For the winter," observed Élodie, "they are making quilted gowns in Lapland style of taffeta and muslin, and coats *à la Zulime*, round-waisted and opening over a stomacher *à la Turque*."

"Nasty cheap things," declared the actress, "you can buy them ready made. Now I have a little seamstress who works like an angel and is not dear; I'll send her to see you, my dear."

So they prattled on trippingly, eagerly discussing and appraising different fine fabrics—striped taffeta, self-coloured china silk, muslin, gauze, nankeen.

And old Brotteaux, as he listened to them, thought with a pensive pleasure of these veils that hide women's charms and change incessantly,—how they last for a few years to be renewed eternally like the flowers of the field. And his eyes, as they wandered from the three pretty women to the cornflowers and the poppies in the wheat, were wet with smiling tears.

They reached Orangis about nine o'clock and stopped before the inn, the *Auberge de la Cloche*, where the Poitrines, husband and wife, offered accommodation for man and beast. The *citoyen* Blaise, who had repaired any disorder in his dress, helped the *citoyennes* to alight. After ordering dinner for midday, they all set off, preceded by their paint-boxes, drawing-boards, easels, and parasols, which were carried by a village lad, for the meadows near the confluence of the

Orge and the Yvette, a charming bit of country giving a view over the verdant plain of Longjumeau and bounded by the Seine and the woods of Sainte-Geneviève.

Jean Blaise, the leader of the troop of artists, was bandying funny stories with the *ci-devant* financier, tales that brought in without rhyme or reason Verboquet the Open-handed, Catherine Cuissot the pedlar, the demoiselles Chaudron, the fortune-teller Galichet, as well as characters of a later time like Cadet-Rousselle and Madame Angot.

Évariste, inspired with a sudden love of nature, as he saw a troop of harvesters binding their sheaves, felt the tears rise to his eyes, while visions of concord and affection filled his heart. For his part, Desmahis was blowing the light down of the seeding dandelions into the *citoyennes'* hair. All three loved posies, as town-bred girls always do, and were busy in the meadows plucking the mullein, whose blossoms grow in spikes close round the stem, the campanula, with its little blue-bells hanging in rows one above another, the slender twigs of the scented vervain, wallwort, mint, dyer's weed, milfoil — all the wild flowers of late summer. Jean-Jacques had made botany the fashion among townswomen, so all three knew the name and symbolism of every flower. As the delicate petals, drooping for want of moisture, wilted in her hands, and fell in a shower about her feet, the *citoyenne* Élodie sighed:

"They are dying already, the poor flowers!"

All set to work and strove to express nature as they saw her; but each saw her through the eyes of a master. In a short time Philippe Dubois had knocked off in the style of Hubert Robert a deserted farm, a clump of storm-riven trees, a dried-up torrent. Évariste Gamelin found a landscape by Poussin ready made on the banks of the Yvette. Philippe Desmahis was at work before a pigeon-cote in the picaresque manner of Callot and Duplessis. Old Brotteaux who piqued himself on imitating the Flemings, was drawing a cow with infinite care. Élodie was sketching a peasant's hut, while her friend Julienne, who was a colourman's daughter, set her palette. A swarm of children pressed about her, watching her paint, whom she would scold out of her light at intervals, calling them pestering gnats and giving them lollipops. The *citoyenne* Thévenin, picking out the pretty ones, would wash their faces, kiss them and put flowers in their hair. She fondled them with a gentle air of melancholy, because she had missed the joy of motherhood,—as well as to heighten her fascinations by a show of tender sentiment and to practise herself in the art of pose and grouping.

She was the only member of the party neither drawing nor painting. She devoted her attention to learning a part and still more to charming her companions, flitting from one to another, book in hand, a bright, entrancing creature.

"No complexion, no figure, no voice, no nothing," declared the women,—and she filled the earth with movement, colour and harmony. Faded, pretty, tired, indefatigable, she was the joy of the expedition. A woman of ever-varying moods, but always gay, sensitive, quick-tempered and yet easy-going and accommodating, a sharp tongue with the most polished utterance, vain, modest, true, false, delightful; if Rose Thévenin enjoyed no triumphant success, if she was not worshipped as a goddess, it was because the times were out of joint and Paris had no more incense, no more altars for the Graces. The *citoyenne* Blaise herself, who made a face when she spoke of her and used to call her "my stepmother," could not see her and not be subjugated by such an array of charms.

They were rehearsing *Les Visitandines* at the Théâtre Feydeau, and Rose was full of self-congratulation at having a part full of "naturalness." It was this quality she strove after, this she sought and this she found.

"Then we shall not see 'Paméla'?" asked Desmahis.

The Théâtre de la Nation was closed and the actors packed off to the Madelonnettes and to Pélagie.

"Do you call that liberty?" cried Rose Thévenin, raising her beautiful eyes to heaven in indignant protest.

"The players of the Théâtre de la Nation are aristocrats," said Gamelin, "and the *citoyen* François' piece tends to make men regret the privileges of the noblesse."

"Gentlemen," said Rose Thévenin, "have you patience to listen only to those who flatter you?"

As midday approached everybody began to feel pangs of hunger and the little band marched back to the inn.

Évariste walked beside Élodie, smilingly recalling memories of their first meetings:

"Two young birds had fallen out of their nests on the roof on to the sill of your window. You brought the little creatures up by hand;

one of them lived and in due time flew away. The other died in the nest of cotton-wool you had made him. 'It was the one I loved best,' I remember you said. That day, Élodie, you were wearing a red bow in your hair."

Philippe Dubois and Brotteaux, a little behind the rest, were talking of Rome, where they had both been, the latter in '72, the other towards the last days of the Academy. Brotteaux indeed had never forgotten the Princess Mondragone, to whom he would most certainly have poured out his plaints but for the Count Altieri, who always followed her like her shadow. Nor did Philippe Dubois fail to mention that he had been invited to dine with Cardinal de Bernis and that he was the most obliging host in the world.

"I knew him," said Brotteaux, "and I may add without boasting that I was for some while one of his most intimate friends; he had a taste for low society. He was an amiable man, and for all his affectation of telling fairy tales, there was more sound philosophy in his little finger than in the heads of all you Jacobins, who are for making us virtuous and God-fearing by Act of Parliament. Upon my word I prefer our simple-minded theophagists who know not what they say nor yet what they do, to these mad law-menders, who make it their business to guillotine us in order to render us wise and virtuous and adorers of the Supreme Being who has created them in His likeness. In former days I used to have Mass said in the Chapel at Les Ilettes by a poor devil of a Curé who used to say in his cups: 'Don't let's speak ill of sinners; we live by 'em, we priests, unworthy as we are!' You must agree, sir, this prayer-monger held sound maxims of government. We should adopt his principles, and govern men as being what they are and not what we should like them to be."

Rose Thévenin had meantime drawn closer to the old man. She knew he had lived on a grand scale, and the thought of this gilded the *ci-devant* financier's present poverty, which she deemed less humiliating as being due to general causes, the result of the public bankruptcy. She saw in him, with curiosity not unmixed with respect, the survival of one of those open-handed millionaires of whom her elder comrades of the stage spoke with sighs of unfeigned regret. Besides, the old fellow in his plum-coloured coat, so threadbare and so well brushed, pleased her by his agreeable address.

"Monsieur Brotteaux," she said to him, "we know how once upon a time, in a noble park, on moonlight nights, you would slip into the

shade of myrtle groves with actresses and dancing-girls to the far-off
shrilling of flutes and fiddles. . . . Alas! they were more lovely, were
they not, your goddesses of the Opera and the Comédie-Française,
than we of to-day, we poor little National actresses?"

"Never think it, Mademoiselle," returned Brotteaux, "but believe me, if one like you had been known in those days, she would
have moved alone, as sovereign queen without a rival (little as she
would have desired such solitude), in the park you are obliging
enough to form so flattering a picture of. . . ."

It was quite a rustic inn, this Hôtel de la Cloche. A branch of
holly hung over the great waggon doors that opened on a courtyard
where fowls were always pecking about in the damp soil. On the far
side of this stood the house itself, consisting of a ground floor and
one storey above, crowned by a high-pitched tiled roof and with
walls almost hidden under old climbing rose-trees covered with
blossom. To the right, trimmed fruit-trees showed their tops above
the low garden wall. To the left was the stable, with an outside
manger and a barn supported by wooden pillars. A ladder leant
against the wall. Here again, under a shed crowded with agricultural
implements and stumps of trees, a white cock was keeping an eye
on his hens from the top of a broken-down cabriolet. The courtyard
was enclosed on this side by cow-sheds, in front of which rose in
mountainous grandeur a dunghill which at this moment a girl as
broad as she was long, with straw-coloured hair, was turning over
with a pitchfork. The liquid manure filled her sabots and bathed
her bare feet, and you could see the heels rise out of her shoes every
now and then as yellow as saffron. Her petticoats were kilted and
revealed the filth on her enormous calves and thick ankles. While
Philippe Desmahis was staring at her, surprised and tickled by the
whimsicalities of nature in framing this odd example of breadth
without length, the landlord shouted:

"Ho there! Tronche, my girl! go fetch some water!"

She turned her head, showing a scarlet face and a vast mouth in
which one huge front tooth was missing. It had needed nothing less
than a bull's horn to effect a breach in that powerful jaw. She stood
there grinning, pitchfork on shoulder. Her sleeves were rolled up
and her arms, as thick as another woman's thighs, gleamed in the
sun.

The table was laid in the farm kitchen, where a brace of fowls was

roasting,—they were almost done to a turn,—under the hood of the open fireplace, above which hung two or three old fowling-pieces by way of ornament. The bare white-washed room, twenty feet long, was lighted only through the panes of greenish glass let into the door and by a single window, framed in roses, near which the grandmother sat turning her spinning-wheel. She wore a coif and a lace frilling in the fashion of the Regency. Her gnarled, earth-stained fingers held the distaff. Flies clustered about her lids without her trying to drive them away. As a child in her mother's arms, she had seen Louis XIV go by in his coach.

Sixty years ago she had made the journey to Paris. In a weak sing-song voice she told the tale to the three young women, standing in front of her, how she had seen the Hôtel de Ville, the Tuileries and the Samaritaine, and how, when she was crossing the Pont-Royal, a barge loaded with apples for the Marché du Mail had broken up, the apples had floated down the current and the river was all red with the rosy-cheeked fruit.

She had been told of the changes that had occurred of late in the kingdom, and in particular of the coil there was betwixt the curés who had taken the oath and the nonjuring curés. She knew likewise there had been wars and famines and portents in the sky. She did not believe the King was dead. They had contrived his escape, she *would* have it, by a subterranean passage, and had handed over to the headsman in his stead a man of the common people.

At the old woman's feet, in his wicker cradle, Jeannot, the last born of the Poitrines, was cutting his teeth. The *citoyenne* Thévenin lifted the cradle and smiled at the child, which moaned feebly, worn out with feverishness and convulsions. It must have been very ill, for they had sent for the doctor, the *citoyen* Pelleport, who, it is true, being a deputy-substitute to the Convention, asked no payment for his visits.

The *citoyenne* Thévenin, an innkeeper's daughter herself, was in her element; not satisfied with the way the farm-girl had washed the plates and dishes, she gave an extra wipe to the crockery and glass, an extra polish to the knives and forks. While the *citoyenne* Poitrine was attending to the soup, which she tasted from time to time as a good cook should, Élodie was cutting up into slices a four-pound loaf hot from the oven. Gamelin, when he saw what she was doing, addressed her:

"A few days ago I read a book written by a young German whose name I have forgotten, and which has been very well translated into French. In it you have a beautiful young girl named Charlotte, who, like you, Élodie, was cutting bread and butter, and like you, cutting it gracefully, and so prettily that at the sight the young Werther fell in love with her."

"And it ended in their marrying?" asked Élodie.

"No," replied Évariste; "it ended in Werther's death by violence."

They dined well, they were all very hungry; but the fare was indifferent. Jean Blaise complained bitterly; he was a great trencherman and made it a rule of conduct to feed well; and no doubt what urged him to elaborate his gluttony into a system was the general scarcity. In every household the Revolution had overturned the cooking pot. The common run of citizens had nothing to chew upon. Clever folks like Jean Blaise, who made big profits amid the general wretchedness, went to the cookshop where they showed their astuteness by stuffing themselves to repletion. As for Brotteaux who, in this year II of liberty, was living on chestnuts and bread-crusts, he could remember having supped at Grimod de la Reynière's at the near end of the Champs Élysées. Eager to win the repute of an accomplished gourmand he reeled off, sitting there before Dame Poitrine's bacon and cabbages, a string of artful kitchen recipes and wise gastronomic maxims. Presently, when Gamelin protested that a Republican scorns the pleasures of the table, the old financier, always a lover of antiquity, gave the young Spartan the true recipe for the famous black broth.

After dinner, Jean Blaise, who never forgot business, set his itinerant academy to make studies and sketches of the inn, which struck him as quite romantic in its dilapidation. While Philippe Desmahis and Philippe Dubois were drawing the cow-houses the girl Tronche came out to feed the pigs. The *citoyen* Pelleport, officer of health, who at the same moment appeared at the door of the farm kitchen where he had been bestowing his professional services on the Poitrine baby, stepped up to the artists and after complimenting them on their talents, which were an honour to the whole nation, pointed to the Tronche girl in the middle of her porkers:

"You see that creature," he said, "it is not one girl, as you might suppose; it is two girls. I speak by the letter, understand that. I was amazed at the extraordinary massiveness of her bony framework and I examined her, to discover she had most of the bones in duplicate—in each thigh two femurs welded together, in each shoulder a double humerus. Some of her muscles are likewise in duplicate. It is a case, in my view, of a pair of twins associated or rather confounded together. It is an interesting phenomenon. I notified Monsieur Saint-Hilaire of the facts, and he thanked me. It is a monster you see before you, *citoyens*. The people call her 'the girl Tronche'; they should say 'the girls Tronche,' for there are two of them. Nature has these freaks. . . . Good evening, *citoyens;* we shall have a storm to-night. . . ."

After supper by candle-light, the Academy Blaise adjourned to the courtyard where they were joined by a son and daughter of the house in a game of blindman's-buff, in which the young folks, both men and women, displayed a feverish energy sufficiently accounted for by the high spirits proper to their age without seeking an explanation in the wild and precarious times in which they lived. When it was quite dark, Jean Blaise proposed children's games in the farm kitchen. Élodie suggested the game of "hunt my heart," and this was agreed to unanimously. Under the girl's direction Philippe Desmahis traced in chalk, on different pieces of furniture, on doors and walls, seven hearts, that is to say one less than there were players, for old Brotteaux had obligingly joined the rest. They danced round in a ring singing "La Tour, prends garde!" and at a signal from Élodie, each ran to put a hand on a heart. Gamelin in his absent-minded clumsiness was too late to find one vacant, and had to pay a forfeit, the little knife he had bought for six sous at the fair of Saint-Germain and with which he had cut the loaf for his mother in her poverty. The game went on, and one after the other Blaise, Élodie, Brotteaux and Rose Thévenin failed to touch a heart; each paid a forfeit in turn—a ring, a reticule, a little morocco-bound book, a bracelet. Then the forfeits were raffled on Élodie's lap, and each player had to redeem his property by showing his society accomplishments—singing a song or reciting a poem. Brotteaux chose the speech of the patron saint of France in the first canto of *La Pucelle:*

> "Je suis Denis et saint de mon métier,
> J'aime la Gaule, . . ." *

---

* "I am Denis, and sainthood is my trade,
   I love the land of Gaul, . . . etc."

The *citoyen* Blaise, though a far less well-read man, replied without hesitation with Richemond's ripost:

> "Monsieur le Saint, ce n'était pas la peine
> D'abandonner le celeste domaine . . ." *

At that time everybody was reading and re-reading with delight the masterpiece of the French Ariosto; the most serious of men smiled over the loves of Jeanne and Dunois, the adventures of Agnès and Monrose and the exploits of the winged ass. Every man of cultivation knew by heart the choice passages of this diverting and philosophical poem. Évariste Gamelin himself, stern-tempered as he was, when he recovered his twopenny knife from Élodie's lap, recited the going down of Grisbourdon into hell, with a good deal of spirit. The *citoyenne* Thévenin sang without accompaniment Nina's ballad:

> *"Quand le bien-aimé reviendra."*

Desmahis sang to the tune of *La Faridondaine:*

> "Quelques-uns prirent le cochon
> De ce bon saint Antoine,
> Et lui mettant un capuchon,
> Ils en firent un moine.
> Il n'en coûtait que la façon . . ." †

All the same Desmahis was in a pensive mood. For the moment he was ardently in love with all the three women with whom he was playing forfeits, and was casting burning looks of soft appeal at each in turn. He loved Rose Thévenin for her grace, her supple figure, her clever acting, her roving glances, and her voice that went straight to a man's heart; he loved Élodie, because he recognized instinctively her rich endowment of temperament and her kind, complaisant humour; he loved Julienne Hasard, despite her colourless hair, her pale eyelashes, her freckles and her thin bust, because, like Dunois in Voltaire's *Pucelle*, he was always ready, in his generosity, to give the least engaging a token of love—and the more so in this instance because she appeared to be for the moment the most

---

> * "Well, well, sir Saint, 'twas hardly worth your pains
> Thus to forsake the heavenly domains. . . ."

> † "Some ribalds took the pig,
> Of the good St. Anthony,
> And clapping a cowl on's head,
> They made the brute a monk.
> 'Twas all a matter of dress. . . ."

neglected, and therefore the most amenable to his attentions. Without a trace of vanity, he was never sure of these being agreeable; nor yet was he ever sure of their not being. So he never omitted to offer them on the chance. Taking advantage of the opportunities offered by the game of forfeits, he made some tender speeches to Rose Thévenin, who showed no displeasure, but could hardly say much in return under the jealous eyes of the *citoyen* Jean Blaise. He spoke more warmly still to the *citoyenne* Élodie, whom he knew to be pledged to Gamelin, but he was not so exacting as to want a heart all to himself. Élodie could never care for him; but she thought him a handsome fellow and did not altogether succeed in hiding the fact from him. Finally, he whispered his most ardent vows in the ear of the *citoyenne* Hasard, which she received with an air of bewildered stupefaction that might equally express abject submission or chill indifference. And Desmahis did not believe she was indifferent to him.

The inn contained only two bedrooms, both on the first floor and opening on the same landing. That to the left, the better of the two, boasted a flowered paper and a looking-glass the size of a man's hand, the gilt frame of which had been blackened by generations of flies since the days when Louis XV was a child. In it, under sprigged muslin curtains, stood two beds with down pillows, coverlets and counterpanes. This room was reserved for the three *citoyennes*.

When the time came to retire, Desmahis and the *citoyenne* Hasard, each holding a bedroom candlestick, wished each other good-night on the landing. The amorous engraver quickly passed a note to the colourman's daughter, beseeching her to come to him, when everybody was asleep, in the garret, which was over the *citoyennes'* chamber.

With judicious foresight, he had taken care in the course of the day to study the lie of the land and explore the garret in question, which was full of strings of onions, apples and pears left there to ripen with a swarm of wasps crawling over them, chests and old trunks. He had even noticed an old bed of sacking, decrepit and now disused, as far as he could see, and a palliasse, all ripped up and jumping with fleas.

Facing the *citoyennes'* room was another of very modest dimensions containing three beds, where the men of the party were to sleep, in such comfort as they might. But Brotteaux, who was a

Sybarite, betook himself to the barn to sleep among the hay. As for Jean Blaise, *he* had disappeared. Dubois and Gamelin were soon asleep. Desmahis went to bed; but no sooner had the silence of night, like a stagnant pool, enveloped the house, than the engraver got up and climbed the wooden staircase, which creaked under his bare feet. The door of the garret stood ajar. From within came a breath of stifling hot air, mingled with the acrid smell of rotting fruit. On the broken-down bed of sacking lay the girl Tronche, fast asleep with her mouth open, her shift pulled up and her legs wide apart. She looked enormous. A moonbeam peeped in at the skylight and threw its pale, blue illumination on her skin, which, between the splotches of filth and splashes of dried dung shone resplendent with the glow of youth and health. Desmahis threw himself upon her. Waking with a start, she gave a cry of alarm; but quite reassured the moment she gathered what he wanted with her, the girl manifested neither surprise nor displeasure and pretended to be still half asleep, in a sort of torpor that absolved her from any precise consciousness of what was happening, but left her senses sufficiently awake. . . .

Desmahis returned to his room, where he slept soundly and peacefully till daybreak.

On the morrow, after a last day's work, the itinerant Academy took the road back to Paris. When Jean Blaise paid mine host in assignats, the *citoyen* Poitrine complained bitterly that he never saw what he called "square money" nowadays, and promised a fine candle to the beggar who'd bring back the "yellow boys" again.

He offered the *citoyennes* their pick of flowers. At his orders, the girl Tronche mounted on a ladder in her sabots and kilted skirts, giving a full view of her noble, much-bespattered calves, and was indefatigable in cutting blossoms from the climbing roses that covered the wall. From her huge hands the flowers fell in showers, in torrents, in avalanches, into the laps of Élodie, Julienne, and Rose Thévenin, who held out their skirts to catch them. The carriage was full of them. The whole party, when they got back at nightfall, carried armfuls home, and their sleeping and waking were perfumed with their fragrance.

Chapter 11

IN THE forenoon of the 7th September the *citoyenne* Rochemaure, on her way to visit Gamelin, the new juror, whose interest she wished to solicit on behalf of an acquaintance, who had been denounced as a suspect, encountered on the landing the *ci-devant* Brotteaux des Ilettes, who had been her lover in the old happy days. Brotteaux was just starting to deliver a gross of dancing-dolls of his manufacture to the toy-merchant in the Rue de la Loi; for their more convenient carriage he had hit on the idea of tying them at the end of a pole, as the street hawkers do with their commodities. His manners were always chivalrous towards women, even to those whose fascination for him had been blunted by long familiarity, as could hardly fail to be the case with Madame de Rochemaure,—unless indeed he found her appetizing with the added seasoning of betrayal, absence, unfaithfulness and fat. Be this as it may, he now greeted her on the sordid stairs with their cracked tiles as courteously as he had ever done on the steps before the entrance-door of Les Ilettes, and begged her to do him the honour of entering his garret. She climbed the ladder nimbly enough and found herself under a timbering, the sloping beams of which supported a tiled roof pierced with a skylight. It was impossible to stand upright. She sat down on the only chair there was in the wretched place; after a brief glance at the broken tiling, she asked in a tone of surprise and sorrow:

"Is this where you live, Maurice? You need have little fear of intruders. One must be an imp or a cat to find you here."

"I am cramped for space," returned the *ci-devant* millionaire; "and I do not deny the fact that sometimes it rains on my pallet. It is a trifling inconvenience. And on fine nights I can see the moon, symbol and confidant of men's loves. For the moon, Madame, since the world began, has been apostrophized by lovers, and at her full, with her pale round face, she recalls to the fond swain's mind the object of his desires."

"I know," sighed the *citoyenne*.

"When their time comes the cats make a fine pandemonium in the rain gutter yonder. But we must forgive love if it makes them caterwaul and swear on the tiles, seeing how it fills the lives of men with torments and villainies."

Both had had the tact to greet each other as friends who had parted the night before to take their night's rest, and though grown strangers to each other, they conversed with a good grace and on a footing of friendliness.

At the same time Madame de Rochemaure seemed pensive. The Revolution, which had for a long while been pleasant and profitable to her, was now a source of anxiety and disquietude; her suppers were growing less brilliant and less merry. The notes of her harp no longer charmed the cloud from sombre faces. Her play-tables were forsaken by the most lavish punters. Many of her cronies, now numbered among the suspects, were in hiding; her lover, Morhardt the financier, was under arrest, and it was on his behalf she had come to sound the juror Gamelin. She was suspect herself. A posse of National Guards had made a search at her house, had turned out the drawers of her cabinets, prised up boards in her floor, thrust their bayonets into her mattresses. They had found nothing, had made their apologies and drunk her wine. But they had come very near lighting on her correspondence with an *émigré*, Monsieur d'Expilly. Certain friends he had among the Jacobins had warned her that Henry, her handsome favourite, was beginning to compromise his party by his violent language, which was too extravagant to be sincere.

Elbows on knees and head on fist, she sat buried in thought; then turning to her old lover sitting on the palliasse, she asked:

"What do you think of it all, Maurice?"

"I think these good gentry give a philosopher and an amateur of the shows of life abundant matter for reflection and amusement; but that it would be better for you, my dear, if you were out of France."

"Maurice, where will it land us?"

"That is what you asked me, Louise, one day we were driving on the banks of the Cher, on the road to Les Ilettes; the horse, you remember, had taken the bit in his teeth and was galloping off with us at a frantic pace. How inquisitive women are! to-day, for the second time, you want to know where we are going to. Ask the fortune-tellers. I am not a wizard, sweetheart. And philosophy, even the soundest, is of small help for revealing the future. These things will have an end; everything has. One may foresee divers issues. The triumph of the Coalition and the entry of the allies into Paris. They are not far off; yet I doubt if they will get there. These soldiers of the Republic take their beatings with a zest nothing can extinguish. It may be Robespierre will marry Madame Royale and have himself proclaimed Protector of the Kingdom during the minority of Louis XVII."

"You think so!" exclaimed the *citoyenne*, agog to have a hand in so promising an intrigue.

"Again it may be," Brotteaux went on, "that La Vendée will win the day and the rule of the priests be set up again over heaps of ruins and piles of corpses. You cannot conceive, dear heart, the empire the clergy still wields over the masses of the foolish, . . . I beg pardon, I meant to say,—of 'the Faithful'; it was a slip of the tongue. The most likely thing, in my poor opinion, is that the Revolutionary Tribunal will bring about the destruction of the régime it has established; it is a menace over too many heads. Those it terrifies are without number; they will unite together, and to destroy it they will destroy the whole system of government. I think you have got our young friend Gamelin posted to this court. He is virtuous; he will be implacable. The more I think of it, fair friend, the more convinced I am that this Tribunal, set up to save the Republic, will destroy it. The Convention has resolved to have, like Royalty, its *Grands Jours*,* its *Chambre Ardente*, and to provide for its security by means of magistrates appointed by itself and by it kept in subjection. But how inferior are the Convention's *Grands Jours* to those of the Monarchy, and its *Chambre Ardente* to that of Louis XIV! The Revolutionary Tribunal is dominated by a sentiment of mean-spirited justice and common equality that will quickly make it odious and ridiculous and will disgust everybody. Do you know, Louise, that this Tribunal, which is about to cite to its bar the Queen of France and twenty-one legislators, yesterday condemned a servant-girl convicted of crying: 'Vive le Roi!' with malicious intent and in

---

* *Grands Jours*,—under the ancien régime, an extraordinary assize held by judges specially appointed by the King and acting in his name.

the hope of destroying the Republic? Our judges, with their black hats and plumes, are working on the model of that William Shakespeare, so dear to the heart of Englishmen, who drags in coarse buffooneries in the middle of his most tragic scenes."

"Ah, well! Maurice," asked the *citoyenne*, "are you still as fortunate as ever with women?"

"Alas!" replied Brotteaux, "the doves flock to the bright new dovecote and light no more on the ruined tower."

"You have not changed. . . . Good-bye, dear friend,—till we meet again."

The same evening the dragoon Henry, paying a visit uninvited at Madame de Rochemaure's, found her in the act of sealing a letter on which he read the address of the *citoyen* Rauline at Vernon. The letter, he knew, was for England. Rauline used to receive Madame de Rochemaure's communications by a postilion of the posting-service and send them on to Dieppe by the hands of a fishwife. The master of a fishing-smack delivered them under cover of night to a British ship cruising off the coast; an *émigré*, Monsieur d'Expilly, received them in London and passed them on, if he thought it advisable, to the Cabinet of Saint James's.

Henry was young and good looking; Achilles was not such a paragon of grace and vigour when he donned the armour Ulysses offered him. But the *citoyenne* Rochemaure, once so enraptured by the charms of the young hero of the Commune, now looked askance at him; her mood had changed since the day she was told how the young soldier had been denounced at the Jacobins as one whose zeal outran discretion and that he might compromise and ruin her. Henry thought it might not break his heart perhaps to leave off loving Madame de Rochemaure; but he was piqued to have fallen in her good graces. He counted on her to meet sundry expenses in which the service of the Republic had involved him. Last but not least, remembering to what extremities women will proceed and how they go in a flash from the most ardent tenderness to the coldest indifference, and how easy they find it to sacrifice what once they held dear and destroy what once they adored, he began to suspect that some day his fascinating mistress might have him thrown into prison to get rid of him. Common prudence urged him to regain his lost ascendancy and to this end he had come armed with all his fascinations. He came near, drew away, came near again, hovered round her, ran from her, in the approved fashion of seduction in the ballet. Then he threw himself in an armchair and in his irresistible voice, his voice that went straight to women's hearts, he extolled the charms of nature and solitude and with a lovelorn sigh proposed an expedition to Ermenonville.

Meanwhile she was striking chords on her harp and looking about her with an expression of impatience and boredom. Suddenly Henry got up with a gesture of gloomy resolution and informed her that he was starting for the army and in a few days would be before Maubeuge.

Without a sign either of scepticism or surprise she nodded her approval.

"You congratulate me on my decision?"

"I do indeed."

She was expecting a new admirer who was infinitely to her taste and from whom she hoped to reap great advantages,—a contrast in every way to the old, a Mirabeau come to life again, a Danton rehabilitated and turned army-contractor, a lion who talked of pitching every patriot into the Seine. She was on tenter-hooks, thinking to hear the bell ring at any moment.

To hasten Henry's departure, she fell silent, yawned, fingered a score, and yawned again. Seeing he made no move to go, she told him she had to go out and withdrew into her dressing-room.

He called to her in a broken voice:

"Farewell, Louise! . . . Shall I ever see you again?"—and his hands were busy fumbling in the open writing-desk.

When he reached the street, he opened the letter addressed to the *citoyen* Rauline and read it with absorbed attention. Indeed it drew a curious picture of the state of public feeling in France. It spoke of the Queen, of the actress Rose Thévenin, of the Revolutionary Tribunal and a host of confidential remarks emanating from that worthy, Brotteaux des Ilettes, were repeated in it.

Having read to the end and restored the missive to his pocket, he stood hesitating a few moments; then, like a man who has made up his mind and says to himself "the sooner the better," he turned his steps to the Tuileries and found his way into the ante-chamber of the Committee of General Security.

The same day, at three o'clock of the afternoon, Évariste Gamelin was seated on the jurors' bench along with fourteen colleagues, most of whom he knew, simple-minded, honest, patriotic folks, savants, artists or artisans,—a painter like himself, an artist in black-and-white, both men of talent, a surgeon, a cobbler, a *ci-devant* marquis, who had given high proofs of patriotism, a printer, two or three small tradesmen, a sample lot in a word of the inhabitants of Paris. There they sat, in the workman's blouse or bourgeois coat, with their hair close-cropped *à la Titus* or clubbed *à la catogan;* there were cocked-hats tilted over the eyes, round hats clapped on the back of the head, red caps of liberty smothering the ears. Some were dressed in coat, flapped waistcoat and breeches, as in olden days, others in the *carmagnole* and striped trousers of the sansculottes. Wearing top-boots or buckled shoes or sabots, they offered in their persons every variety of masculine attire prevalent at that date. Having all of them occupied their places on several previous occasions, they seemed very much at their ease, and Gamelin envied them their un-concern. His own heart was thumping, his ears roaring; a mist was before his eyes and everything about him took on a livid tinge.

When the usher announced the opening of the sitting, three judges took their places on a raised platform of no great size in front of a green table. They wore hats cockaded and crowned with great black plumes and the official cloak with a tricolour riband from which a heavy silver medal was suspended on the breast. In front of them at the foot of the daïs, sat the Deputy of the Public Prosecutor, simi-larly attired. The clerk of the court had a seat between the judges' bench and the prisoner's chair, at present unoccupied. To Gamelin's eyes these men wore a different aspect from that of every day; they seemed nobler, graver, more alarming, albeit their bearing was com-monplace enough as they turned over papers, beckoned to an usher or leant back to listen to some communication from a juryman or an officer of the court.

Above the judges' heads hung the Tables of the Rights of Man; to their right and left, against the old feudal walls, the busts of Le Pel-tier Saint-Fargeau and Marat. Facing the jury bench, at the lower end of the hall, rose the public gallery. The first row of seats was filled by women, who all, fair, brown and grey-haired alike, wore the high coif with the pleated tucker shading their cheeks; the breast, which invariably, as decreed by the fashion of the day, showed the amplitude of the nursing mother's bosom, was covered with a crossed white kerchief or the rounded bib of a blue apron. They sat with folded arms resting on the rail of the tribune. Behind them, scattered about the rising tiers, could be seen a sprinkling of citizens dressed in the varied garb which at that date gave every gathering so striking and picturesque a character. On the right hand, near the doors, behind a broad barrier, a space was reserved where the public could stand. On this occasion it was nearly empty. The business that was to occupy the attention of this particular Section of the Tribunal interested only a few spectators, while doubtless the other Sections sitting at the same hour would be hearing more exciting cases.

This fact somewhat reassured Gamelin; his heart was like to fail him as it was, and he could not have endured the heated atmosphere of one of the great days. His eyes took in the most trifling details of the scene,—the cotton-wool in the *greffier's* ear and a blot of ink on the Deputy Prosecutor's papers. He could see, as through a magnifying glass, the capitals of the pillars sculptured at a time when all knowledge of the classical orders was forgotten and which crowned the Gothic columns with wreaths of nettle and holly. But wherever he looked, his gaze came back again and again to the fatal chair; this was of an antiquated make, covered in red Utrecht velvet, the seat worn and the arms blackened with use. Armed National Guards stood guarding every door.

At last the accused appeared, escorted by grenadiers, but with limbs unbound, as the law directed. He was a man of fifty or thereabouts, lean and dry, with a brown face, a very bald head, hollow cheeks and thin livid lips, dressed in an out-of-date coat of a sanguine red. No doubt it was fever that made his eyes glitter like jewels and gave his cheeks their shiny, varnished look. He took his seat. His legs, which he crossed, were extraordinarily spare and his great knotted hands met round the knees they clasped. His name was Marie-Adolphe Guillergues, and he was accused of malversation in the supply of forage to the Republican troops. The act of indictment laid to his charge numerous and serious offences, of which no single one was positively certain. Under examination, Guillergues denied the majority of the charges and explained the rest in a light favourable to himself. He spoke in a cold, precise way, with a marked ability and gave the impression of being a dangerous man to have business dealings with. He had an answer for everything. When the judge asked him an embarrassing question, his face remained unmoved and his voice confident, but his two hands, folded on his breast, kept twitching in an agony. Gamelin was struck by this and whispered to the colleague sitting next him, a painter like himself: "Watch his thumbs!"

The first witness to depose alleged a number of most damaging facts. He was the mainstay of the prosecution. Those on the other hand who followed showed themselves well disposed to the prisoner. The Deputy of the Public Prosecutor spoke strongly, but did not go beyond generalities. The advocate for the defence adopted a tone of bluff conviction of his client's innocence that earned the accused a sympathy he had failed to secure by his own efforts. The sitting was suspended and the jury assembled in the room set apart for deliberation. There, after a confused and confusing discussion, they found themselves divided in two groups about equal in number. On the one side were the unemotional, the lukewarm, the men of reason, whom no passion could stir, on the other the kind who let their feelings guide them, who prove all but inaccessible to argument and only consult their heart. These always voted guilty. They were the true metal, pure and unadulterated; their only thought was to save the Republic and they cared not a straw for anything else. Their attitude made a strong impression on Gamelin who felt he was of the same kidney himself.

"This Guillergues," he thought to himself, "is a cunning scamp, a villain who has speculated in the forage supplied to our cavalry. To acquit him is to let a traitor escape, to be false to the fatherland, to devote the army to defeat." And in a flash Gamelin could see the Hussars of the Republic, mounted on stumbling horses, sabred by the enemy's cavalry. . . . "But if Guillergues was innocent . . . ?"

Suddenly he remembered Jean Blaise, likewise suspected of bad faith in the matter of supplies. There were bound to be many others acting like Guillergues and Blaise, contriving disaster, ruining the Republic! An example must be made. But if Guillergues was innocent . . . ?

"There are no proofs," said Gamelin, aloud.

"There never are," retorted the foreman of the jury, shrugging his shoulders; he was good metal, pure metal!

In the end, there proved to be seven votes for condemnation, eight for acquittal.

The jury re-entered the hall and the sitting was resumed. The jurors were required to give reasons for their verdict, and each spoke in turn facing the empty chair. Some were prolix, others confined themselves to a sentence; one or two talked unintelligible gabble.

When Gamelin's turn came, he rose and said:

"In presence of a crime so heinous as that of robbing the defenders of the fatherland of the sinews of victory, we need formal proofs which we have not got."

By a majority of votes the accused was declared not guilty.

Guillergues was brought in again and stood before his judges amid a hum of sympathy from the spectators which conveyed the news of his acquittal to him. He was another man. His features had lost their harshness, his lips were relaxed again. He looked venerable; his face bore the impression of innocence. The President read out in tones of emotion the verdict releasing the prisoner; the audience broke into applause. The gendarme who had brought Guillergues in threw himself into his arms. The President called him to the daïs and gave him the embrace of brotherhood. The jurors kissed him, while Gamelin's eyes rained hot tears.

The courtyard of the Palais, dimly lighted by the last rays of the setting sun, was filled with a howling, excited crowd. The four Sections of the Tribunal had the day before pronounced thirty sentences of death, and on the steps of the Great Stairway a throng of *tricoteuses* squatted to see the tumbrels start. But Gamelin, as he descended the steps among the press of jurors and spectators, saw nothing, heard nothing, but his own act of justice and humanity and the self-congratulation he felt at having recognized innocence. In the courtyard stood Élodie, all in white, smiling through her tears; she threw herself into his arms and lay there half fainting. When she had recovered her voice, she said to him:

"Évariste, you are noble, you are good, you are generous! In the hall there, your voice, so gentle and manly, went right through me with its magnetic waves. It electrified me. I gazed at you on your bench, I could see no one but you. But you, dear heart, you never guessed I was there? Nothing told you I was present? I sat in the gallery in the second row to the right. By heaven! how sweet it is to do the right! you saved that unhappy man's life. Without you, it was all over with him; he was as good as dead. You have given him back to life and the love of his friends. At this moment he must bless you. Évariste, how happy I am and how proud to love you!"

Arm in arm, pressed close to one another, they went along the streets; their bodies felt so light they seemed to be flying.

They went to the *Amour peintre*. On reaching the Oratoire:

"Better not go through the shop," Élodie suggested.

She made him go in by the main coach-door and mount the stairs with her to the suite of rooms above. On the landing she drew out of her reticule a heavy iron key.

"It might be the key of a prison," she exclaimed, "Évariste, you are going to be my prisoner."

They crossed the dining-room and were in the girl's bed-chamber.

Évariste felt upon his the ardent freshness of Élodie's lips. He pressed her in his arms; with head thrown back and swooning eyes, her hair flowing loose over her relaxed form, half fainting, she escaped his hold and ran to shoot the bolt. . . .

The night was far advanced when the *citoyenne* Blaise opened the outer door of the flat for her lover and whispered to him in the darkness.

"Good-bye, sweetheart! it is the hour my father will be coming home. If you hear a noise on the stairs, go up quick to the higher floor and don't come down till all danger is over of your being seen. To have the street-door opened, give three raps on the *concierge's* window. Good-bye, my life, good-bye, my soul!"

When he found himself in the street, he saw the window of Élodie's chamber half unclose and a little hand pluck a red carnation, which fell at his feet like a drop of blood.

Chapter 12

ONE evening when old Brotteaux arrived in the Rue de la Loi bringing a gross of dancing-dolls for the *citoyen* Caillou, the toy-merchant, the latter, a soft-spoken, polite man as a rule, stood there stiff and stern among his dolls and punch-and-judies and gave him a far from gracious welcome.

"Have a care, *citoyen* Brotteaux," he began, "have a care! There is a time to laugh and a time to be serious; jokes are not always in good taste. A member of the Committee of Security of the Section, who inspected my establishment yesterday, saw your dancing-dolls and deemed them anti-revolutionary."

"He was jesting!" declared Brotteaux.

"Not so, *citoyen*, not at all. He is not the man to joke. He said in these little fellows the National representatives were insidiously mimicked, that in particular one could discover caricatures of Couthon, Saint-Just and Robespierre, and he seized the lot. It is a dead loss to me, to say nothing of the grave risks to which I am exposed."

"What! these Harlequins, these Gilles, these Scaramouches, these Colins and Colinettes, which I have painted the same as Boucher used to fifty years ago, how should they be parodies of Couthon and Saint-Just? No sensible man could imagine such a thing."

"It is possible," replied the *citoyen* Caillou, "that you acted without malice, albeit we must always distrust a man of parts like you. But it is a dangerous game. Shall I give you an instance? Natoile, who runs a little outdoor theatre in the Champs Élysées, was arrested the day before yesterday for anti-patriotism, because he made Polichinelle poke fun at the Convention."

"Now listen to me," Brotteaux urged, raising the cloth that covered his little dangling figures; "just look at these masks and faces, are they anything else whatever but characters in plays and pastorals? How could you let yourself be persuaded, *citoyen* Caillou, that I was making fun of the National Convention?"

Brotteaux was dumfounded. While allowing much for human folly, he had not thought it possible it could ever go so far as to suspect his Scaramouches and Colinettes. Repeatedly he protested their innocence and his; but the *citoyen* Caillou would not hear a word.

"*Citoyen* Brotteaux, take your dolls away. I esteem you, I honour you, but I do not mean to incur blame or get into trouble because of you. I intend to remain a good citizen and to be treated as such. Good evening, *citoyen* Brotteaux; take your dolls away."

The old man set out again for home, carrying his suspects over his shoulder at the end of a pole, an object of derision to the children, who took him for the hawker of rat-poison. His thoughts were gloomy. No doubt, he did not live only by his dancing-dolls; he used to paint portraits at twenty *sols* apiece, under the archways of doors or in one of the market halls, among the darners and old-clothes menders, where he found many a young recruit starting for the front and wanting to leave his likeness behind for his sweetheart. But these petty tasks cost him endless pains, and he was a long way from making as good portraits as he did dancing-dolls. Sometimes, too, he acted as amanuensis for the Market dames, but this meant mixing himself up in Royalist plots, and the risks were heavy. He remembered there lived in the Rue Neuve-des-Petits-Champs, near the erstwhile Place Vendôme, another toy-merchant, Joly by name, and he resolved to go next day to offer him the goods the chicken-hearted Caillou had declined.

A fine rain began to fall. Brotteaux who feared its effects on his marionettes, quickened his pace. As he crossed the dark and deserted Pont-Neuf and was turning the corner of the Place de Thionville, he saw by the light of a street-lamp, sitting on a stone post, a lean old man who seemed utterly exhausted with fatigue and hunger, but still preserved his venerable appearance. He was dressed in a tattered surtout, had no hat and appeared over sixty. Approaching the poor wretch, Brotteaux recognized the Père Longuemare, the same he had saved from hanging six months before while both of them were waiting in queue in front of the bakery in the Rue de Jérusalem. Feeling bound to the monk by the service he had already done him, Brotteaux stepped up to him and made himself known as the publican who had stood beside him among the common herd, one day of great scarcity, and asked him if he could not be of some use to him.

"You seem wearied, Father. Take a taste of cordial,"—and Brotteaux drew from the pocket of his plum-coloured coat a flask of brandy, which lay there alongside his Lucretius.

"Drink. And I will help you to get back to your house."

The Père Longuemare pushed away the flask with his hand and tried to rise, but only to fall back again in his seat.

"Sir," he said in a weak but firm voice, "for three months I have been living at Picpus. Being warned they had come to arrest me at my lodging, yesterday at five o'clock of the afternoon, I did not return home. I have no place to go to; I am wandering the streets and am a little fatigued."

"Very well, Father," proposed Brotteaux, "do me the honour to share my garret."

"Sir," replied the Barnabite, "you know, I suppose, I am a suspect."

"I am one too," said Brotteaux, "and my marionettes into the bargain, which is the worst thing of all. You see them exposed under this flimsy cloth to the fine rain that chills our bones. For, I must tell you, Father, that after having been a publican, I now make dancing-dolls for a living."

The Père Longuemare took the hand the *ci-devant* financier extended to him and accepted the hospitality offered. Brotteaux, in his garret, served him a meal of bread and cheese and wine, which last he had put to cool in the rain-gutter, for was he not a Sybarite?

Having appeased his hunger:

"Sir," said the Père Longuemare, "I ought to inform you of the circumstances that led to my flight and left me to die on yonder post where you found me. Driven from my cloister, I lived on the scanty allowance the Assembly had assigned to me; I gave lessons in Latin and Mathematics and I wrote pamphlets on the persecution of the Church of France. I have even composed a work of some length, to prove that the Constitutional oath of the Priests is subversive of Ecclesiastical discipline. The advances made by the Revolution deprived me of all my pupils, while I could not get my pension because I had not the certificate of citizenship required by law. This certificate I went to the Hôtel de Ville to claim, in the conviction I was well entitled to it. Member of an order founded by the Apostle Paul himself, who boasted the title of Roman citizen, I always piqued myself on behaving after his example as a good French citizen, a re-

107

specter of all human laws which are not in opposition to the Divine. I presented my demand to Monsieur Colin, pork-butcher and Municipal officer, in charge of the delivery of certificates of the sort. He questioned me as to my calling. I told him I was a Priest. He asked me if I was married, and on my answering that I was not, he told me that was the worse for me. Finally, after a variety of questions, he asked me if I had proved my citizenship on the 10th August, the 2nd September and the 31st May. 'No certificates can be given,' he added, 'except to such as have proved their patriotism by their behaviour on these three occasions.' I could not give him an answer that would satisfy him. However, he took down my name and address and promised me to make prompt enquiry into my case. He kept his word, and as the result of his enquiry two Commissioners of the Committee of General Security of Picpus, supported by an armed band, presented themselves at my lodging in my absence to conduct me to prison. I do not know of what crime I am accused. But you will agree with me one must pity Monsieur Colin, whose wits are so clouded he holds it a reproach to an ecclesiastic not to have made display of his patriotism on the 10th August, the 2nd September, and the 31st May. A man capable of such a notion is surely deserving of commiseration."

"*I* am in the same plight, I have no certificate," observed Brotteaux. "We are both suspects. But you are weary. To bed, Father. We will discuss plans to-morrow for your safety."

He gave the mattress to his guest and kept the palliasse for himself; but the monk in his humility demanded the latter with so much urgency that his wish had to be complied with; otherwise he would have slept on the boards.

These arrangements completed, Brotteaux blew out the candle both to save tallow and as a wise precaution.

"Sir," the monk addressed him, "I am thankful for what you are doing for me; but alas! it is of small moment to you whether I am grateful or no. May God account your act meritorious! *That* is of infinite concern for you. But God pays no heed to what is not done for his glory and is merely the outcome of purely natural virtue. Wherefore I beseech you, sir, to do for Him what you were led to do for me."

"Father," answered Brotteaux, "never trouble yourself on this head and do not think of gratitude. What I am doing now, the merit of which you exaggerate,—is not done for any love of you; for indeed, albeit you are a lovable man, Father, I know you too little to love you. Nor yet do I act so for love of humanity; for I am not so simple as to think with 'Don Juan' that humanity has rights; indeed this prejudice, in a mind so emancipated as his, grieves me. I do it out of that selfishness which inspires mankind to perform all their deeds of generosity and self-sacrifice, by making them recognize themselves in all who are unfortunate, by disposing them to commiserate their own calamities in the calamities of others and by inciting them to offer help to a mortal resembling themselves in nature and destiny, so that they think they are succouring themselves in succouring him. I do it also for lack of anything better to do; for life is so desperately insipid we must find distraction at any cost, and benevolence is an amusement, of a mawkish sort, one indulges in for want of any more savoury; I do it out of pride and to get an advantage over you; I do it, in a word, as part of a system and to show you what an atheist is capable of."

"Do not calumniate yourself, sir," replied the Père Longuemare. "I have received of God more marks of grace than He has accorded you hitherto; but I am not as good a man as you, and am greatly your inferior in natural merits. But now let me take an advantage too over you. Not knowing me, you cannot love me. And I, sir, without knowing you, I love you better than myself; God bids me do so."

Having so said, the Père Longuemare knelt down on the floor, and after repeating his prayers, stretched himself on his palliasse and fell peacefully asleep.

Chapter 13

ÉVARISTE GAMELIN occupied his place as juror of the Tribunal for the second time. Before the opening of the sitting, he discussed with his colleagues the news that had arrived that morning. Some of it was doubtful, some untrue; but part was authentic—and appalling; the armies of the coalition in command of all the roads and marching *en masse* on Paris, La Vendée triumphant, Lyons in insurrection, Toulon surrendered to the English, who were landing fourteen thousand men there.

For him and his fellow magistrates these were not only events of interest to all the world, but so many matters of domestic concern. Foredoomed to perish in the ruin of the fatherland, they made the public salvation their own proper business. The Nation's interests, thus entangled with their own, dictated their opinions and passions and conduct.

Gamelin, where he sat on the jury bench, was handed a letter from Trubert, Secretary of the Committee of Defence; it was to notify his appointment as Commissioner of Supplies of Powder and Saltpetre:

"You will excavate all the cellars in the Section in order to extract the substances necessary for the manufacture of powder. To-morrow perhaps the enemy will be before Paris; the soil of the fatherland must provide us with the lightning we shall launch against our aggressors. I send you herewith a schedule of instructions from the Convention regarding the manipulation of saltpetres. Farewell and brotherly greeting."

At that moment the accused was brought in. He was one of the last of the defeated Generals whom the Convention delivered over one after the other to the Tribunal, and the most insignificant. At sight of him Gamelin shuddered; once again he seemed to see the same soldier whom three weeks before, looking on as a spectator, he had seen sentenced and sent to the guillotine. The man was the same, with his obstinate, opinionated look; the procedure was the same. He gave his answers in a cunning, brutish way that ruined the effect

110

even of the most convincing. His cavilling and chicanery and the accusations he levelled against his subordinates, made you forget he was fulfilling the honourable task of defending his honour and his life. Everything was uncertain, every statement disputed,—position of the armies, total of forces engaged, munitions of war, orders given, orders received, movements of troops; nobody knew anything. It was impossible to make head or tail of these confused, nonsensical, aimless operations which had ended in disaster; defending counsel and the accused himself were as much in the dark as were accuser, judges, and jury, and strange to say, not a soul would admit, whether to himself or to other people, that this was the case. The judges took a childish delight in drawing plans and discussing problems of tactics and strategy, while the prisoner constantly betrayed his inborn predilection for crooked ways.

The arguments dragged on endlessly. And all the time Gamelin could see on the rough roads of the north the ammunition waggons stogged in the mire and the guns capsized in the ruts, and along all the ways the broken and beaten columns flying in disorder, while from all sides the enemy's cavalry was debouching by the abandoned defiles. And from this host of men betrayed he could hear a mighty shout going up in accusation of the General. When the hearing closed, darkness was falling on the hall, and the head of Marat gleamed half-seen like a phantom above the President's head. The jury was called upon to give judgment, but was of two minds. Gamelin, in a hoarse, strangled voice, but in resolute accents, declared the accused guilty of treason against the Republic, and a murmur of approval rose from the crowd, a flattering unction to his youthful virtue. The sentence was read by the light of torches which cast a lurid, uncertain gleam on the prisoner's hollow temples beaded with drops of sweat. Outside the doors, on the steps crowded with the customary swarm of cockaded harridans, Gamelin could hear his name, which the habitués of the Tribunal were beginning to know, passed from mouth to mouth, and was assailed by a bevy of *trico-teuses* who shook their fists in his face, demanding the head of *the Austrian*.

The next day Évariste had to give judgment on the fate of a poor woman, the widow Meyrion. She distributed bread from house to house and tramped the streets pushing a little hand-cart and carrying a wooden tally hung at her waist, on which she cut notches with her knife representing the number of the loaves she had delivered. Her gains amounted to eight sous a day. The Deputy of the Public Prosecutor displayed an extraordinary virulence towards the wretched creature, who had, it appears, shouted "Vive le Roi!" on several occasions, uttered anti-revolutionary remarks in the houses where she called to leave the daily dole of bread, and been mixed up in a plot for the escape of the woman Capet. In answer to the Judge's question she admitted the facts, alleged against her; whether fool or fanatic, she professed Royalist sentiments of the most enthusiastic sort and waited her doom.

The Revolutionary Tribunal made a point of proving the triumph of Equality by showing itself just as severe for street-porters and servant maids as for the aristocrats and financiers. Gamelin could conceive no other system possible under a popular government. He would have deemed it a mark of contempt, an insult to the people, to exclude it from punishment. That would have been to consider it, so to speak, as unworthy of chastisement by the law. Reserved for aristocrats only, the guillotine would have appeared to him in the light of an iniquitous privilege. In his thoughts he was beginning to erect chastisement into a religious and mystic dogma, to assign it a virtue, a merit of its own; he conceived that society owes punishment to criminals and that it is doing them an injustice to cheat them of this right. He declared the woman Meyrion guilty and deserving of death, only regretting that the fanatics, more culpable than herself, who had brought her to her ruin, were not there to share her fate.

Every evening almost Évariste attended the meetings of the Jacobins, who assembled in the former chapel of the Dominicans, commonly known as Jacobins, in the Rue Honoré. In a courtyard, in which stood a tree of Liberty, a poplar whose leaves shook and rustled all day in the wind, the chapel, built in a poor, clumsy style and surmounted by a heavy roof of tiles, showed its bare gable, pierced by a round window and an arched doorway, above which floated the National colours, the flagstaff crowned with the cap of Liberty. The Jacobins, like the Cordeliers and the Feuillants, had appropriated the premises and taken the name of the dispossessed monks. Gamelin, once a regular attendant at the sittings of the Cordeliers, did not find at the Jacobins the familiar sabots, *carmagnoles* and rallying cries of the Dantonists. In Robespierre's club administrative reserve and bourgeois gravity were the order of the day. The Friend of the People was no more, and since his death Évariste had followed the lessons of Maximilien whose thought ruled the Jacobins, and thence, through a thousand affiliated societies was disseminated over all France. During the reading of the minutes, his eyes wandered over the bare, dismal walls, which, after sheltering the spiritual sons of the arch-inquisitor of heresy, now looked down on the assemblage of zealous inquisitors of crimes against the fatherland.

There, without pomp or ceremony, sat the body that was the chiefest power of the State and ruled by force of words. It governed the city, the empire, dictated its decrees to the Convention itself. These artisans of the new order of things, so respectful of the law that they continued Royalists in 1791 and would fain have been Royalists still on the King's return from Varennes, so obstinate in their attachment to the Constitution, friends of the established order of the State even after the massacres of the Champ de Mars, and never revolutionaries against the Revolution, heedless of popular agitation, cherished in their dark and puissant soul a love of the fatherland that had given birth to fourteen armies and set up the guillotine. Évariste was lost in admiration of their vigilance, their suspicious temper, their reasoned dogmatism, their love of system, their supremacy in the art of governing, their sovereign sanity.

The public that formed the audience gave no token of their presence save a low, long-drawn murmur as of one voice, like the rustling of the leaves of the tree of Liberty that stood outside the threshold.

That day, the 11th Vendémiaire, a young man, with a receding brow, a piercing eye, a sharp prominent nose, a pointed chin, a pock-marked face, a look of cold self-possession, mounted the tribune slowly. His hair was white with powder and he wore a blue coat that displayed his slim figure. He showed the precise carriage and moved with the cadenced step that made some say in mockery that he was like a dancing-master and earned him from others the name of the "French Orpheus." Robespierre, speaking in a clear voice, delivered an eloquent discourse against the enemies of the Republic. He belaboured with metaphysical and uncompromising arguments Brissot and his accomplices. He spoke at great length, in free-flowing har-

113

monious periods. Soaring in the celestial spheres of philosophy, he launched his lightnings at the base conspirators crawling on the ground.

Évariste heard and understood. Till then he had blamed the Gironde; were they not working for the restoration of the monarchy or the triumph of the Orleans faction, were they not planning the ruin of the heroic city that had delivered France from her fetters and would one day deliver the universe? Now, as he listened to the sage's voice, he discerned truths of a higher and purer compass; he grasped a revolutionary metaphysic which lifted his mind above coarse, material conditions into a region of absolute, unqualified convictions, untrammelled by the errors of the senses. Things are in their nature involved and full of confusion; the complexity of circumstances is such that we lose our way amongst them. Robespierre simplified them to his mind, put good and evil before him in clear and precise formulas. Federalism,—indivisibility; unity and indivisibility meant salvation, Federalism damnation. Gamelin tasted the ineffable joy of a believer who knows the word that saves and the word that destroys the soul. Henceforth the Revolutionary Tribunal, as of old the ecclesiastical courts, would take cognizance of crime absolute, of crime definable in a word. And, because he had the religious spirit, Évariste welcomed these revelations with a sombre enthusiasm; his heart swelled and rejoiced at the thought that, henceforth, he had a talisman to discern betwixt crime and innocence, he possessed a creed! Ye stand in lieu of all else, oh, treasures of faith!

The sage Maximilien enlightened him further as to the perfidious intent of those who were for equalizing property and partitioning the land, abolishing wealth and poverty and establishing a happy mediocrity for all. Misled by their specious maxims, he had originally approved their designs, which he deemed in accord with the principles of a true Republican. But Robespierre, in his speeches at the Jacobins, had unmasked their machinations and convinced him that these men, disinterested as their intentions appeared, were working to overthrow the Republic, that they were alarming the rich only to rouse against the lawful authority powerful and implacable foes. Once private property was threatened, the whole population, the more ardently attached to its possessions the less of these it owned, would turn suddenly against the Republic. To terrify vested interests is to conspire against the State. These men who, under pretence of securing universal happiness and the reign of justice, proposed a system of equality and community of goods as a worthy object of good citizens' endeavours, were traitors and malefactors more dangerous than the Federalists.

But the most startling revelation he owed to Robespierre's wisdom was that of the crimes and infamies of atheism. Gamelin had never denied the existence of God; he was a deist and believed in a Providence that watches over mankind; but, admitting that he could form only a very vague conception of the Supreme Being and deeply attached to the principle of freedom of conscience, he was quite ready to allow that right-thinking men might follow the example of Lamettrie, Boulanger, the Baron d'Holbach, Lalande, Helvetius, the *citoyen* Dupuis, and deny God's existence, on condition they formulated a natural morality and found in themselves the sources of justice and the rules of a virtuous life. He had even felt himself in sympathy with the atheists, when he had seen them vilified and persecuted. Maximilien had opened his mind and unsealed his eyes. The great man by his virtuous eloquence had taught him the true character of atheism, its nature, its objects, its effects; he had shown him how this doctrine, conceived in the drawing-rooms and boudoirs of the aristocracy, was the most perfidious invention the enemies of the people had ever devised to demoralize and enslave it; how it was a criminal act to uproot from the heart of the unfortunate the consoling thought of a Providence to reward and compensate and give them over without rein or bit to the passions that degrade men and make vile slaves of them; how, in fine, the monarchical Epicureanism of a Helvetius led to immorality, cruelty, and every wickedness. Now that he had learnt these lessons from the lips of a great man and a great citizen, he execrated the atheists — especially when they were of an open-hearted, joyous temper, like his old friend Brotteaux.

In the days that followed Évariste had to give judgment one after the other on a *ci-devant* convicted of having destroyed wheat-stuffs in order to starve the people, three *émigrés* who had returned to foment civil war in France, two ladies of pleasure of the Palais-Égalité, fourteen Breton conspirators, men, women, old men, youths, masters, and servants. The crime was proven, the law explicit. Among the guilty was a girl of twenty, adorable in the heyday of her young beauty under the shadow of the doom so soon to overwhelm her, a fascinating figure. A blue bow bound her golden locks, her lawn kerchief revealed a white, graceful neck.

Évariste was consistent in casting his vote for death, and all the accused, with the one exception of an old gardener, were sent to the scaffold.

The following week Évariste and his Section mowed down sixty-three heads — forty-five men and eighteen women.

The judges of the Revolutionary Tribunal drew no distinction between men and women, in this following a principle as old as justice itself. True, the President Montané, touched by the bravery and beauty of Charlotte Corday, had tried to save her by paltering with the procedure of the trial and had thereby lost his seat, but women as a rule were shown no favour under examination, in strict accordance with the rule common to all the Tribunals. The jurors feared them, distrusting their artful ways, their aptitude for deception, their powers of seduction. They were the match of men in resolution, and this invited the Tribunal to treat them in the same way. The majority of those who sat in judgment, men of normal sensuality or sensual on occasion, were in no wise affected by the fact that the prisoner was a woman. They condemned or acquitted them as their conscience, their prejudices, their zeal, their love, lukewarm or vehement, for the Republic dictated. Almost always they appeared before the court with their hair carefully dressed and attired with as much elegance as the unhappy conditions allowed. But few of them were young and still fewer pretty. Confinement and suspense had blighted them, the harsh light of the hall betrayed their weariness and the anguish they had endured, beating down on faded lids, blotched and pimpled cheeks, white, drawn lips. Nevertheless, the fatal chair more than once held a young girl, lovely in her pallor, while a shadow of the tomb veiled her eyes and made her beauty the more seductive. That the sight had the power to melt some jurymen and irritate others, who should deny! That, in the secret depraved heart of him, one of these magistrates may have pried into the most sacred intimacies of the fair body that was to his morbid fancy at the same moment a living and a dead woman's, and that, gloating over voluptuous and ghoulish imaginings he may have found an atrocious pleasure in giving over to the headsman those dainty, desirable limbs,— this is perhaps a thing better left unsaid, but one which no one can deem impossible who knows what men are. Évariste Gamelin, cold and pedantic in his artistic creed, could see no beauty but in the Antique; he admired beauty, but it hardly stirred his senses. His classical taste was so severe he rarely found a woman to his liking; he was as insensible to the charms of a pretty face as he was to Fragonard's colouring and Boucher's drawing. He had never known desire save under the form of deep passion.

Like the majority of his colleagues in the Tribunal, he thought women more dangerous than men. He hated the *ci-devant* princesses, the creatures he pictured to himself in his horrified dreams in company with Elisabeth and *the Austrian* weaving plots to assassinate good patriots; he even hated all those fair mistresses of financiers, philosophers, and men of letters whose only crime was having enjoyed the pleasures of the senses and the mind and lived at a time when it was sweet to live. He hated them without admitting the feeling to himself, and when he had one before him at the bar, he condemned her out of pique, convinced all the while that he was dooming her justly and rightly for the public good. His sense of honour, his manly modesty, his cold, calculated wisdom, his devotion to the State, his virtues in a word, pushed under the knife heads that might well have moved men's pity.

But what is this, what is the meaning of this strange prodigy? Once the difficulty was to find the guilty, to search them out in their lair, to drag the confession of their crime from reluctant lips. Now, there is no hunting with a great pack of sleuth-hounds, no pursuing a timid prey; lo! from all sides come the victims to offer themselves a voluntary sacrifice. Nobles, virgins, soldiers, courtesans, flock to the Tribunal, dragging their condemnation from dilatory judges, claiming death as a right which they are impatient to enjoy. Not enough the multitude with which the zeal of the informers has crowded the prisons and which the Public Prosecutor and his myrmidons are wearing out their lives in haling before the Tribunal; punishment must likewise be provided for those who refuse to wait. And how many others, prouder and more pressing yet, begrudging their judges and headsmen their death, perish by their own hand! The mania of killing is equalled by the mania to die. Here, in the Conciergerie, is a young soldier, handsome, vigorous, beloved; he leaves behind him in the prison an adorable mistress; she bade him "Live for me!"—he will live neither for her nor love nor glory. He lights his pipe with his act of accusation. And, a Republican, for he breathes liberty through every pore, he turns Royalist that he may die. The Tribunal tries its best to save him, but the accused proves the stronger; judges and jury are forced to let him have his way.

Évariste's mind, naturally of an anxious, scrupulous cast, was filled to overflowing through the lessons he learned at the Jacobins and the contemplation of life with suspicions and alarms. At night, as he paced the ill-lighted streets on his way to Élodie's, he fancied through every cellar-grating he passed he caught a glimpse of a plate for printing off forged assignats; in the dark recesses of the baker's and grocer's empty shops he imagined storerooms bursting with provisions fraudulently held back for a rise in prices; looking in at the glittering windows of the eating-houses, he seemed to hear the talk of the speculators plotting the ruin of the country as they drained bottles of Beaune and Chablis; in the evil-smelling alleys he could see the very prostitutes trampling underfoot the National cockade to the applause of elegant young roisterers; everywhere he beheld conspirators and traitors. And he thought: "Against so many foes, secret or declared, O Republic, thou hast but one succour; Saint Guillotine, save the fatherland! . . ."

Élodie would be waiting for him in her little blue chamber above the *Amour peintre*. To let him know he might come in, she used to set on the window-sill her little watering-can beside the pot of carnations. Now he filled her with horror, he seemed like a monster to her; she was afraid of him,—and she adored him. All the night, clinging together in a frantic embrace, the bloody-minded lover and the amorous girl exchanged in silence frenzied kisses.

Chapter 14

RISING at dawn, the Père Longuemare, after sweeping out the room, departed to say his Mass in a chapel in the Rue d'Enfer served by a nonjuring priest. There were in Paris thousands of similar retreats, where the refractory clergy gathered together clandestinely little troops of the faithful. The police of the Sections, vigilant and suspicious as they were, kept their eyes shut to these hidden folds, from fear of the exasperated flock and moved by some lingering veneration for holy things. The Barnabite made his farewells to his host who had great difficulty in persuading him to come back to dine, and only succeeded in the end by promising that the cheer would be neither plentiful nor delicate.

Brotteaux, when left to himself, kindled a little earthenware stove; then, while he busied himself with preparations for the Monk's and the Epicurean's meal, he read in his Lucretius and meditated on the condition of human beings.

As a sage and a philosopher, he was not surprised that these wretched creatures, silly playthings of the forces of nature, found themselves more often than not in absurd and painful situations; but he was weak and illogical enough to believe that the Revolutionaries were more wicked and more foolish than other men, thereby falling into the error of the metaphysician. At the same time he was no pessimist and did not hold that life was altogether bad. He admired Nature in several of her departments, especially the celestial mechanism and physical love, and accommodated himself to the labours of life, pending the arrival of the day, which could not be far off, when he would have nothing more either to fear or to desire.

He coloured some dancing-dolls with painstaking care and made a Zerline that was very like Rose Thévenin. He liked the girl and his Epicureanism highly approved of the arrangement of the atoms of which she was composed.

These tasks occupied him till the Barnabite's return.

"Father," he announced, as he opened the door to admit him, "I told you, you remember, that our fare would be meagre. We have nothing but chestnuts. The more reason, therefore, they should be well seasoned."

"Chestnuts!" cried Père Longuemare, smiling, "there is no more delicious dish. My father, sir, was a poor gentleman of the Limousin, whose whole estate consisted of a pigeon-cote in ruins, an orchard run wild and a clump of chestnut-trees. He fed himself, his wife and his twelve children on big green chestnuts, and we were all strong and sturdy. I was the youngest and the most turbulent; my father used to declare, by way of jesting, he would have to send me to America to be a filibuster. . . . Ah! sir, how fragrant your chestnut soup smells! It takes me back to the table where my mother sat smiling, surrounded by her troop of little ones."

The repast ended, Brotteaux set out for Joly's the toy-merchant in the Rue Neuve-des-Petits-Champs, who took the dancing-dolls Caillou had refused, and ordered—not another gross of them like the latter, but a round twenty-four dozen to begin with.

On reaching the erstwhile Rue Royale and turning into the Place de la Révolution, Brotteaux caught sight of a steel triangle glittering between two wooden uprights; it was the guillotine. An immense crowd of light-hearted spectators pressed round the scaffold, waiting the arrival of the loaded carts. Women were hawking Nanterre cakes on a tray hung in front of them and crying their wares; sellers of cooling drinks were tinkling their little bells; at the foot of the Statue of Liberty an old man had a peep-show in a small booth surmounted by a swing on which a monkey played its antics. Underneath the scaffold some dogs were licking yesterday's blood. Brotteaux turned back towards the Rue Honoré.

Regaining his garret, where the Barnabite was reading his breviary, he carefully wiped the table and arranged his colour-box on it alongside the materials and tools of his trade.

"Father," he said, "if you do not deem the occupation unworthy of the sacred character with which you are invested, I will ask you to help me make my marionettes. A worthy tradesman, Joly by name, has this very morning given me a pretty heavy order. Whilst I am painting these figures already put together, you will do me a great service by cutting out heads, arms, legs, and bodies from the patterns here. Better you could not find; they are after Watteau and Boucher."

"I agree with you, sir," replied Longuemare, "that Watteau and Boucher were well fitted to create such-like baubles; it had been more to their glory if they had confined themselves to innocent figures like these. I should be delighted to help you, but I fear I may not be clever enough for that."

The Père Longuemare was right to distrust his own skill; after sundry unsuccessful attempts, the fact was patent that his genius did not lie in the direction of cutting out pretty shapes in thin cardboard with the point of a penknife. But when, at his suggestion, Brotteaux gave him some string and a bodkin, he showed himself very apt in endowing with motion the little creatures he had failed to make and teaching them to dance. He had a happy knack, by way of trying them afterwards, of making them each execute three or four steps of a gavotte, and when they rewarded his pains, a smile would flicker on his stern lips.

One time when he was pulling the string of a Scaramouch to a dance tune:

"Sir," he observed, "this little travesty reminds me of a quaint story. It was in 1746, when I was completing my noviciate under the care of the Père Magitot, a man well on in years, of deep learning and austere morals. At that period, you perhaps remember, dancing figures, intended in the first instance to amuse children, exercised over women and even over men, both young and old, an extraordinary fascination; they were all the rage in Paris. The fashionable shops were crammed with them; they were to be found in the houses of people of quality, and it was nothing out of the way to see a grave and reverend senior dancing his doll in the streets and public gardens. The Père Magitot's age, character, and sacred profession did not avail to guard him against infection. Every time he saw anyone busy jumping his cardboard mannikin, his fingers itched with impatience to be at the same game,—an impatience that soon grew well-nigh intolerable. One day when he was paying a visit of importance on a matter involving the interests of the whole Order to Monsieur Chauvel, advocate in the courts of the Parlement, noticing one of these dancers hanging from the chimney-piece, he felt a terrible temptation to pull its string, which he only resisted at the cost of a tremendous effort. But this frivolous ambition pursued him everywhere and left him no peace. In his studies, in his meditations, in his prayers, at church, at chapter, in the confessional and in the pulpit, he was possessed by it. After some days of dreadful agony of mind, he laid bare his extraordinary case to the General of the Order, who happened fortunately to be in Paris at the moment. He was an eminent ecclesiastic of Milan, a Doctor and Prince of the Church. His counsel to the Père Magitot was to satisfy a craving, innocent in its inception, importunate in its consequences and inordinate in its excess, which threatened to superinduce the gravest disorders in the soul which was afflicted with it. On the advice, or more strictly by the order of the General, the Père Magitot returned to Monsieur Chauvel's house, where the advocate received him, as on the first occasion, in his cabinet. There, finding the dancing figure still fastened in the same place, he ran excitedly to the chimney-piece and begged his host to do him a favour,—to let him pull the string. The lawyer gave him his permission very readily, and informed him in confidence that sometimes he set Scaramouch (that was the doll's name) dancing while he was studying his briefs, and that, only the night before, he had modulated on Scaramouch's movements the peroration of his speech in defence of a woman falsely accused of poisoning her husband. The Père Magitot seized the string with trembling fingers and saw Scaramouch throw his limbs wildly about under his manipulation like one possessed of devils in the agonies of exorcism. When he had satisfied his caprice in this way, his obsession left him."

"Your tale does not surprise me, Father," Brotteaux told him. "We see such cases of obsession; but it is not always cardboard figures that occasion it."

The Père Longuemare, who was religious by profession, never talked about religion, while Brotteaux was for ever harping on the subject. He was conscious of a bond of sympathy between himself and the Barnabite, and took a delight in embarrassing and disturbing his peace of mind with objections against divers articles of the Christian faith.

Once when they were working together making Zerlines and Scaramouches:

"When I consider," remarked Brotteaux, "the events which have brought us to the point at which we stand, I am in doubt as to which party, in the general madness, has been the most insane; sometimes, I am greatly tempted to believe it was that of the Court."

"Sir," answered the monk, "all men lose their wits like Nebuchadnezzar, when God forsakes them; but no man in our days ever plunged so deep in ignorance and error as the Abbé Fauchet, no man was so fatal as he to the kingdom. God must needs have been sorely exasperated against France to send her Monsieur l'Abbé Fauchet!"

"I imagine we have seen other evil-doers besides poor, unhappy Fauchet."

"The Abbé Grégoire too, was full of malice."

"And Brissot, and Danton, and Marat, and a hundred others, what of them, Father?"

"Sir, they are laics; the laity could never incur the same responsibilities as the clergy. They do not work evil from so high a standpoint, and their crimes are not of universal bearing."

"And your God, Father, what say you of His behaviour in the present Revolution?"

"I do not understand you, sir."

"Epicurus said: Either God wishes to hinder evil and cannot, or He can and does not wish to, or He cannot nor does He wish to, or He does wish to and can. If He wishes to and cannot, He is impotent; if He can and does not wish to, He is perverse; if He cannot nor does He wish to, He is impotent and perverse; if He does wish to and can, why does He not, tell me that, Father!"—and Brotteaux cast a look of triumph at his interlocutor.

"Sir," retorted the monk, "there is nothing more contemptible than these difficulties you raise. When I look into the reasoning of infidels, I seem to see ants piling up a few blades of grass as a dam against the torrent that sweeps down from the mountains. With your leave, I had rather not argue with you; I should have too many excellent reasons and too few wits to apply them. Besides, you will find your refutation in the Abbé Guénée and twenty other apologists. I will only say that what you quote from Epicurus is foolishness; because God is arraigned in it as if he was a man, with a man's moral code. Well! sir, the sceptics, from Celsus down to Bayle and Voltaire, have cajoled fools with such-like paradoxes."

"See, Father," protested Brotteaux, "to what lengths your faith makes you go. Not satisfied with finding all truth in your Theology, you likewise refuse to discover any in the works of so many noble intellects who thought differently from yourselves."

"You are entirely mistaken, sir," replied Longuemare. "On the contrary, I believe that nothing could ever be altogether false in a man's thoughts. The atheists stand on the lowest rung of the ladder of knowledge; but even there, gleams of sense are to be found and flashes of truth, and even when darkness is thick about him, a man may lift up his eyes to God, and He will put understanding in his heart; was it not so with Lucifer?"

"Well, sir," said Brotteaux, "I cannot match your generosity, and I am bound to tell you I cannot find in all the works of the Theologians one atom of good sense."

At the same time he would repudiate any desire to attack religion, which he deemed indispensable for the nations; he could only wish it had for its ministers philosophers instead of controversialists. He deplored the fact that the Jacobins were for replacing it by a newer and more pestilent religion, the cult of liberty, equality, the republic, the fatherland. He had observed this, that it is in the vigour of their youth religions are the fiercest and most cruel, and grow milder as they grow older. He was anxious, therefore, to see Catholicism preserved; it had devoured many victims in the times of its vigour, but nowadays, burdened by the weight of years and with enfeebled appetite, it was content with roasting four or five heretics in a hundred years.

"As a matter of fact," he concluded, "I have always got on very well with your God-eaters and Christ-worshippers. I kept a chaplain at Les Ilettes, where Mass was said every Sunday and all my guests attended. The philosophers were the most devout while the opera girls showed the most fervour. I was prosperous then and had crowds of friends."

"Friends," exclaimed the Père Longuemare, "friends! Ah! sir, do you really think they loved you, all these philosophers and all these courtesans, who have degraded your soul in such wise that God himself would find it hard to know it for one of the temples built by Him for His glory?"

The Père Longuemare lived for a week longer at the publican's without being interfered with. As far as possible he observed the discipline of his House and every night at the canonical hours would rise from his palliasse to kneel on the bare boards and recite the Offices. Though both were reduced to a diet of wretched scraps, he duly observed fasts and abstinence. A smiling but pitiful spectator of these austerities, Brotteaux one day asked him:

"Do you really believe that God finds any satisfaction in seeing you endure cold and hunger as you do?"

"God himself," was the monk's answer, "has given us the example of suffering."

On the ninth day since the Barnabite had come to share the philosopher's garret, the latter sallied forth at twilight to deliver his dancing-dolls to Joly, the toy-merchant of the Rue Neuve-des-Petits-Champs. He was on his way back overjoyed at having sold them all, when, as he was crossing the erstwhile Place du Carrousel, a girl in a blue satin pelisse trimmed with ermine, running by with a limping gait, threw herself into his arms and held him fast in the way suppliants have had since the world began.

She was trembling, and her heart was beating so fast and loud it could be plainly heard. Wondering to see one of her common sort look so pathetic, Brotteaux, a veteran amateur of the stage, thought how Mademoiselle Raucourt, if she could have seen her, might have learnt something from her bearing.

She spoke in breathless tones, lowering her voice to a whisper for fear of being overheard by the passers-by:

"Take me with you, *citoyen*, and hide me, for the love of pity! . . . They are in my room in the Rue Fromenteau. While they were coming upstairs, I ran for refuge into Flora's room,—she is my next-door neighbour,—and leapt out of the window into the street, that is how I sprained my ankle. . . . They are coming; they want to put me in prison and kill me. . . . Last week they killed Virginie."

Brotteaux understood, of course, that the child was speaking of the delegates of the Revolutionary Committee of the Section or else the Commissaries of the Committee of General Security. At that time the Commune had as Procureur a man of virtue, the *citoyen* Chaumette, who regarded the ladies of pleasure as the direct foes of the Republic and harassed them unmercifully in his efforts to re-generate the Nation's morals. To tell the truth, the young ladies of the Palais-Égalité were no great patriots. They regretted the old

125

state of things and did not always conceal the fact. Several had been guillotined already as conspirators, and their tragic fate had excited no little emulation among their fellows.

The *citoyen* Brotteaux asked the suppliant what offence she had been guilty of to bring down on herself a warrant of arrest.

She swore she had no notion, that she had done nothing anyone could blame her for.

"Well then, my girl," Brotteaux told her, "you are not suspect; you have nothing to fear. Be off with you to bed and leave me alone."

At this she confessed everything:

"I tore out my cockade and shouted: 'Vive le roi!'"

He walked down to the river-side and she kept by his side along the deserted *quais*. Clinging to his arm she went on:

"It is not that I care for him particularly, the King, you know; I never knew him, and I daresay he wasn't very much different from other men. But they are bad people. They are cruel to poor girls. They torment and vex and abuse me in every kind of way; they want to stop me following my trade. I have no other trade. You may be sure, if I had, I should not be doing what I do. . . . What is it they want? They are so hard on poor humble folks, the milkman, the charcoalman, the water carrier, the laundress. They won't rest content till they've set all poor people against them."

He looked at her; she seemed a mere child. She was no longer afraid; she was almost smiling, as she limped along lightly at his side. He asked her her name. She said she was called Athenaïs and was sixteen.

Brotteaux offered to see her safe to anywhere she wished to go. She did not know a soul in Paris; but she had an aunt, in service at Palaiseau, who would take her in.

Brotteaux made up his mind at once.

"Come with me, my child," he ordered, and led the way home, with her hanging on his arm.

On his arrival, he found the Père Longuemare in the garret reading his breviary.

Holding Athenaïs by the hand, he drew the other's attention to her:

"Father," he said, "here is a girl from the Rue Fromenteau who has been shouting: 'Vive le roi!' The Revolutionary police are on her track. She has nowhere to lay head. Will you allow the girl to pass the night here?"

The Père Longuemare closed his breviary.

"If I understand you right," he said, "you ask me, sir, if this young girl, who is like myself subject to be molested under a warrant of arrest, may be suffered, for her temporal salvation, to spend the night in the same room as I?"

"Yes, Father."

"By what right should I object? and why must I suppose myself affronted by her presence? am I so sure that I am any better than she?"

He established himself for the night in an old broken-down armchair, declaring he should sleep excellently in it. Athenaïs lay on the mattress. Brotteaux stretched himself on the palliasse and blew out the candle.

The hours and half-hours sounded one after the other from the church towers, but the old man could not sleep; he lay awake listening to the mingled breathing of the man of religion and the girl of pleasure. The moon rose, symbol and witness of his old-time loves, and threw a silvery ray into the attic, illuminating the fair hair and golden lashes, the delicate nose and round, red mouth of Athenaïs, who lay sound asleep.

"Truly," he thought to himself, "a terrible enemy for the Republic!"

When Athenaïs awoke, the day was breaking. The monk had disappeared. Brotteaux was reading Lucretius under the skylight, learning from the maxims of the Latin poet to live without fears and without desires; but for all this he felt himself at the moment devoured with regrets and disquietudes.

Opening her eyes, Athenaïs was dumfounded to see the roof beams of a garret above her head. Then she remembered, smiled at her preserver and extended towards him with a caressing gesture her pretty little dirty hands.

Rising on her elbow, she pointed to the dilapidated armchair in which the monk had passed the night.

"He is not there? . . . He has not gone to denounce me, has he?"

"No, no, my child. You could not find a more honest soul than that old madman."

Athenaïs asked in what the old fellow's madness consisted; and when Brotteaux informed her it was religion, she gravely reproached him for speaking so, declaring that men without faith were worse than the beasts that perish and that for her part she often prayed to God, hoping He would forgive her her sins and receive her in His blessed mercy.

Then, noticing that Brotteaux held a book in his hand, she thought it was a book of the Mass and said:

"There you see, you too, you say your prayers! God will reward you for what you have done for me."

Brotteaux having told her that it was not a Massbook, and that it had been written before ever the Mass had been invented in the world, she opined it was an *Interpretation of Dreams*, and asked if it did not contain an explanation of an extraordinary dream she had had. She could not read, and these were the only two sorts of books she had heard tell of.

Brotteaux informed her that this book was only by way of explaining the dream of life. Finding this a hard saying, the pretty child did not try to understand it and dipped the end of her nose in the earthenware crock that replaced the silver basins Brotteaux had once been accustomed to use. Next, she arranged her hair before her host's shaving-glass with scrupulous care and gravity. Her white arms raised above her head, she let fall an observation from time to time with long intervals between:

"You, you were rich once."

"What makes you think that?"

"I don't know. But you *were* rich,—and you are an aristocrat, I am certain of it."

She drew from her pocket a little Blessed Virgin of silver in a round ivory shrine, a bit of sugar, thread, scissors, a flint and steel, two or three cases for needles and the like, and after selecting what she required, sat down to mend her skirt, which had got torn in several places.

"For your own safety, my child, put this in your cap!" Brotteaux bade her, handing her a tricolour cockade.

"I will do that gladly, sir," she agreed, "but it will be for the love of you and not for the love of the Nation."

When she was dressed and had made herself look her best, taking her skirt in both hands, she dropped a curtsey as she had been taught to do in her village, and addressing Brotteaux:

128

"Sir," she said, "I am your very humble servant."

She was prepared to oblige her benefactor in all ways he might wish, but she thought it more becoming that he asked for no favour and she offered none; it seemed to her a pretty way to part so, and what good manners required.

Brotteaux slipped a few assignats into her hand to pay her coach-hire to Palaiseau. It was the half of his fortune, and, albeit he was notorious for his lavishness towards women, it was the first time he had ever made so equal a partition of his goods with any of the sex.

She asked him his name.

"I am called Maurice."

It was with reluctance he opened the garret door for her:

"Good-bye, Athenaïs."

She kissed him. "Monsieur Maurice," she said, "when you think of me, if ever you do, call me Marthe; that is the name I was christened, the name they called me by in the village. . . . Good-bye and thank you. . . . Your very humble servant, Monsieur Maurice."

Chapter 15

THE prisons were full to bursting and must be emptied; the work of judging, judging, must go on without truce or respite. Seated against the walls tapestried with fasces and red caps of Liberty, like their fellows of the fleurs-de-lis, the judges preserved the same gravity, the same dreadful calm, as their Royal predecessors. The Public Prosecutor and his Deputies, worn out with fatigue, consumed with the fever of sleeplessness and brandy, could only shake off their exhaustion by a violent effort; their broken health made them tragic figures to look upon. The jurors, diverse in character and origin, some educated, others ignorant, craven or generous, gentle or violent, hypocritical or sincere, but all men who, knowing the fatherland and the Republic in danger, suffered or feigned to suffer the same anguish, to burn with the same ardour; all alike primed to atrocities of virtue or of fear, they formed but one living entity, one single head, dull and irritable, one single soul, a beast of the apocalypse that by the mere exercise of its natural functions produced a teeming brood of death. Kind-hearted or cruel by caprice of sensibility, when shaken momentarily by a sudden pang of pity, they would acquit with streaming eyes a prisoner whom an hour before they would have condemned to the guillotine with taunts. The further they proceeded with their task, the more impetuously did they follow the impulses of their heart.

Judge and jury toiled, fevered and half asleep with overwork, distracted by the excitement outside and the orders of the sovereign people, menaced by the threats of the *sansculottes* and *tricoteuses* who crowded the galleries and the public enclosure, relying on insane evidence, acting on the denunciations of madmen, in a poisonous atmosphere that stupefied the brain, set ears hammering and temples beating and darkened the eyes with a veil of blood. Vague rumours were current among the public of jurors bought by the gold of the accused. But to these the jury as a body replied with indignant protest and merciless condemnations. In truth they were men neither worse nor better than their fellows. Innocence more often than not is a piece of good fortune rather than a virtue; any other who should have consented to put himself in their place would have acted as they did and accomplished to the best of his commonplace soul these appalling tasks.

Antoinette, so long expected, sat at last in the fatal chair, in a black gown, the centre of such a concentration of hate that only the certainty of what the sentence would be made the court observe the forms of law. To the deadly questions the accused replied sometimes with the instinct of self-preservation, sometimes with her wonted haughtiness, and once, thanks to the hideous suggestion of one of her accusers, with the noble dignity of a mother. The witnesses were confined to outrage and calumny; the defence was frozen with terror. The Tribunal, forcing itself to respect the rules of procedure, was only waiting till all formalities were completed to hurl the head of *the Austrian* in the face of Europe.

Three days after the execution of Marie Antoinette Gamelin was called to the bedside of the *citoyen* Fortuné Trubert, who lay dying within thirty paces of the Military Bureau where he had worn out his life, on a pallet of sacking, in the cell of some expelled Barnabite father. His livid face was sunk in the pillow. His eyes, which already were almost sightless, turned their glassy pupils upon his visitor; his parched hand grasped Évariste's and pressed it with unexpected vigour. Three times he had vomited blood in two days. He tried to speak; his voice, at first hoarse and feeble as a whisper, grew louder, deeper:

"Wattignies! Wattignies! . . . Jourdan has forced the enemy into their camp . . . raised the blockade at Maubeuge. . . . We have retaken Marchiennes, *ça ira . . . ça ira . . .* " and he smiled.

These were no dreams of a sick man, but a clear vision of the truth that flashed through the brain so soon to be shrouded in eternal darkness. Hereafter the invasion seemed arrested; the Generals were terrorized and saw that the one best thing for them to do was to be victorious. Where voluntary recruiting had failed to produce what was needed, a strong and disciplined army, compulsion was succeeding. One effort more, and the Republic would be saved.

After a half hour of semi-consciousness, Fortuné Trubert's face, hollow-cheeked and worn by disease, lit up again and his hands moved.

He lifted his finger and pointed to the only piece of furniture in the room, a little walnut-wood writing-desk. The voice was weak and breathless, but the mind quite unclouded:

"Like Eudamidas," he said, "I bequeath my debts to my friend— three hundred and twenty livres, of which you will find the account . . . in that red book yonder . . . good-bye, Gamelin. Never rest; wake and watch over the defence of the Republic. *Ça ira*."

The shades of night were deepening in the cell. The difficult breathing of the dying man was the only sound, and his hands scratching on the sheet.

At midnight he uttered some disconnected phrases:

"More saltpetre. . . . See the muskets are delivered. Health? Oh! excellent. . . . Get down the church-bells. . . ."

He breathed his last at five in the morning.

By order of the Section his body lay in state in the nave of the erstwhile church of the Barnabites, at the foot of the Altar of the Fatherland, on a camp bed, covered with a tricolour flag and the brow wreathed with an oak crown.

Twelve old men clad in the Roman toga, with palms in their hands, twelve young girls wearing long veils and carrying flowers, surrounded the funeral couch. At the dead man's feet stood two children, each holding an inverted torch. One of them Évariste recognized as his *concierge's* little daughter Joséphine, who in her childish gravity and beauty reminded him of those charming genii of Love and Death the Romans used to sculpture on their tombs.

The funeral procession made its way to the Cemetery of Saint-André-des-Arts to the strains of the *Marseillaise* and the *Ça-ira*.

As he laid the kiss of farewell on Fortuné Trubert's brow, Évariste wept. His tears flowed in self-pity, for he envied his friend who was resting there, his task accomplished.

On reaching home, he received notice that he was posted a member of the Council General of the Commune. After standing as candidate for four months, he had been elected unopposed, after several ballots, by some thirty suffrages. No one voted nowadays; the Sections were deserted; rich and poor alike only sought to shirk the performance of public duties. The most momentous events had ceased to rouse either enthusiasm or curiosity; the newspapers were left unread. Out of the seven hundred thousand inhabitants of the capital Évariste doubted if as many as three or four thousand still preserved the old Republican spirit.

The same day the Twenty-one came up for trial. Innocent or guilty of the calamities and crimes of the Republic, vain, incautious, ambitious and impetuous, at once moderate and violent, feeble in their fear as in their clemency, quick to declare war, slow to carry it out, haled before the Tribunal to answer for the example they had given, they were not the less the first and the most brilliant children of the Revolution, whose delight and glory they had been. The judge who will question them with artful bias; the pallid accuser yonder who, where he sits behind his little table, is planning their death and dishonour; the jurors who will presently try to stifle their defence; the public in the galleries which overwhelms them with howls of insult and abuse,—all, judge, jury, people, have applauded their eloquence in other days, extolled their talents and their virtues. But judge, jury, people have short memories now.

Once Évariste had made Vergniaud his god, Brissot his oracle. But he had forgotten; if any vestige of his old wonder still lingered in his memory, it was to think that these monsters had seduced the noblest citizens.

Returning to his lodging after the sitting, Gamelin heard heartbreaking cries as he entered the house. It was little Joséphine; her mother was whipping her for playing in the Place with good-fornothing boys and dirtying the fine white frock she had worn for the obsequies of the *citoyen* Trubert.

Chapter 16

AFTER three months during which he had made a daily holocaust of victims, illustrious or insignificant, to the fatherland, Évariste had a case that interested him personally; there was one prisoner he made it his special business to track down to death.

Ever since he had sat on the juror's bench, he had been eagerly watching, among the crowd of culprits who appeared before him, for Élodie's seducer; of this man he had elaborated in his busy fancy a portrait, some details of which were accurate. He pictured him as young, handsome, haughty, and felt convinced he had fled to England. He thought he had discovered him in a young *émigré* named Maubel, who, having come back to France and been denounced by his host, had been arrested in an inn at Passy; Fouquier-Tinville was in charge of the prosecution,—among a thousand others. Letters had been found on him which the accusation regarded as proofs of a plot concocted between Maubel and the agents of Pitt, but which were in fact only letters written to the *émigré* by a banking-house in London which he had entrusted with certain funds. Maubel, who was young and good-looking, seemed to be mainly occupied in affairs of gallantry. His pocket-book afforded a clue to some correspondence with Spain, then at war with France; but these communications were really of a purely private nature, and if the court of preliminary enquiry did not ignore the bill, it was only in virtue of the maxim that justice should never be in too great a hurry to release a prisoner.

Gamelin was handed a report of Maubel's first semi-private examination and he was struck by what it revealed of the young man's character, which he took to agree with what he believed to be that of Élodie's betrayer. Thereafter he spent long hours in the private room of the Clerk of the Court, poring eagerly over the papers relating to this case. His suspicion received a remarkable confirmation on his discovering in a note-book belonging to the *émigré*, but long out of date, the address of the *Amour peintre*, in company, it is true, with those of the *Green Monkey*, the *Dauphin's Head*, and several more print and picture shops. But when he was informed that in this same note-book had been found three or four petals of a red carnation carefully wrapped in a piece of silk paper, remembering how the red carnation was Élodie's favourite flower, the one she cultivated on her window-sill, wore in her hair and used to give (he had reason to know) as a love-token, Évariste's last doubts vanished. Being now convinced he knew the facts, he resolved to question Élodie, though without letting her know the circumstances that had led him to discover the culprit.

As he was climbing the stairs to his lodgings, he perceived even on the lower landings a stifling smell of fruit, and on reaching the studio, found Élodie helping the *citoyenne* Gamelin to make quince preserve. While the old housewife was kindling the stove and turning over in her mind ways of saving the fuel and moist sugar without prejudicing the quality of the preserves, the *citoyenne* Blaise, seated in a straw-bottomed chair, with an apron of brown holland and her lap full of the golden fruit, was peeling the quinces, quartering and throwing them into a shallow copper basin. The strings of her coif were thrown back over her shoulders, the meshes of her black hair coiled above her moist forehead; from her whole person breathed a domestic charm and an intimate grace that induced gentle thoughts and voluptuous dreams of tranquil pleasures.

Without stirring from her seat, she lifted her beautiful eyes, that gleamed like molten gold, to her lover's face, and said:

"See, Évariste, we are working for you. We mean you to have a store of delicious quince jelly to last you the winter; it will settle your stomach and make your heart merry."

But Gamelin, stepping nearer, uttered a name in her ear:

"Jacques Maubel . . ."

At that moment Combalot the cobbler showed his red nose at the half-open door. He had brought, along with some pairs of shoes he had re-heeled, the bill for the repairs.

For fear of being taken for a bad citizen, he made a point of using the new calendar. The *citoyenne* Gamelin, who liked to see clearly what was what in her accounts, was all astray among the *Fructidors* and *Vendémiaires*. She heaved a sigh.

"Jesus!" she complained, "they want to alter everything,—days, months, seasons of the year, the sun and the moon! Lord God, Monsieur Combalot, what ever is this pair of over-shoes down for the 8 Vendémiaire?"

"*Citoyenne*, just cast your eye over your almanac, and you'll get the hang of it."

She took it down from the wall, glanced at it and immediately turning her head another way:

"It hasn't a Christian look!" she cried in a shocked tone.

"Not only that, *citoyenne*," said the cobbler, "but now we have only three Sundays in the month instead of four. And that's not all; we shall soon have to change our ways of reckoning. There will be no more farthings and half-farthings, everything will be regulated by distilled water."

At the words the *citoyenne* Gamelin, whose lips were trembling, threw up her eyes to the ceiling and sighed out:

"They are going too far!"

And, while she was lost in lamentations, looking like the holy women in a wayside calvary, a bad coal that had caught alight in the fire when her attention was diverted, began to fill the studio with a poisonous smother which, added to the stifling smell of quinces, was like to make the air unbreathable.

Élodie complained that her throat was tickling her and begged to have the window opened. But, directly the *citoyen* Combalot had taken his leave and the *citoyenne* Gamelin had gone back to her stove, Évariste repeated the same name in the girl's ear:

"Jacques Maubel," he reiterated.

She looked up at him in some surprise, and very quietly, still going on cutting a quince in quarters:

"Well! . . . Jacques Maubel . . .?"

"He is the man."

"The man! what man?"

"You once gave him a red carnation."

She declared she did not understand and asked him to explain himself.

"That aristocrat! that *émigré!* that scoundrel!"

She shrugged her shoulders, and denied with the most natural air that she had never known a Jacques Maubel.

It was true; she *had* never known anyone of the name.

She denied she had ever given red carnations to anybody but Évariste; but perhaps, on this point, her memory was not very good.

He had little experience of women and was far from having fully fathomed Élodie's character; still, he deemed her quite capable of cajoling and deceiving a cleverer man than himself.

"Why deny?" he asked. "I know all."

Again she asseverated she had never known anybody called Maubel. And, having done peeling the quinces, she asked for a basin of water, because her fingers were sticky. This Gamelin brought her, and, as she washed her hands, she repeated her denials.

Again he repeated that he knew, and this time she made no reply.

She did not guess the object of her lover's question and she was a thousand miles from suspecting that this Maubel, whom she had never heard spoken of before, was to appear before the Revolutionary Tribunal; she could make nothing of the suspicions with which she was assailed, but she knew them to be unfounded. For this reason, having very little hope of dissipating them, she had very little wish to do so either. She ceased to deny having known Maubel, preferring to leave her jealous lover to go astray on a false trail, when from one moment to the next, the smallest incident might start him on the right road. Her little lawyer's clerk of former days, now grown into a patriot dragoon and lady-killer, had quarrelled by now with his aristocratic mistress. Whenever he met Élodie in the street, he would gaze at her with a glance that seemed to say:

"Come, my beauty! I feel sure I am going to forgive you for having betrayed you, and I am really quite ready to take you back into favour." She made no further attempt therefore to cure what she called her lover's crotchets, and Gamelin remained firm in the conviction that Jacques Maubel was Élodie's seducer.

Through the days that ensued the Tribunal devoted its undivided attention to the task of crushing Federalism, which, like a hydra, had threatened to devour Liberty. They were busy days; and the jurors, worn out with fatigue, dispatched with the utmost possible expedition the case of the woman Roland, instigator and accomplice of the crimes of the Brissotin faction.

Meantime Gamelin spent every morning at the Courts to press

on Maubel's trial. Some important pieces of evidence were to be found at Bordeaux; he insisted on a Commissioner being sent to ride post to fetch them. They arrived at last. The Deputy of the Public Prosecutor read them, pulled a face and told Évariste:

"It is not good for much, your new evidence! there is nothing in it! mere fiddle-faddle. . . . If only it was certain that this *ci-devant* Comte de Maubel ever really emigrated . . . !"

In the end Gamelin succeeded. Young Maubel was served with his act of accusation and brought before the Revolutionary Tribunal on the 19 Brumaire.

From the first opening of the sitting the President showed the gloomy and dreadful face he took care to assume for the hearing of cases where the evidence was weak. The Deputy Prosecutor stroked his chin with the feather of his pen and affected the serenity of a conscience at ease. The Clerk read the act of accusation; it was the hollowest sham the Court had ever heard so far.

The President asked the accused if he had not been aware of the laws passed against the *émigrés*.

"I was aware of them and I observed them," answered Maubel, "and I left France provided with passports in proper form."

As to the reasons for his journey to England and his return to France he had satisfactory explanations to offer. His face was pleasant, with a look of frankness and confidence that was agreeable. The women in the galleries looked at the young man with a favourable eye. The prosecution maintained that he had made a stay in Spain at the time that nation was at war with France; he averred he had never left Bayonne at that period. One point alone remained obscure. Among the papers he had thrown in the fire at the time of his arrest, and of which only fragments had been found, some words in Spanish had been deciphered and the name of "Nieves."

On this subject Jacques Maubel refused to give the explanations demanded; and, when the President told him that it was in the accused's own interest to clear up the point, he answered that a man ought not always to do what his own interest requires.

Gamelin only thought of convicting Maubel of a crime; three times over he pressed the President to ask the accused if he could explain about the carnation the dried petals of which he hoarded so carefully in his pocket-book.

Maubel replied that he did not consider himself obliged to answer a question that had no concern with the case at law, as no letter had been found concealed in the flower.

The jury retired to the hall of deliberations, favourably impressed towards the young man whose mysterious conduct appeared chiefly connected with a lover's secrets. This time the good patriots, the purest of the pure themselves, would gladly have voted for acquittal. One of them, a *ci-devant* noble, who had given pledges to the Revolution, said:

"Is it his birth they bring up against him? I, too, I have had the misfortune to be born in the aristocracy."

"Yes, but you have left them," retorted Gamelin, "and he has not."

And he spoke with such vehemence against this conspirator, this emissary of Pitt, this accomplice of Coburg, who had climbed the mountains and sailed the seas to stir up enemies to Liberty, he demanded the traitor's condemnation in such burning words, that he awoke the never-resting suspicions, the old stern temper of the patriot jury.

One of them told him cynically:

"There are services that cannot well be refused between colleagues."

The verdict of death was recorded by a majority of one.

The condemned man heard his sentence with a quiet smile. His eyes, which had been gazing unconcernedly about the hall, as they fell on Gamelin's face, took on an expression of unspeakable contempt.

No one applauded the decision of the court.

Jacques Maubel was taken back to the Conciergerie; here he wrote a letter while he waited the hour of execution, which was to take place the same evening, by torchlight:

My dear sister,— The tribunal sends me to the scaffold, affording me the only joy I have been able to appreciate since the death of my adored Nieves. They have taken from me the only relic I had left of her, a pomegranate flower, which they called, I cannot tell why, a carnation.

I loved the arts; at Paris, in happier times, I made a collection of paintings and engravings, which are now in a sure place, and which will be delivered to you so soon as this is possible. I pray you, dear sister, to keep them in memory of me.

He cut a lock of his hair, enclosed it in the letter, which he folded and wrote outside:

The Gods are A-thirst

To the citoyenne Clémence Dezeimeries, née Maubel,
La Réole.

He gave all the silver he had on him to the turnkey, begging him to forward this letter to its destination, asked for a bottle of wine, which he drank in little sips while waiting for the cart. . . .

After supper Gamelin ran to the *Amour peintre* and burst into the blue chamber where every night Élodie was waiting for him.

"You are avenged," he told her. "Jacques Maubel is no more. The cart that took him to his death has just passed beneath your window, escorted by torch-bearers."

She understood:

"Wretch! it is you have killed him, and he was not my lover. I did not know him. . . . I have never seen him . . . What was this man? He was young, amiable . . . innocent. And you have killed him, wretch! wretch!"

She fell in a faint. But, amid the shadows of this momentary death, she felt herself overborne by a flood at once of horror and voluptuous ecstasy. She half revived; her heavy lids lifted to show the whites of the eyes, her bosom swelled, her hands beat the air, seeking for her lover. She pressed him to her in a strangling embrace, drove her nails into the flesh, and gave him with her bleeding lips, without a word, without a sound, the longest, the most agonized, the most delicious of kisses.

She loved him with all her flesh, and the more terrible, cruel, atrocious she thought him, the more she saw him reeking with the blood of his victims, the more consuming was her hunger and thirst for him.

Chapter 17

THE 24 Frimaire, at ten in the forenoon, under a clear bright sun that was melting the ice formed in the night, the *citoyens* Guénot and Delourmel, delegates of the Committee of General Security, proceeded to the Barnabites and asked to be conducted to the Committee of Surveillance of the Section, in the Capitular hall, whose only occupant for the moment was the *citoyen* Beauvisage, who was piling logs on the fire. But they did not see him just at first because of his short, thickset stature.

In a hunchback's cracked voice the *citoyen* Beauvisage begged the delegates to seat themselves and put himself entirely at their service.

Guénot then asked him if he knew a *ci-devant* Monsieur des Ilettes, residing near the Pont-Neuf.

"It is an individual," he added, "whose arrest I am instructed to effect,"—and he exhibited the order from the Committee of General Security.

Beauvisage, after racking his memory for a while, replied that he knew no individual of that name, that the suspect in question might not be an inhabitant of his Section, certain portions of the *Sections du Muséum, de l'Unité, de Marat-et-Marseille* being likewise in the near neighbourhood of the Pont-Neuf; that, if he did live in the Section, it must be under another name than that borne on the Committee's order; that, nevertheless, it would not be long before they laid hands on him.

"Let's lose no time," urged Guénot. "Our vigilance was aroused in this case by a letter from one of the man's accomplices that was intercepted and put into the hands of the Committee a fortnight ago, but which the *citoyen* Lacroix took action upon only yesterday evening. We are overdone with business; denunciations flow in from

141

every quarter in such abundance one does not know which to attend to."

"Denunciations," replied Beauvisage proudly, "are coming in freely, too, to the Committee of Vigilance of our Section. Some make these revelations out of patriotism, others lured by the bait of a bank-bill for a hundred *sols*. Many children denounce their parents, whose property they covet."

"This letter," resumed Guénot, "emanates from a *ci-devant* called Rochemaure, a woman of gallantry, at whose house they played *biribi*, and is addressed to one *citoyen* Rauline; but is really for an *émigré* in the service of Pitt. I have brought it with me to communicate to you the portion relating to this man des Ilettes."

He drew the letter from his pocket.

"It begins with copious details as to those members of the Convention who might, according to the woman's tale, be gained over by the offer of a sum of money or the promise of a well-paid post under a new Government, more stable than the present. Then comes the following passage:

> "*I have just returned from a visit to Monsieur des Ilettes, who lives near the Pont-Neuf in a garret where you must be either a cat or an imp to get at him; he is reduced to earning a living by making punch-and-judies. He is a man of judgment, for which reason I report to you, sir, the main gist of his conversation. He does not believe that the existing state of things will last long. Nor does he foresee its being ended by the victory of the coalition, and events appear to justify his opinion; for, as you are aware, sir, for some time past tidings from the front have been bad. He would rather seem to believe in the revolt of the poor and the women of the humbler classes, who remain still deeply attached to their religion. He holds that the wide-spread alarm caused by the Revolutionary Tribunal will soon reunite all France against the Jacobins. 'This tribunal,' he said, in his joking way, 'which sentences the Queen of France and a bread-hawker, is like that William Shakespeare the English admire so much, etc. . . .' He thinks it not impossible that Robespierre may marry Madame Royale and have himself named Protector of the Kingdom.*
>
> "*I should be grateful to you, sir, if you would transmit me the amount owing to me, that is to say one thousand pounds sterling, by the channel you are in the habit of using; but whatever you do, do not write to Monsieur Morhardt; he has lately been arrested, thrown into prison, etc., etc. . . ."*

"This worthy des Ilettes makes dancing-dolls, it appears," observed Beauvisage, "that is a valuable clue . . . though certainly there are many petty trades of the sort carried on in the Section."

"That reminds me," said Delourmel, "I promised to bring home a doll for my little girl Nathalie, my youngest, who is ill with scarlatina. The spots came out yesterday. The fever is not a dangerous one, but it demands careful nursing, and Nathalie, a very forward child for her age, and with a very active brain, has but delicate health."

"I," remarked Guénot, "I have only a boy. He plays hoop with barrel-hoops and makes little montgolfier balloons by inflating paper bags."

"Very often," Beauvisage put in his word, "it is with articles that are not toys at all that children like best to play. My nephew Émile, a little chap of seven, a very intelligent child, amuses himself all day long with little wooden bricks with which he builds houses. . . . Do you take snuff, *citoyens?*"—and Beauvisage held out his open snuff-box to the two delegates.

"Now we must set about nabbing our rascal," said Delourmel, who had long moustaches and great eyes that rolled in his head. "I feel quite in the mood this morning for a dish of aristocrat's lights and liver, washed down with a glass of white wine."

Beauvisage suggested to the delegates going to the Place Dauphine to see if his colleague Dupont senior was at his shop there; he would be sure to know this man, des Ilettes.

So they set off in the keen morning air, accompanied by four grenadiers of the Section.

"Have you seen *'The Last Judgment of Kings'* played?" Delourmel asked his companions; "the piece is worth seeing. The author shows you all the Kings of Europe on a desert island where they have taken refuge, at the foot of a volcano which swallows them up. It is a patriotic work."

At the corner of the Rue du Harlay Delourmel's eye was caught by a little cart, as brilliantly painted as a reliquary, which an old woman was pushing, wearing over her coif a hat of waxed cloth.

"What is that old woman selling?" he asked.

The old dame answered for herself:

"Look, gentlemen, make your choice. I have beads and rosaries, crosses, St. Anthonys, holy cerecloths, St. Veronica handkerchiefs, *Ecce homos*, *Agnus Deis*, hunting-horns and rings of St. Hubert, and articles of devotion of every sort and kind."

"Why, it is the very arsenal of fanaticism!" cried Delourmel in horror,—and he proceeded to a summary examination of the poor woman, who made the same answer to every question:

143

"My son, it's forty years I have been selling articles of devotion."

Another delegate of the Committee of General Security, noticing a blue-coated National Guard passing, directed him to convey the astonished old woman to the Conciergerie.

The *citoyen* Beauvisage pointed out to Delourmel that it would have been more in the competence of the Committee of Surveillance to arrest the woman and bring her before the Section; that in any case, one never knew nowadays what attitude to take up towards the old religion so as to act up to the views of the Government, and whether it was best to allow everything or forbid everything.

On nearing the joiner's shop, the delegates and the commissary could hear angry shouts mingling with the hissing of the saw and the grinding of the plane. A quarrel had broken out between the joiner, Dupont senior, and his neighbour Remacle, the porter, because of the *citoyenne* Remacle, whom an irresistible attraction was for ever drawing into the recesses of the workshop, whence she would return to the porter's lodge all covered with shavings and saw-dust. The injured porter bestowed a kick on Mouton, the carpenter's dog, which at that very moment his own little daughter Joséphine was nursing lovingly in her arms. Joséphine was furious and burst into a torrent of imprecations against her father, while the carpenter shouted in a voice of exasperation:

"Wretch! I tell you you shall not beat my dog."

"And I," retorted the porter brandishing his broom, "I tell you you shall *not* . . ."

He did not finish the sentence; the joiner's plane had hurtled close past his head.

The instant he caught sight of the *citoyen* Beauvisage and the attendant delegates, he rushed up to him and cried:

"*Citoyen* Commissary, you are my witness, this villain has just tried to murder me."

The *citoyen* Beauvisage, in his red cap, the badge of his office, put out his long arms in the attitude of a peacemaker, and addressing the porter and the joiner:

"A hundred *sols*," he announced, "to whichever of you will inform us where to find a suspect, wanted by the Committee of General Security, a *ci-devant* named des Ilettes, a maker of dancing-dolls."

With one accord porter and carpenter designated Brotteaux's

lodging, the only quarrel now between them being who should have the assignat for a hundred *sols* promised the informer.

Delourmel, Guénot, and Beauvisage, followed by the four grenadiers, Remacle the porter, Dupont the carpenter, and a dozen little scamps of the neighbourhood filed up the stairs, which shook under their tread, and finally mounted the ladder to the attics.

Brotteaux was in his garret busy cutting out his dancing figures, while the Père Longuemare sat facing him, stringing their scattered limbs on threads, smiling to himself to see rhythm and harmony thus growing under his fingers.

At the sound of muskets being grounded on the landing, the monk trembled in every limb, not that he was a whit less courageous than Brotteaux, who never moved a muscle, but the habit of respect for human conventions had never disciplined him to assume an attitude of self-composure. Brotteaux gathered from the *citoyen* Delourmel's questions the quarter from which the blow had come, and saw too late how unwise it is to confide in women. He obeyed the *citoyen* Commissary's order to go with him, first picking up his Lucretius and his three shirts.

"The *citoyen*," he said, "pointing to the Père Longuemare, "is an assistant I have taken to help me make my marionettes. His home is here."

But the monk failing to produce a certificate of citizenship was put under arrest along with Brotteaux.

As the procession filed past the porter's door, the *citoyenne* Remacle, leaning on her broom, looked at her lodger with the eyes of virtue beholding crime in the clutches of the law. Little Joséphine, dainty and disdainful, held back Mouton by his collar when the dog tried to fawn on the friend who had often given him a lump of sugar. A gaping crowd filled the Place de Thionville.

At the foot of the stairs Brotteaux came face to face with a young peasant woman who was on the point of going up. She carried a basket on her arm full of eggs and in her hand a flat cake wrapped in a napkin. It was Athenaïs, who had come from Palaiseau to present her saviour with a token of her gratitude. When she observed a posse of magistrates and four grenadiers and "Monsieur Maurice" being led away a prisoner, she stopped in consternation and asked if it was really true; then she stepped up to the Commissary and said in a gentle voice:

"You are not taking him to prison? it can't be possible. . . . Why! you don't know him! God himself is not better or kinder."

The *citoyen* Delourmel pushed her away and beckoned to the grenadiers to come forward. Then Athenaïs let loose a torrent of the foulest abuse, the filthiest and most abominable invective, at the magistrates and soldiers, who thought that all the rinsings of the Palais-Royal and the Rue Fromenteau were being emptied over their devoted heads. After which, in a voice that filled the whole Place de Thionville and sent a shudder through the throng of curious onlookers:

"Vive le roi! Vive le roi!" she yelled.

Chapter 18

THE *citoyenne* Gamelin was devoted to old Brotteaux, and taking him altogether, thought him the best and greatest man she had ever known. She had not bidden him good-bye when he was arrested, because she would not have dared to defy the powers that be and because in her lowly estate she looked upon cowardice as a duty. But she had received a blow she could not recover from.

She could not eat and lamented she had lost her appetite just when she had at last the means to satisfy it. She still admired her son; but she durst not let her mind dwell on the appalling duties he was engaged upon and congratulated herself she was only an ignorant woman who had no call to judge his conduct.

The poor mother had found a rosary at the bottom of a trunk; she hardly knew how to use it, but often fumbled the beads in her trembling fingers. She had lived to grow old without any overt exercise of her religion, but she now became a pious woman, and she would pray to God all day long, in the chimney corner, to save her boy and that good, kind Monsieur Brotteaux. Élodie often came to see her; they durst not look each other in the eyes, and sitting side by side they would talk at random of indifferent matters.

One day in Pluviose, when the snow, falling in heavy flakes, darkened the sky and deadened the noises of the city, the *citoyenne* Gamelin, who was alone in the lodging, heard a knock at the door. She started violently; for months now the slightest noise had set her trembling. She opened the door. A young man of eighteen or twenty walked in, his hat on his head. He was dressed in a bottle-green box-coat, the triple collar of which covered his bust and descended to the waist. He wore top-boots of an English cut. His chestnut hair fell in ringlets about his shoulders. He stepped into the middle of the studio, as if wishful that all the light admitted by the snow-encumbered skylight might fall on him, and stood there some moments without moving or speaking.

At last, in answer to the *citoyenne* Gamelin's look of amazement:

"Don't you know your daughter?"

The old dame clasped her hands:

"Julie! . . . It is you. . . . Good God! is it possible? . . ."

"Why, yes, it is I. Kiss me, mother."

The *citoyenne* Gamelin pressed her daughter to her bosom, and dropped a tear on the collar of the box-coat. Then she began again in an anxious voice:

"You, in Paris! . . ."

"Ah! mother, but why did I not come alone! For myself, they will never know me in this dress."

It was a fact that the box-coat sufficiently disguised her shape, and she did not look very different from a great many very young men, who, like her, wore their hair long and parted in two masses on the forehead. Her features, which were delicately cut and charming, but burnt by the sun, drawn with fatigue, worn with anxiety, had a bold, masculine expression. She was slim, with long straight limbs and an easy carriage; only the clear treble of her voice could have betrayed her sex.

Her mother asked her if she was hungry. She said she would be glad of something to eat, and when bread, wine and ham had been set before her, she fell to, one elbow on the table, with a pretty gluttony, like Ceres in the hut of the old woman Baubo.

Then, the glass still at her lips:

"Mother," she asked, "do you know when my brother will be back? I have come to speak to him."

The good woman looked at her daughter in embarrassment and said nothing.

"I must see him. My husband was arrested this morning and taken to the Luxembourg."

By this name of "husband" she designated Fortuné de Chassagne, a *ci-devant* noble and officer in Bouillé's regiment. He had first loved her when she was a work-girl at a milliner's in the Rue des Lombards, and had carried her away with him to England, whither he had fled after the 10th August. He was her lover; but she thought it more becoming to speak of him as her husband before her mother. Indeed, she told herself that the hardships they

148

had shared had surely united them in a wedlock consecrated by suffering.

More than once they had spent the night side by side on a bench in one of the London parks and gathered up scraps of broken bread under the table in the taverns in Piccadilly.

Her mother could find no answer and gazed at her mournfully.

"Don't you hear what I say, mother? Time presses, I must see Évariste at once; he, and he only, can save Fortuné's life."

"Julie," answered her mother at last, "it is better you should not speak to your brother."

"Why, what do you mean, mother?"

"I mean what I say, it is better you do not speak to your brother about Monsieur de Chassagne."

"But, mother, I must!"

"My child, Évariste can never forgive Monsieur de Chassagne for his treatment of you. You know how angrily he used to speak of him, what names he called him."

"Yes, he called him seducer," said Julie with a little hissing laugh, shrugging her shoulders.

"My child, it was a mortal blow to his pride. Évariste has vowed never again to mention Monsieur de Chassagne's name, and for two years now he has not breathed one word of him or of you. But his feelings have not altered; you know him, he can never forgive you."

"But, mother, as Fortuné has married me . . . in London. . . ."

The poor mother threw up her eyes and hands:

"Fortuné is an aristocrat, an *émigré*, and that is cause enough to make Évariste treat him as an enemy."

"Mother, give me a direct answer. Do you mean that if I ask him to go to the Public Prosecutor and the Committee of General Security and take the necessary steps to save Fortuné's life, do you mean that he will not consent? . . . But, mother, he would be a monster if he refused!"

"My child, your brother is an honest man and a good son. But do not ask him, oh! do not ask him to intercede for Monsieur de Chassagne. . . . Listen to me, Julie. He does not confide his thoughts to me and, no doubt, I should not be competent to understand them . . . but he is a juror; he has principles; he acts as his conscience dictates. Do not ask him anything, Julie."

149

"Ah! I see you know him now. You know that he is cold, callous, that he is a bad man, that ambition and vainglory are his only guides. And you always loved him better than me. When we lived together, all three of us, you set him up as my pattern to copy. His staid demeanour and grave speech impressed you; you thought he possessed all the virtues. And me, me you always blamed, you gave me all the vices, because I was frank and free, and because I climbed trees. You could never endure me. You loved nobody but him. There, I hate him, your model Évariste; he is a hypocrite."

"Hush, Julie! I have been a good mother to you as well as to him. I had you taught a trade. It has been no fault of mine that you are not an honest woman and did not marry in your station. I loved you tenderly and I love you still. I forgive you and I love you. But do not speak ill of Évariste. He is a good son. He has always taken care of me. When you left me, my child, when you abandoned your trade and forsook your shop, to go and live with Monsieur de Chassagne, what would have become of me without him? I should have died of hunger and wretchedness."

"Do not talk so, mother; you know very well we would have cherished you with all affection, Fortuné and I, if you had not turned your face from us, at Évariste's instigation. Never tell me! he is incapable of a kindly action. It was to make me odious in your eyes that he made a pretence of caring for you. He! love you? . . . Is he capable of loving anyone? He has neither heart nor head. He has no talent, not a scrap. To paint, a man must have a softer, tenderer nature than his."

She threw a glance round the canvases in the studio, which she found to be no better and no worse than when she left her home.

"There you see his soul! he has put it in his pictures, cold and sombre as it is. His Orestes, his Orestes with the dull eye and cruel mouth, and looking as if he had been impaled, is himself all over. . . . But, mother, cannot you understand at all? I cannot leave Fortuné in prison. You know these Jacobins, these patriots, all Évariste's crew. They will kill him. Mother, little mother, darling mother, I cannot have them kill him. I love him! I love him! He has been so good to me, and we have been so unhappy together. Look, this box-coat is one of his coats. I had never a shift left. A friend of Fortuné's lent me a jacket and I got a post with an eating-house keeper at Dover, while he worked at a barber's. We knew quite well that to return to France was to risk our lives; but we were asked if we would go to Paris to carry out an important mission. . . . We agreed,—we would have accepted a mission to hell! Our travelling expenses were paid and we were given a letter of exchange on a Paris banker. We found the offices closed; the banker is in prison and going to be guillotined. We had not a brass farthing. All the individuals with whom we were in correspondence and to whom we could appeal are fled or imprisoned. Not a door to knock at. We slept in a stable in the Rue de la Femme-sans-tête. A charitable boot-black, who slept on the same straw with us there, lent my lover one of his boxes, a brush and a pot of blacking three quarters empty. For a fortnight Fortuné made his living and mine by blacking shoes in the Place de Grève.

"But on Monday a Member of the Commune put his foot on the box to have his boots polished. He had been a butcher once, a man Fortuné once gave a kick in the behind for selling meat of short weight. When Fortuné raised his head to ask for his two sous, the rascal recognized him, called him aristocrat, and threatened to have him arrested. A crowd collected, made up of honest folks and a few blackguards, who began to shout '*Death to the émigré!*' and called for the gendarmes. At that moment I came up with Fortuné's bowl of soup. I saw him taken off to the Section and shut up in the church of Saint-Jean. I tried to kiss him, but they hustled me away. I spent the night like a dog on the church steps. . . . They took him away this morning. . . ."

Julie could not finish, her sobs choked her.

She threw her hat on the floor and fell on her knees at her mother's feet.

"They took him away this morning to the Luxembourg prison. Mother, mother, help me to save him; have pity on your child!"

Drowned in her tears, she threw open her box-coat and, the better to prove herself a woman and a wife, bared her bosom; seizing her mother's hands, she held them close over her throbbing breasts.

"My darling, my daughter, Julie, my Julie!" sobbed the widow Gamelin,—and pressed her streaming cheeks to the girl's.

For some moments they clung together without a word. The poor mother was racking her brains for some way of helping her daughter, and Julie was watching the kind look in those tearful eyes.

"Perhaps," thought Évariste's mother, "perhaps, if I speak to him, he will be melted. He is good, he is tender-hearted. If politics had not hardened him, if he had not been influenced by the Jacobins, he would never have had these cruel feelings, that terrify me because I cannot understand them."

She took Julie's head in her two hands:

"Listen, my child. I will speak to Évariste. I will sound him, get him to see you and hear your story. The sight of you might anger him; his first impulse might be to turn against you. . . . And then, I know him; this costume would offend him; he is uncompromising in everything that touches morals, that shocks the proprieties. *I* was a bit startled to see my Julie dressed as a man."

"Oh! mother, the emigration and the fearful disorders of the kingdom have made these disguises quite a common thing. They are adopted in order to follow a trade, to escape recognition, to get a borrowed passport or a certificate approved. In London I saw young Girey dressed as a girl,—and he made a very pretty girl; you must own, mother, *that* is a more scandalous disguise than mine."

"My poor child, you have no need to justify yourself in my eyes, whether in this or any other thing. I am your mother; for me you will always be blameless. I will speak to Évariste, I will say . . ."

She broke off. She knew what her son was; she felt it in her heart, but she would not believe it, she *would* not know it.

"He is kind-hearted. He will do it for my sake . . . for your sake, he will do what I ask him."

The two women, weary to the death, fell silent. Julie sank asleep, her head pillowed on the knees where she had rested as a child, while the mother, the rosary between her hands, wept, like another *mater dolorosa*, over the calamities she felt drawing stealthily nearer and nearer in the silence of this day of snow when everything was hushed, footsteps and carriage wheels and the very heaven itself.

Suddenly, with a keenness of hearing sharpened by anxiety, she caught the sound of her son's steps on the stairs.

"Évariste!" she cried. "Hide"—and she hurried the girl into the bedroom.

"How are you to-day, mother dear?"

Évariste hung up his hat on its peg, changed his blue coat for a working jacket and sat down before his easel. For some days he had been working at a sketch in charcoal of a Victory laying a wreath on the brow of a dead soldier, who had died for the fatherland. Once the subject would have called out all his enthusiasm, but the Tribunal consumed all his days and absorbed his whole soul, while his hand had lost its knack from disuse and had grown heavy and inert.

He hummed over the *Ça ira*.

"I hear you singing," said the *citoyenne* Gamelin; "you are lighthearted, Évariste?"

"We have reason to be glad, mother; there is good news. La Vendée is crushed, the Austrians beaten, the Army of the Rhine has forced the lines of Lautern and of Wissembourg. The day is at hand when the Republic triumphant will show her clemency. Why must the conspirators' audacity increase the mightier the Republic waxes in strength, and traitors plot to strike the fatherland a blow in the dark at the very moment her lightnings overwhelm the enemies that assail her openly?"

The *citoyenne* Gamelin, as she sat knitting a stocking, was watching her son's face over her spectacles.

"Berzélius, your old model, has been to ask for the ten livres you owed him; I paid him. Little Joséphine has had a belly-ache from eating too much of the preserves the carpenter gave her. So I made her a drop of herb tea. . . . Desmahis has been to see you; he was sorry he did not find you in. He wanted to engrave a design by you. He thinks you have great talent. He is a fine fellow; he looked at your sketches and admired them."

"When peace is re-established and conspiracy suppressed," said the painter, "I shall begin on my Orestes again. It is not my way to flatter myself; but that head is worthy of David's brush."

He outlined with a majestic sweep the arm of his Victory.

"She holds out palms," he said. "But it would be finer if her arms themselves were palms."

"Évariste!"

"Mother?"

"I have had news . . . guess, of whom . . ."

"I do not know."

"Of Julie . . . of your sister. . . . She is not happy."

"It would be a scandal if she were."

"Do not speak so, my son, she is your sister. Julie is not a bad woman; she has a good disposition, which misfortune has developed. She loves you. I can assure you, Évariste, that she only desires a hard-working, exemplary life, and her fondest wish is to be reconciled to her friends. There is nothing to prevent your seeing her again. She has married Fortuné Chassagne."

"She has written to you?"

"No."

"How, then, have you had news of her, mother?"

"It was not by letter, Évariste; it was . . ."

He sprang up and stopped her with a savage cry:

"Not another word, mother! Do not tell me they have both returned to France. . . . As they are doomed to perish, at least let it not be at my hands. For their own sake, for yours, for mine, let me not know they are in Paris. . . . Do not force the knowledge on me; otherwise . . ."

"What do you mean, my son? you would think, you would dare . . . ?"

"Mother, hear what I say; if I knew my sister Julie to be in that room . . ." (and he pointed at the closed door), "I should go instantly to denounce her to the Committee of Vigilance of the Section."

The poor mother, her face as white as her coif, dropped her knitting from her trembling hands and sighed in a voice fainter than the faintest whisper:

"I would not believe it, but I see it now; my boy is a monster. . ."

As pale as she, the froth gathering on his lips, Évariste fled from the house and ran to find at Élodie's side forgetfulness, sleep, the delicious foretaste of extinction.

Chapter 19

WHILE the Père Longuemare and the girl Athenaïs were examined at the Section, Brotteaux was led off between two gendarmes to the Luxembourg, where the door-keeper refused to admit him, declaring he had no room left. The old financier was next taken to the Conciergerie and brought into the gaoler's office, quite a small room, divided in two by a glazed partition. While the clerk was inscribing his name in the prison registers, Brotteaux could see through the panes two men lying each on a tattered mattress, both as still as death and with glazed eyes that seemed to see nothing. Plates, bottles and bits of broken bread and meat littered the floor round them. They were prisoners condemned to death and waiting for the cart to arrive.

The *ci-devant* Monsieur des Ilettes was thrust into a dungeon, where by the light of a lantern he could just make out two figures stretched on the ground, one savage-looking and hideously muti-lated, the other graceful and pleasing. The two prisoners offered him a share of their straw, and this, rotten and swarming with ver-min as it was, was better than having to lie on the earth, which was befouled with excrement. Brotteaux sank down on a bench in the pestiferous darkness and sat there, his head against the wall, speech-less and motionless. So intense was his agony of mind he would have dashed out his brains against the stones if he had had the strength. He could not breathe. His eyes swam, and a long-drawn murmur, as soft as silence, filled his ears. He felt his whole being bathed in a delicious semi-consciousness. For one incomparable moment every-thing was harmony, serenity, light, fragrance, sweetness. Then he ceased to know or feel anything.

When he returned to himself, the first notion that entered his head was to regret his coma and, a philosopher even in the stupor of de-spair, he reflected how he had had to plunge to the depths of an un-derground dungeon, there to await execution, to enjoy the most ex-

quisite of all voluptuous sensations he had ever tasted. He tried hard
to lose consciousness again, but without success; on the contrary,
little by little he felt the poisonous air of the dungeon fill his lungs
and bring with it, along with the fever of life, a full consciousness of
his intolerable wretchedness.

Meantime his two companions regarded his silence as a cruel personal insult. Brotteaux, who was of a social turn, endeavoured to
satisfy their curiosity; but when they discovered he was only what
they called "a political," one of the mild sort whose crime was only
a matter of words and opinions, they lost all respect and sympathy
for him. The offences charged against these two prisoners had more
grit; the older of the men was a murderer, the other had been manu-
facturing forged assignats. Both made the best of their situation and
even found some alleviations in it. Brotteaux's thoughts suddenly
turned to the world above him,—how over his head all was noise and
bustle, light and life, while the pretty shopwomen in the Palais de
Justice behind their counters, loaded with perfumery and pretty
knickknacks, smiled on their customers, happy people free to go
where they pleased,—and the picture doubled his despair.

Night fell, unmarked in the darkness and silence of the dungeon,
but yet gloomy and oppressive. One leg extended on his bench and
his back propped against the wall, Brotteaux fell into a doze. And
lo! he saw himself seated at the foot of a leafy beech, in which the
birds were singing; the setting sun bathed the river in liquid fire and
the clouds were edged with purple. The night wore through. A burning fever consumed him and he greedily drained his pitcher to the
dregs, but the fetid water only increased his distress.

Next day the gaoler who brought the food promised Brotteaux, if
he could afford the cost, to give him the privileges of a prisoner who
pays for his accommodation, so soon as there should be room, and
the wait was not likely to be long. And so it turned out; two days
later he invited the old financier to leave his dungeon. At every step
he took upwards, Brotteaux felt life and vigour coming back to him,
and when he saw a room with a red-tiled floor and in it a bed of sacking covered with a dingy woollen counterpane, he wept for joy. The
gilded bed carved with doves billing and cooing that he had once had
made for the prettiest of the dancers at the Opera had not seemed so
desirable or promised him such delights.

This bed of sacking was in a large hall, very fairly clean, which

held seventeen others like it, separated by high partitions of planks. The company that occupied these quarters, composed of ex-nobles, tradesmen, bankers, working-men, hit the old publican's taste well enough, for he could accommodate himself to persons of all qualities. He noticed that these, cut off like himself from every opportunity of pleasure and foredoomed to perish at the hand of the executioner, were of a very merry humour and showed a marked taste for wit and raillery. His bent was to think lightly of mankind, so he attributed the high spirits of his companions to the frivolity of their minds, which prevented them from looking seriously at their situation. Moreover, he was strengthened in his opinion by observing how the more intelligent among them were profoundly sad. He remarked before long, that, for the most part, wine and brandy supplied the inspiration of a gaiety that betrayed its source by its violent and sometimes almost insane character. They did not all possess courage; but all made a display of it. This caused Brotteaux no surprise; he was well aware how men will readily enough avow cruelty, passion, even avarice, but never cowardice, because such an admission would bring them, among savages and even in civilized society, into mortal danger. That is the reason, he reflected, why all nations are nations of heroes and all armies are made up of brave men only.

More potent, even, than wine and brandy were the rattle of weapons and keys, the clash of locks and bolts, the cry of sentries, the stamping of feet at the door of the Tribunal, to intoxicate the prisoners and fill their minds with melancholy, insanity, or frenzy. Some there were who cut their throat with a razor or threw themselves from a window.

Brotteaux had been living for three days in these privileged quarters when he learned through the turnkey that the Père Longuemare was languishing on the rotten verminous straw of the common prison with the thieves and murderers. He had him put on paying terms in the same room as himself, where a bed had fallen vacant. Having promised to pay for the monk, the old publican, who had no large sum of money about him, struck out the idea of making portraits at a crown apiece. By the help of a gaoler, he procured a supply of small black frames in which to put pretty little designs in hair which he executed with considerable cleverness. These productions sold well, being highly appreciated among people whose thoughts were set on leaving souvenirs to their friends.

The Père Longuemare kept a good heart and a high spirit. While waiting his summons to appear before the Revolutionary Tribunal, he was preparing his defence. Drawing no distinction between his own case and that of the Church, he promised himself to expose to his judges the disorders and scandals to which the Spouse of Christ was exposed by the Civil Constitution of the Clergy; he proposed to depict the eldest daughter of the Church waging sacrilegious war upon the Pope, the French clergy robbed, outraged, subjected to the odious domination of laics; the regulars, Christ's true army, despoiled and scattered. He cited St. Gregory the Great and St. Irenæus, quoted numerous articles of the Canon Law and whole paragraphs from the Decretals.

All day long he sat scribbling on his knees, at the foot of his bed, dipping stumps of pens worn to the feathers in ink, soot, coffee-grounds, covering with illegible writing candle-wrappers, packing-paper, newspapers, book covers, playing cards, even thinking of using his shirt for the same purpose after starching it. Leaf by leaf the pile grew; pointing to this mass of undecipherable scrawls, he would say:

"Ah! when I appear before my judges, I will inundate them with light."

Another day, casting a look of satisfaction on his defence, which grew bulkier day by day, and thinking of these magistrates he was burning to confound, he cried:

"I wouldn't like to be in *their* shoes!"

The prisoners whom fate had brought together in this prison-room were Royalists or Federalists, there was even a Jacobin amongst the rest; they held widely different views as to the right way of conducting the business of the State, but not one of them all preserved the smallest vestige of Christian beliefs. Feuillants, Constitutionals, Girondists, all, like Brotteaux, considered the Christians' God a very bad thing for themselves and an excellent one for the people; as for the Jacobins, they were for installing in the place of Jehovah a Jacobin god, anxious to refer the dispensation of Jacobinism on earth to a higher source. But as they could not conceive, either one or the other, of anybody being so absurd as to believe in any revealed religion, seeing that the Père Longuemare was no fool, they took him to be a knave. By way, no doubt, of preparing for martyrdom, he made confession of faith at every opportunity, and the more sincerity he displayed, the more like an impostor he seemed.

In vain Brotteaux stood surety for the monk's good faith; Brotteaux himself was reputed to believe only a part of what he said. His ideas were too singular not to appear affected and satisfied nobody entirely. He dubbed Jean-Jacques a dull, paltry rascal. Voltaire, on the other hand, he accounted among the divinely-gifted men, though not on the same level as the amiable Helvetius, or Diderot, or the Baron d'Holbach. In his opinion the greatest genius of the century was Boulanger. He also thought highly of the astronomer Lalande and of Dupuis, author of a *Memoir on the origin of the Constellations*.

The wits of the company made a thousand jokes at the poor Barnabite's expense, the point of which he never saw; his simplicity saved him from every pitfall. To drown the suspense that racked them and escape the torments of idleness, the prisoners played at draughts, cards, and backgammon. No instrument of music was allowed. After supper they would sing, or recite verses. Voltaire's *La Pucelle* brought a little cheerfulness to these aching hearts, and the company never wearied of hearing the telling passages repeated. But, unable to distract their thoughts from the appalling vision that always loomed before their mind's eye, they strove sometimes to make a diversion of it, and in the chamber of the eighteen beds, before turning in for the night, they would play at Revolutionary Tribunal. The parts were distributed according to tastes and aptitudes. While some represented the judges and prosecutor, others were the accused or the witnesses, others again the headsman and his men. The trials invariably wound up with the execution of the condemned, who were laid at full length on a bed, the neck underneath a plank. The scene then shifted to the infernal regions. The most agile of the troop, wrapped in white sheets, played spectres. There was a young *avocat* from Bordeaux, a man named Dubosc, short, dark, one-eyed, humpbacked, bandy-legged, the very black deuce in person, who used to come all horned and hoofed, to drag the Père Longuemare feet first out of his bed, announcing to the culprit that he was condemned to the everlasting flames of hell and doomed past redemption for having made of the Creator of the Universe a jealous being, a blockhead, and a bully, an enemy of human happiness and love.

"Ah! ha! ha!" the devil would scream discordantly, "so you taught, you old bonze, that God delights to see His creatures languish in contrition and deny themselves His dearest gifts. Impostor, hypocrite, sneak, sit on nails and eat egg-shells for all eternity!"

The Père Longuemare, for all reply, would observe that the speech showed the philosopher's cloven hoof behind the devil's, and that the meanest imp of hell would never have talked such foolishness, having at least rubbed shoulders with Theology and for certain being less ignorant than an Encyclopædist.

But when the Girondist *avocat* called him a Capuchin, he turned scarlet with anger and declared that a man incapable of distinguishing a Barnabite from a Franciscan was too blind to see a fly in milk.

The Revolutionary Tribunal was always draining the prisons, which the Committees were as unceasingly replenishing; in three months the chamber of the eighteen was half full of new faces. The Père Longuemare lost his tormentor. The *avocat* Dubosc was haled before the Revolutionary Tribunal and condemned to death as a Federalist and for having conspired against the unity of the Republic. On leaving the court, he returned, as the prisoners always did, by a corridor that ran through the prison and opened on the room he had enlivened for three months with his gaiety. As he made his farewells to his companions, he maintained the same light tone and cheerful air that were habitual with him.

"Forgive me, sir," he said to the Père Longuemare, "for having hauled you feet foremost from your bed. I will never do it again."

Then, turning to old Brotteaux:

"Good-bye, I go before you into the land of nowhere. I gladly return to Nature the atoms of my composition, only hoping she will make a better use of them for the future, for it must be owned she did not make much of a job of me."

So he went on his way to the gaoler's room, leaving Brotteaux sorrowful and the Père Longuemare trembling and green as a leaf, more dead than alive to see the impious wretch laugh on the brink of the abyss.

When Germinal brought back the bright days, Brotteaux, who was of an ardent temperament, tramped down several times every day to the courtyard giving on the women's quarters, near the fountain where the female prisoners used to come of a morning to wash their linen. An iron railing separated the two barracks; but the bars were not so close together as to hinder hands joining and lips meeting. Under the kindly shade of night loving couples would press against the obstacle. At such times Brotteaux would retire discreetly to the staircase and, sitting on a step, would draw from the pocket of his plum-coloured surtout his little Lucretius and read, by the light of a lantern, some of the author's sternly consolatory maxims: *"Sic ubi non erimus. . . .* When we shall have ceased to be, nothing will have power to move us, not even the heavens and earth and sea confounding their shattered fragments. . . ."* But, in the act of enjoying his exalted wisdom, Brotteaux would find himself envying the Barnabite this craze that veiled the universe from his eyes.

Month by month terror grew more intense. Every night the tipsy gaolers, their watch-dogs at their heels, would march from cell to cell, delivering acts of accusation, howling out names they mutilated, waking the prisoners and for twenty victims marked on their list terrifying two hundred. Along these corridors, reeking with bloody memories, passed every day, without a murmur, twenty, thirty, fifty condemned prisoners, old men, women, young men and maidens, so widely different in rank and character and opinion that the question rose involuntarily to the lips,—had they not been chosen by lot?

And the card playing went on, the Burgundy drinking, the making of plans, the assignations for after dark at the rails. The company, new almost to a man, now consisted in great part of "extremists" and "irreconcilables." But still the room of the eighteen beds remained the home of elegance and good breeding; barring two prisoners recently transferred from the Luxembourg to the Conciergerie and added to the company, by whom they were suspected of being spies, the *citoyens* Navette and Bellier by name, there were none but honest folk there who reposed a mutual trust in each other. Glass in hand, the victories of the Republic were celebrated by all. Amongst the rest were several poets, as there always are in any gathering of people with nothing to do. The most accomplished composed odes on the triumphs of the Army of the Rhine, which they recited with much mouthing. They were uproariously applauded. Brotteaux was the only lukewarm admirer of the victors and the bards who sang their victories.

"Since Homer began it," he observed one day, "it has always been a mania with poets, this extolling the powers of fighting-men. War is not an art, and luck alone decides the fate of battles. With two generals, both blockheads, face to face, one of them must inevitably be victorious. Wait till some day one of these warriors you make gods of swallows you all up like the stork in the fable who gobbles up the frogs. Ah! then he would be really and truly a God! For you can always tell the gods by their appetite."

Brotteaux's head had never been turned by the glamour of arms. He felt no triumph at the victories of the Republic, which he had foreseen. He did not like the new régime, which military success confirmed. He was a malcontent. Another would have been the same for less cause.

One morning it was announced that the Commissaries of the Committee of General Security were going to institute a search in the prisoners' quarters, that they would seize assignats, articles of gold and silver, knives, scissors; that similar proceedings had been taken at the Luxembourg, where letters, papers, and books had been taken possession of.

Thereupon everyone tried to think of some hiding place in which to secure whatever he held most precious. The Père Longuemare carried away his defence in armfuls to a rain-gutter, while Brotteaux slipped his Lucretius among the ashes on the hearth.

When the Commissaries, wearing tricolour ribands at their necks, arrived to carry out their perquisition, they found scarcely anything but such trifles as it had been deemed judicious to let them discover. On their departure, the Père Longuemare ran to his rain-pipe and rescued as much of his defence as wind and water had spared. Brotteaux pulled out his Lucretius from the fireplace all black with soot.

"Let us make the best of the present," he thought, "for I augur from sundry tokens that our time is straitly measured from henceforth."

One soft night in Prairial, while over the prison yard the moon riding high in a pale sky showed her two silver horns, the ex-financier, who, as his way was, sat reading Lucretius on a step of the stone stairs, heard a voice call him, a woman's voice, a delightful voice, which he did not know. He went down into the court and saw behind the railing a form which he recognized as little as he did the voice, but which reminded him, in its half-seen fascinating outlines, of all the women he had loved. A flood of silvery blue moonlight fell on it. Next instant Brotteaux recognized the pretty actress of the Rue Feydeau, Rose Thévenin.

"You here, my child! It is a joy to see you, but it stabs my heart. Since when have you been here, and why?"

"Since yesterday,"—and she added very low:

162

"I have been denounced as a Royalist. They accuse me of conspiring to set free the Queen. Knowing you were here, I tried at once to see you. Listen to me, dear friend . . . you will let me call you so? . . . I know people in power; I have sympathizers, I am sure of it, on the Committee of Public Safety itself. I will set my friends to work; they will deliver me, and *I* will deliver you."

But Brotteaux in a voice that took on an accent of urgency:

"By everything you hold dear, my child, do nothing of the sort! Do not write, do not petition; ask nothing of anybody, I conjure you, let yourself be forgotten."

As she appeared unconvinced by what he said, he went on more beseechingly still:

"Not a word, Rose, let them forget you; there lies safety. Anything your friends might attempt would only hasten your undoing. Time is everything; only a short delay, a very short one, I hope, is needed to save you. . . . Above all, never try to melt the judges, the jurors, a Gamelin. They are not men, they are things; there is no arguing with things. Let them forget you; if you take my advice, sweetheart, I shall die happy, happy to have saved your life."

She answered:

"I will do as you say. . . . Never talk of dying. . . ."

He shrugged his shoulders.

"My life is ended, my child. Do you live and be happy."

She took his hands and laid them on her bosom:

"Hear what I say, dear friend. . . . I have only seen you once for a day, and yet you are not indifferent to me. And if what I am going to tell you can renew your attachment to life, oh! believe my promise,—I will be for you . . . whatever you shall wish me to be."

And they exchanged a kiss on the mouth through the bars.

Chapter 20

ÉVARISTE GAMELIN, as he sat, one day that a long, tedious case was before the Tribunal, on the jury-bench in the stifling court, closed his eyes and thought:

"Evil-doers, by forcing Marat to hide in holes and corners, had turned him into a bird of night, the bird of Minerva, whose glance pierced the dark recesses where conspirators lurked. Now it is a blue eye, cold and calm, that discovers the enemies of the State and denounces traitors with a subtlety unknown even to the Friend of the People, now asleep for ever in the garden of the Cordeliers. The new saviour of the country, as zealous and more keen-sighted than the first, sees what no man before had seen and with a lifted finger spreads terror broadcast. He discerns the fine, imperceptible shades of difference that divide evil from good, vice from virtue, which but for him would have been confounded, to the hurt of the fatherland and freedom, he marks out before him the thin, inflexible line outside which lies, to the right hand and to the left, only error, crime, and wickedness. The Incorruptible teaches how men serve the foreigner equally by excess of zeal and by supineness, by persecuting the religious in the name of reason no less than by fighting in the name of religion against the laws of the Republic. Every whit as much as the villains who immolated Le Peltier and Marat, do they serve the foreigner who decree them divine honours, to compromise their memory. Agent of the foreigner whosoever repudiates the ideas of order, wisdom, opportunity; agent of the foreigner whosoever outrages morals, scandalizes virtue, and, in the foolishness of his heart, denies God. Yes, fanatic priests deserve to die; but there is an anti-revolutionary way of combating fanaticism; abjurers, too, may be guilty of a crime. By moderation men destroy the Republic; by violence they do the same.

"August and terrible the functions of a judge,—functions defined by the wisest of mankind! It is not aristocrats alone, Federalists, scoundrels of the Orleans faction, open enemies of the fatherland, that we must strike down. The conspirator, the agent of the foreigner, is a Proteus, he assumes all shapes; he puts on the guise of a patriot, a revolutionary, an enemy of Kings; he affects the boldness of a heart that beats only for freedom; his voice swells, and the foes of the Republic tremble. His name is Danton; his violence is a poor cloak to his odious moderatism, and his base corruption is manifest at last. The conspirator, the agent of the foreigner, is that fluent stammerer, the man who clapped the first cockade of revolution in his hat, that pamphleteer who, in his ironical and cruel patriotism, nicknamed himself, 'The procureur of the Lantern.' *His* name is Camille Desmoulins. He threw off the mask by defending the Generals, traitors to their country, and demanding measures of clemency criminal at such a time. There was Philippeaux, there was Hérault, there was the despicable Lacroix. There was the Père Duchesne, he, too, a conspirator and agent of the foreigner, the vile demagogue who degraded liberty, and whose filthy calumnies stirred sympathy for Antoinette herself. There was Chaumette, who yet was a mild man, popular, moderate, well-intentioned, and virtuous in the administration of the Commune; but he was an atheist! Conspirators, agents of the foreigner,—such were all those *sansculottes* in red cap and *carmagnole* and sabots who recklessly outbid the Jacobins in patriotism. Conspirator and agent of the foreigner was Anacharsis Clootz, 'orator of the human race,' condemned to die by all the monarchies of the world; but everything was to be feared of him,—he was a Prussian.

"Now, violent or moderate, all these evil-doers, all these traitors, —Danton, Desmoulins, Hébert, Chaumette,—have perished under the axe. The Republic is saved; a chorus of praises rises from all the Committees and the popular assemblies one and all to greet Maximilien and *the Mountain*. Good citizens cry aloud: 'Worthy representatives of a free people, in vain have the sons of the Titans lifted their proud heads; O mountain of blessing, O protecting Sinai, from thy tumultuous bosom has issued the saving lightning. . . . '

"In this chorus the Tribunal has its meed of praise. How sweet a thing it is to be virtuous, and how dear is public gratitude to the heart of the upright judge!

"Meanwhile, for a patriot heart, what food for amazement, what

165

motives for anxiety! What! to betray the people's cause, it was not enough to have a Mirabeau, a La Fayette, a Bailly, a Pétion, a Brissot? We must likewise have the men who denounced these traitors. Can it be that all the patriots who made the Revolution only wrought to ruin her? that these heroes of the great days were but contriving with Pitt and Coburg to give the kingdom to the Orleans and set up a Regency under Louis XVII? What! Danton was another Monk! What! Chaumette and the Hébertists, falser than the Federalists whom they sent to the guillotine, had conspired to destroy the State! But among those who hurried to their death the traitor Danton and the traitor Chaumette, will not the blue eye of Robespierre discover anon more perfidious traitors yet? What will be the end of this hideous concatenation of traitors betrayed and the revelations of the keen-sighted Incorruptible? . . ."

Chapter 21

MEANTIME Julie Gamelin, in her bottle-green box-coat, went every day to the Luxembourg Gardens and there, on a bench at the end of one of the avenues, sat waiting for the moment when her lover should show his face at one of the dormers of the Palace. Then they would beckon to each other and talk together in a language of signs they had invented. In this way she learned that the prisoner occupied a fairly good room and had pleasant companions, that he wanted a blanket for his bed and a kettle and loved his mistress fondly.

She was not the only one to watch for the sight of a dear face at a window of the Palace now turned into a prison. A young mother not far from her kept her eyes fixed on a closed casement; then directly she saw it open, she would lift her little one in her arms above her head. An old lady in a lace veil sat for long hours on a folding-chair, vainly hoping to catch a momentary glimpse of her son, who, for fear of breaking down, never left his game of quoits in the courtyard of the prison till the hour when the gardens were closed.

During these long hours of waiting, whether the sky were blue or overcast, a man of middle age, rather stout and very neatly dressed, was constantly to be seen on a neighbouring bench, playing with his snuff-box and the charms on his watch-guard or unfolding a newspaper, which he never read. He was dressed like a bourgeois of the old school in a gold-laced cocked hat, a plum-coloured coat and blue waistcoat embroidered in silver. He looked well-meaning enough, and was something of a musician to judge by a flute, one end of which peeped from his pocket. Never for a moment did his eyes wander from the supposed stripling, on whom he bestowed continual smiles, and when he saw him leave his seat, he would get up himself and follow him at a distance. Julie, in her misery and loneliness, was touched by the discreet sympathy the good man manifested.

167

One day, as she was leaving the gardens, it began to rain; the old fellow stepped up to her and, opening his vast red umbrella, asked permission to offer her its shelter. She answered sweetly, in her clear treble, that she would be very glad. But at the sound of her voice and warned perhaps by a subtle scent of womanhood, he strode rapidly away, leaving the girl exposed to the rain-storm; she took in the situation, and, despite her gnawing anxieties, could not restrain a smile.

Julie lived in an attic in the Rue du Cherche-Midi and represented herself as a draper's shop-boy in search of employment; the widow Gamelin, at last convinced that the girl was running smaller risks anywhere else than at her home, had got her away from the Place de Thionville and the Section du Pont-Neuf, and was giving her all the help she could in the way of food and linen. Julie did her trifle of cooking, went to the Luxembourg to see her beloved prisoner and back again to her garret; the monotony of the life was a balm to her grief, and, being young and strong, she slept well and soundly the night through. She was of a fearless temper and broken in to an adventurous life; the costume she wore added perhaps a further spice of excitement, and she would sometimes sally out at night to visit a restaurateur's in the Rue du Four, at the sign of the Red Cross, a place frequented by men of all sorts and conditions and women of gallantry. There she read the papers or played backgammon with some tradesman's clerk or citizen-soldier, who smoked his pipe in her face. Drinking, gambling, love-making were the order of the day, and scuffles were not unfrequent. One evening a customer, hearing a trampling of hoofs on the paved roadway outside, lifted the curtain, and recognizing the Commandant-in-Chief of the National Guard, the *citoyen* Hanriot, who was riding past with his Staff, muttered between his teeth:

"There goes Robespierre's jackass!"

Julie overheard and burst into a loud guffaw.

But a moustachioed patriot took up the challenge roundly:

"Whoever says that," he shouted, "is a bl . . . sted aristocrat, and I should like to see the fellow sneeze into Samson's basket. I tell you General Hanriot is a good patriot who'll know how to defend Paris and the Convention at a pinch. That's why the Royalists can't forgive him."

Glaring at Julie, who was still laughing, the patriot added:

"You there, greenhorn, have a care I don't land you a kick in the backside to learn you to respect good patriots."

But other voices were joining in:

"Hanriot's a drunken sot and a fool!"

"Hanriot's a good Jacobin! Vive Hanriot!"

Sides were taken, and the fray began. Blows were exchanged, hats battered in, tables overturned, and glasses shivered; the lights went out and the women began to scream. Two or three patriots fell upon Julie, who seized hold of a settle in self-defence; she was brought to the ground, where she scratched and bit her assailants. Her coat flew open and her neckerchief was torn, revealing her panting bosom. A patrol came running up at the noise, and the girl aristocrat escaped between the gendarmes' legs.

Every day the carts were full of victims for the guillotine.

"But I cannot, I cannot let my lover die!" Julie would tell her mother.

She resolved to beg his life, to take what steps were possible, to go to the Committees and Public Departments, to canvas Representatives, Magistrates, to visit anyone who could be of help. She had no woman's dress to wear. Her mother borrowed a striped gown, a kerchief, a lace coif from the *citoyenne* Blaise, and Julie, attired as a woman and a patriot, set out for the abode of one of the judges, Renaudin, a damp, dismal house in the Rue Mazarine.

With trembling steps she climbed the wooden, tiled stairs and was received by the judge in his squalid cabinet, furnished with a deal table and two straw-bottomed chairs. The wall-paper hung in strips. Renaudin, with black hair plastered on his forehead, a lowering eye, tucked-in lips, and a protuberant chin, signed to her to speak and listened in silence.

She told him she was the sister of the *citoyen* Chassagne, a prisoner at the Luxembourg, explained as speciously as she could the circumstances under which he had been arrested, represented him as an innocent man, the victim of mischance, pleaded more and more urgently; but he remained callous and unsympathetic.

She fell at his feet in supplication and burst into tears.

No sooner did he see her tears than his face changed; his dark blood-shot eyes lit up, and his heavy blue jowl worked as if pumping up the saliva in his dry throat.

"*Citoyenne*, we will do what is necessary. You need have no anxiety,"—and opening a door, he pushed the petitioner into a little sitting-room, with rose-pink hangings, painted panels, Dresden china figures, a time-piece and gilt candelabra; for furniture it contained settees, and a sofa covered in tapestry and adorned with a pastoral group after Boucher. Julie was ready for anything to save her lover.

Renaudin had his way,—rapidly and brutally. When she got up, readjusting the *citoyenne* Élodie's pretty frock, she met the man's cruel mocking eye; instantly she knew she had made her sacrifice in vain.

"You promised me my brother's freedom," she said.

He chuckled.

"I told you, *citoyenne*, we would do what was necessary,—that is to say, we should apply the law, neither more nor less. I told you to have no anxiety,—and why should you be anxious? The Revolutionary Tribunal is always just."

She thought of throwing herself upon the man, biting him, tearing out his eyes. But, realizing she would only be consummating Fortuné Chassagne's ruin, she rushed from the house, and fled to her garret to take off Élodie's soiled and desecrated frock. All night she lay, screaming with grief and rage.

Next day, on returning to the Luxembourg, she found the gardens occupied by gendarmes, who were turning out the women and children. Sentinels were posted in the avenues to prevent the passers-by from communicating with the prisoners. The young mother, who used to come every day, carrying her child in her arms, told Julie that there was talk of plotting in the prisons and that the women were blamed for gathering in the gardens in order to rouse the people's pity in favour of aristocrats and traitors.

Chapter 22

A MOUNTAIN has suddenly sprung up in the garden of the Tuileries. Under a cloudless sky, Maximilien heads the procession of his colleagues in a blue coat and yellow breeches, carrying in his hand a bouquet of wheat-ears, cornflowers and poppies. He ascends the mountain and proclaims the God of Jean-Jacques to the Republic, which hears and weeps. O purity! O sweetness! O faith! O antique simplicity! O tears of pity! O fertilizing dew! O clemency! O human fraternity!

In vain Atheism still lifts its hideous face; Maximilien grasps a torch; flames devour the monster and Wisdom appears, with one hand pointing to the sky, in the other holding a crown of stars.

On the platform raised against the façade of the Tuileries, Évariste, standing amid a throng of deeply-stirred spectators, sheds tears of joy and renders thanks to God. An era of universal felicity opens before his eyes.

He sighs:

"At last we shall be happy, pure, innocent, if the scoundrels suffer it."

Alas! the scoundrels have not suffered it. There must be more executions; more torrents of tainted blood must be shed. Three days after the festival celebrating the new covenant and the reconciliation of heaven and earth, the Convention promulgates the Law of Prairial which suppresses, with a sort of ferocious good-nature, all the traditional forms of Law, whatever has been devised since the time of the Roman jurisconsults for the safeguarding of innocence under suspicion. No more sifting of evidence, no more questioning of the accused, no more witnesses, no more counsel for the defence; love of the fatherland supplies everything that is needful. The prisoner, who bears locked up in his bosom his guilt or innocence, passes without a word allowed before the patriot jury, and it is in this brief moment

171

they must unravel his case, often complicated and obscure. How is justice possible? How distinguish in an instant between the honest man and the villain, the patriot and the enemy of the fatherland . . .?

Disconcerted for the moment, Gamelin quickly learned his new duties and accommodated himself to his new functions. He recognized that this curtailment of formalities was genuinely characteristic of the new justice, at once salutary and terrifying, the administrators of which were no longer ermined pedants leisurely weighing the *pros* and *contras* in their Gothic balances, but good *sansculottes* judging by patriotic inspiration and seeing the whole truth in a flash. When guarantees and precautions would have undone everything, the impulses of an upright heart saved the situation. We must follow the promptings of Nature, the good mother who never deceives; the heart must teach us to do judgment, and Gamelin made invocation to the manes of Jean-Jacques:

"Man of virtue, inspire me with the love of men, the ardent desire to regenerate humankind!"

His colleagues, for the most part, felt with him. They were, first and foremost, simple people; and when the forms of law were simplified, they felt more comfortable. Justice thus abbreviated satisfied them; the pace was quickened, and no obstacles were left to fret them. They limited themselves to an enquiry into the opinions of the accused, not conceiving it possible that anyone could think differently from themselves except in pure perversity. Believing themselves the exclusive possessors of truth, wisdom, the quintessence of good, they attributed to their opponents nothing but error and evil. They felt themselves all-powerful; they saw God.

They saw God, these jurors of the Revolutionary Tribunal. The Supreme Being, acknowledged by Maximilien, flooded them with His flames of light. They loved, they believed.

The chair of the accused had been replaced by a vast platform able to accommodate fifty persons; the court only dealt with batches now. The Public Prosecutor would often confound under the same charge or implicate as accomplices individuals who met each other for the first time before the Tribunal. The latter, taking advantage of the terrible facilities accorded by the law of Prairial, sat in judgment on those supposed prison plots which, coming after the proscriptions of the Dantonists and the Commune, were made to seem their outcome by the insinuations of cunning adversaries. In fact, to let the world appreciate the two essential characteristics of a conspiracy fomented by foreign gold against the Republic, to wit, inopportune moderation on the one hand and self-interested excess of zeal on the other, and to display the wickedness of Hébertism and of Dantonism side by side, they had united in the same condemnation two very different women, the widow of Camille Desmoulins, poor lovable Lucille, and the widow of the Hébertist Momoro, goddess of a day and jolly companion all her life. Both, to make the analogy complete, had been shut up in the same prison, where they had mingled their tears on the same bench; both, to round off the resemblance, had climbed the scaffold. Too ingenious the symbol,—a masterpiece of equilibrium, conceived doubtless by a lawyer's brain, and the honour of which was given to Maximilien. This representative of the people was credited with every eventuality, happy or unhappy, that came about in the Republic, every change that was effected in the laws, in manners and morals, the very course of the seasons, the harvests, the incidence of epidemics. Unjust of course, but not unmerited the injustice, for indeed the man, the little, spruce, cat-faced dandy, was all-powerful with the people. . . .

That day the Tribunal was clearing off a batch of prisoners involved in the great plot, thirty or more conspirators from the Luxembourg, submissive enough in gaol, but Royalists or Federalists of the most pronounced type. The prosecution relied almost entirely on the evidence of a single informer. The jurors did not know one word of the matter,—not so much as the conspirators' names. Gamelin, casting his eye over the prisoners' bench, recognized Fortuné Chassagne among the accused. Julie's lover, pale-faced and emaciated by long confinement and his features showing coarser in the glare of light that flooded the hall, still retained traces of his old grace and proud bearing. His eyes met Gamelin's and filled with scorn.

Gamelin, possessed by a calm fury, rose, asked leave to speak, and, fixing his eyes on the bust of Roman Brutus, which looked down on the Tribunal:

"*Citoyen* President," he said, "although there may exist between one of the accused and myself ties which, if they were made public, would be ties of married kinship, I hereby declare I do not decline to act. The two Bruti did not decline their duty, when, for the salvation of the state and the cause of freedom, the one had to condemn a son, the other to strike down an adoptive father."

He resumed his seat.

"A fine scoundrel that," muttered Chassagne between his teeth.

The public remained cold, whether because it was tired of high-flown characters, or thinking that Gamelin had triumphed too easily over his feelings of family affection.

"*Citoyen* Gamelin," said the President, "by the terms of the law, every refusal must be formulated in writing within the twenty-four hours preceding the opening of the trial. In any case, you have no reason to refuse; a patriot jury is superior to human passions."

Each prisoner was questioned for three or four minutes, the examination resulting in a verdict of death in every instance. The jurors voted without a word said, by a nod of the head or by exclamation. When Gamelin's turn came to pronounce his opinion:

"All the accused," he declared, "are convicted, and the law is explicit."

As he was descending the stairway of the Palais de Justice, a young man dressed in a bottle-green box-coat, and who looked seventeen or eighteen years of age, stopped him abruptly as he went by. The lad wore a round hat, tilted on the back of his head, the brim framing his fine pale face in a dark aureole. Facing the juror, in a terrible voice vibrating with passion and despair:

"Villain, monster, murderer!" he screamed. "Strike me, coward! I am a woman! Have me arrested, have me guillotined, Cain! I am your sister,"—and Julie spat in his face.

The throng of *tricoteuses* and *sansculottes* was relaxing by this time in its Revolutionary vigilance; its civic zeal had largely cooled; Gamelin and his assailant found themselves the centre of nothing worse than uproar and confusion. Julie fought a way through the press and disappeared in the dark.

Chapter 23

ÉVARISTE GAMELIN was worn out and could not rest; twenty times in the night he would awake with a start from a sleep haunted by nightmares. It was only in the blue chamber, in Élodie's arms, that he could snatch a few hours' slumber. He talked and cried out in his sleep and used often to awake her; but she could make nothing of what he said.

One morning, after a night when he had seen the Eumenides, he started awake, broken with terror and weak as a child. The dawn was piercing the window curtains with its wan arrows. Évariste's hair, lying tangled on his brow, covered his eyes with a black veil; Élodie, by the bedside, was gently parting the wild locks. She was looking at him, now, with a sister's tenderness, while with her handkerchief she wiped away the icy sweat from the unhappy man's forehead. Then he remembered that fine scene in the *Orestes* of Euripides, which he had essayed to represent in a picture that, if he could have finished it, would have been his masterpiece—the scene where the unhappy Electra wipes away the spume that sullies her brother's lips. And he seemed to hear Élodie also saying in a gentle voice:

"Hear me, beloved brother, while the Furies leave you master of your reason . . ."

And he thought:

"And yet I am no parricide. Far from it, it is filial piety has made me shed the tainted blood of the enemies of my fatherland."

175

Chapter 24

THERE seemed no end to these trials for conspiracy in the prisons. Forty-nine accused crowded the tiers of seats. Maurice Brotteaux occupied the right-hand corner of the topmost row,—the place of honour. He was dressed in his plum-coloured surtout, which he had brushed very carefully the day before and mended at the pocket where his little Lucretius had ended by fretting a hole. Beside him sat the woman Rochemaure, painted and powdered and patched, a brilliant and ghastly figure. They had put the Père Longuemare between her and the girl Athenaïs, who had recovered her look of youthful freshness at the Madelonnettes.

On the platform the gendarmes massed a number of other prisoners unknown to any of our friends, and who, as likely as not, knew nothing of each other,—yet accomplices one and all,—lawyers, journalists, *ci-devant* nobles, citizens, and citizens' wives. The *citoyenne* Rochemaure caught side of Gamelin on the jurors' bench. He had not answered her urgent letters and repeated messages; still she had not abandoned hope, and threw him a look of supplication, trying to appear fascinating and pathetic for him. But the young juror's cold glance robbed her of any illusion she might have entertained.

The Clerk read the act of accusation, which, succinct as was its reference to each individual, was a lengthy document because of the great number accused. It began by exposing in general outline the plot concocted in the prisons to drown the Republic in the blood of the Representatives of the nation and the people of Paris; then, coming to each severally, it went on:

"One of the most mischievous authors of this abominable conspiracy is the man Brotteaux, once known as des Ilettes, receiver of imposts under the tyrant. This person, who was remarkable, even in the days of tyranny, for his libertine behaviour, is a sure proof how dissoluteness and immorality are the greatest enemies of the liberty

176

and happiness of peoples; as a fact, after misappropriating the public revenues and wasting in debauchery a noticeable part of the people's patrimony, the person in question connived with his former concubine, the woman Rochemaure, to enter into correspondence with the *émigrés* and traitorously keep the faction of the foreigner informed of the state of our finances, the movements of our troops, the fluctuations of public opinion.

"Brotteaux, who, at this period of his despicable life, was living in concubinage with a prostitute he had picked up in the mud of the Rue Fromenteau, the girl Athenaïs, easily suborned her to his purposes and made use of her to foment the counter-revolution by impudent and unpatriotic cries and indecent and traitorous speeches.

"Sundry remarks of this ill-omened individual will afford you a clear indication of his abject views and pernicious purpose. Speaking of the patriotic Tribunal now called upon to punish him, he declared insultingly,—'The Revolutionary Tribunal is like a play of William Shakespeare, who mixes up with the most bloodthirsty scenes the most trivial buffooneries.' Then he was forever preaching atheism, as the surest means of degrading the people and driving it into immorality. In the prison of the Conciergerie, where he was confined, he used to deplore as among the worst of calamities the victories of our valiant armies, and tried to throw suspicion on the most patriotic Generals, crediting them with designs of tyrannicide. 'Only wait,' he would say in atrocious language which the pen is loath to reproduce, 'only wait till, some day, one of these warriors, to whom you owe your salvation, swallows you all up as the stork in the fable gobbled up the frogs.'

"The woman Rochemaure, a *ci-devant* noble, concubine of Brotteaux, is not less culpable than he. Not only was she in correspondence with the foreigner and in the pay of Pitt himself, but in complicity with swindlers, such as Julien (of Toulouse) and Chabot, associates of the *ci-devant* Baron de Batz, she seconded that reprobate in all sorts of cunning machinations to depreciate the shares of the Company of the Indies, buy them in at a cheap price, and then raise the quotation by artifices of an opposite tendency, to the confusion and ruin of private fortunes and of the public funds. Incarcerated at La Bourbe and the Madelonnettes, she never ceased in prison to conspire, to dabble in stocks and shares and to devote herself to attempts at corruption, to suborn judges and jury.

"Louis Longuemare, ex-noble, ex-Capuchin, had long been practised in infamy and crime before committing the acts of treason for
which he has to answer here. Living in a shameful promiscuity with
the girl Gorcut, known as Athenaïs, under Brotteaux's very roof, he
is the accomplice of the said girl and the said *ci-devant* nobleman.
During his imprisonment at the Conciergerie he has never ceased for
one single day writing pamphlets aimed at the subversion of public
liberty and security.

"It is right to say, with regard to Marthe Gorcut, known as
Athenaïs, that prostitutes are the greatest scourge of public morality, which they insult, and the approbrium of the society which they
disgrace. But why speak at length of revolting crimes which the accused confesses shamelessly . . . ?"

The accusation then proceeded to pass in review the fifty-four
other prisoners, none of whom either Brotteaux, or the Père Longuemare, or the *citoyenne* Rochemaure, were acquainted with, except
for having seen several of them in the prisons, but who were one and
all included with the first named in "this odious plot, with which
the annals of nations can furnish nothing to compare."

The piece concluded by demanding the penalty of death for all
the culprits.

Brotteaux was the first to be examined:

"You were in the plot?"

"No, I have been in no plots. Every word is untrue in the act of
accusation I have just heard read."

"There, you see; you are plotting still, at this moment, to dis-
credit the Tribunal,"—and the President went on to the woman
Rochemaure, who answered with despairing protestations of innocence, tears and quibblings.

The Père Longuemare referred himself purely and entirely to
God's will. He had not even brought his written defence with him.

All the questions put to him he answered in a spirit of resignation.
Only, when the President spoke of him as a Capuchin, did the old
Adam wake again in him:

"I am not a Capuchin," he said, "I am a priest and a religious of
the Order of the Barnabites."

"It is the same thing," returned the President good-naturedly.

The Père Longuemare looked at him indignantly:

"One cannot conceive a more extraordinary error," he cried,

178

"than to confound with a Capuchin a religious of this Order of the Barnabites which derives its constitutions from the Apostle Paul himself."

The remark was greeted with a burst of laughter and hooting from the spectators, at which the Père Longuemare, taking this derision to betoken a denial of his proposition, announced that he would die a member of this Order of St. Barnabas, the habit of which he wore in his heart.

"Do you admit," asked the President, "entering into plots with the girl Gorcut, known as Athenaïs, the same who accorded you her despicable favours?"

At the question, the Père Longuemare raised his eyes sorrowfully to heaven, but made no answer; his silence expressed the surprise of an unsophisticated mind and the gravity of a man of religion who fears to utter empty words.

"You, the girl Gorcut," the President asked, turning to Athenaïs, "do you admit plotting in conjunction with Brotteaux?"

Her answer was softly spoken:

"Monsieur Brotteaux, to my knowledge, has done nothing but good. He is a man of the sort we should have more of; there is no better sort. Those who say the contrary are mistaken. That is all I have to say."

The President asked her if she admitted having lived in concubinage with Brotteaux. The expression had to be explained to her, as she did not understand it. But, directly she gathered what the question meant, she answered, that would only have depended on him, but he had never asked her.

There was a laugh in the public galleries, and the President threatened the girl Gorcut to refuse her a hearing if she answered in such a cynical sort again.

At this she broke out, calling him sneak, sour face, cuckold, and spewing out over him, judges, and jury a torrent of invective, till the gendarmes dragged her from her bench and hustled her out of the hall.

The President then proceeded to a brief examination of the rest of the accused, taking them in the order in which they sat on the tiers of benches.

One, a man named Navette, pleaded that he could not have plotted in prison where he had only spent four days. The President observed that the point deserved to be considered, and begged the *citoyens* of the jury to make a note of it. A certain Bellier said the same, and the President made the same remark to the jury in his favour. This mildness on the judge's part was interpreted by some as the result of a praiseworthy scrupulosity, by others as payment due in recognition of their talents as informers.

The Deputy of the Public Prosecutor spoke next. All he did was to amplify the details of the act of accusation and then to put the question:

"Is it proven that Maurice Brotteaux, Louise Rochemaure, Louis Longuemare, Marthe Gorcut, known as Athenaïs, Eusèbe Rocher, Pierre Guyton-Fabulet, Marcelline Descourtis, etc., etc., are guilty of forming a conspiracy, the means whereof are assassination, starvation, the making of forged assignats and false coin, the depravation of morals and public spirit, the emptying of the prisons; the aim and object, civil war, the abolition of the National representation, the re-establishment of Royalty?"

The jurors withdrew into the chamber of deliberation. They voted unanimously in the affirmative, only excepting the cases of the afore-named Navette and Bellier, whom the President, and following his lead, the Public Prosecutor, had put, as it were, in a separate class by themselves.

Gamelin stated the motives for his decision thus:

"The guilt of the accused is self-evident; the safety of the Nation demands their chastisement, and they ought themselves to desire their punishment as the only means of expiating their crimes."

The President pronounced sentence in the absence of those it concerned. On these great days, contrary to what the law prescribed, the condemned were not called back again to hear their judgment read, no doubt for fear of the effects of despair on so large a number of prisoners. A needless apprehension, so extraordinary and so general was the submissiveness of the victims in those days! The Clerk of the Court came down to the cells to read the verdict, which was listened to with such silence and impassivity as made it a common comparison to liken the condemned of Prairial to trees marked down for felling.

The *citoyenne* Rochemaure declared herself pregnant. A surgeon, who was likewise one of the jury, was directed to see her. She was carried out fainting to her dungeon.

"Ah!" sighed the Père Longuemare, "these judges and jurors are men very deserving of pity: their state of mind is truly deplorable. They mix up everything and confound a Barnabite with a Franciscan."

The execution was to take place the same day at the Barrière du Trône-Renversé. The condemned, their toilet completed, hair cropped and shirt cut down at the neck, waited for the headsman, packed like cattle in the small room separated off from the gaoler's office by a glazed partition.

When presently the executioner and his men arrived, Brotteaux, who was quietly reading his Lucretius, put the marker at the page he had begun, shut the book, stuffed it in the pocket of his coat, and said to the Barnabite:

"What enrages me, Reverend Father, is that I shall never convince you. We are going both of us to sleep our last sleep, and I shall not be able to twitch you by the sleeve and wake you to hear me say: 'There, you see; you have neither sensation nor consciousness left; you are inanimate. What comes after life is like what goes before.'"

He tried to smile; but an atrocious spasm of pain wrung his heart and vitals, and he came near fainting.

He resumed, however:

"Father, I let you see my weakness. I love life and I do not leave it without regret."

"Sir," replied the monk gently, "take heed, you are a braver man than I, and nevertheless death troubles you more. What does that mean, if not that I see the light, which you do not see yet?"

"Might it not also be," said Brotteaux, "that I regret life because I have enjoyed it better than you, who have made it as close a copy of death as possible?"

"Sir," said the Père Longuemare, his face paling, "this is a solemn moment. God help me! It is plain we shall die without spiritual aid. It must be that in other days I have received the sacraments lukewarmly and with a thankless heart, for Heaven to refuse me them today, when I have such pressing need of them."

The carts were waiting. The condemned were loaded into them pell-mell, with hands tied. The woman Rochemaure, whose pregnancy had not been verified by the surgeon, was hoisted into one of the tumbrels. She recovered a little of her old energy to watch the crowd of onlookers, hoping against hope to find rescuers amongst them. Her eyes were imploring. The throng was less dense than formerly, and the excitement less extreme. Only a few women screamed, "Death! death!" or mocked those who were to die. The men mostly shrugged their shoulders, looked another way, and said nothing, whether out of prudence or from respect for the laws.

A shudder went through the crowd when Athenaïs emerged from the wicket. She looked a mere child.

She bowed her head before the religious:

"Monsieur le Curé," she asked him, "give me absolution."

The Père Longuemare gravely recited the sacramental words in muttered tones; then:

"My daughter!" he added, "you have fallen into great disorders of living; but would I could offer the Lord a heart as simple as yours."

She climbed lightly into the cart. And there, throwing out her bosom and proudly lifting her girlish head, she cried "Vive le Roi!"

She made a little sign to Brotteaux to show him there was a vacant place beside her. Brotteaux helped the Barnabite to get in and came and placed himself between the religious and the simple-hearted girl.

"Sir," said the Père Longuemare to the Epicurean philosopher, "I ask you a favour; this God in whom you do not yet believe, pray to Him for me. It is far from sure you are not nearer to Him than I am myself; a moment can decide this. A second, and you may be called by the Lord to be His highly favoured son. Sir, pray for me."

While the wheels were grinding over the pavement of the long Faubourg Antoine, the monk was busy, with heart and lips, reciting the prayers for the dying. Brotteaux's mind was fixed on recalling the lines of the poet of nature: *Sic ubi non erimus.* . . . Bound as he was and shaken in the vile, jolting cart, he preserved his calm and even showed a certain solicitude to maintain an easy posture. At his side, Athenaïs, proud to die like the Queen of France, surveyed the crowd with haughty looks, and the old financier, noting as a connoisseur the girl's white bosom, was filled with regret for the light of day.

Chapter 25

WHILE the carts, escorted by gendarmes, were rumbling along on their way to the Place du Trône Renversé, carrying to their death Brotteaux and his "accomplices," Évariste sat pensive on a bench in the garden of the Tuileries. He was waiting for Élodie. The sun, nearing its setting, shot its fiery darts through the leafy chestnuts. At the gate of the garden, Fame on her winged horse blew her everlasting trumpet. The newspaper hawkers were bawling the news of the great victory of Fleurus.

"Yes," thought Gamelin, "victory is ours. We have paid full price for it."

He could see the beaten Generals, disconsolate shades, trailing in the blood-stained dust of yonder Place de la Révolution where they perished. And he smiled proudly, reflecting that, but for the severities in which he had borne his share, the Austrian horses would to-day be gnawing the bark of the trees beside him.

He soliloquized:

"Life-giving terror, O blessed terror! Last year at this time, our heroic defenders were beaten and in rags, the soil of the fatherland was invaded, two-thirds of the departments in revolt. Now our armies, well equipped, well trained, commanded by able generals, are taking the offensive, ready to bear liberty through the world. Peace reigns over all the territory of the Republic. . . . Life-giving terror, O blessed terror! O saintly guillotine! Last year at this time, the Republic was torn by factions, the hydra of Federalism threatened to devour her. Now a united Jacobinism spreads over the empire its might and its wisdom. . . ."

Nevertheless, he was gloomy. His brow was deeply lined, his mouth bitter. His thoughts ran: "We used to say: *To conquer or to die*. We were wrong; it is *to conquer and to die* we ought to say."

He looked about him. Children were building sand-castles. *Citoy-*

183

ennes in their wooden chairs under the trees were sewing or embroidering. The passers-by, in coat and breeches of elegant cut and strange fashion, their thoughts fixed on their business or their pleasures, were making for home. And Gamelin felt himself alone amongst them; he was no compatriot, no contemporary of theirs. What was it had happened? How came the enthusiasm of the great years to have been succeeded by indifference, weariness, perhaps disgust? It was plain to see, these people never wanted to hear the Revolutionary Tribunal spoken of again and averted their eyes from the guillotine. Grown too painful a sight in the Place de la Révolution, it had been banished to the extremity of the Faubourg Antoine. There even, the passage of the tumbrels was greeted with murmurs. Voices, it was said, had been heard to shout: "Enough!"

Enough, when there were still traitors, conspirators! Enough, when the Committees must be reformed, the Convention purged! Enough, when scoundrels disgraced the National representation! Enough, when they were planning even in the Revolutionary Tribunal the downfall of *The Just!* For, dreadful thought, but only too true! Fouquier himself was weaving plots, and it was to ruin Maximilien that he had sacrificed with solemn ceremony fifty-seven victims haled to death in the red sheet of parricides. France was giving way to pity — and pity was a crime! Then we should have saved her in spite of herself, and when she cried for mercy, stopped our ears and struck! Alas! the fates had decided otherwise; the fatherland was for cursing its saviours. Well, let it curse, if only it may be saved!

"It is not enough to immolate obscure victims, aristocrats, financiers, publicists, poets, a Lavoisier, a Roucher, an André Chénier. We must strike these all-puissant malefactors who, with hands full of gold and dripping with blood, are plotting the ruin of *the Mountain* — the Fouchés, Talliens, Rovères, Carriers, Bourdons. We must deliver the State from all its enemies. If Hébert had triumphed, the Convention was overthrown, the Republic hastening to the abyss; if Desmoulins and Danton had triumphed, the Convention had lost its virtue, ready to surrender the Republic to the aristocrats, the money-jobbers and the Generals. If men like Tallien and Fouché, monsters gorged with blood and rapine, triumph, France is overwhelmed in a welter of crime and infamy . . . Robespierre, awake; when criminals, drunken with fury and affright, plan your death

and the death of freedom! Couthon, Saint-Just, make haste; why tarry ye to denounce the plots?

"Why! the old-time state, the Royal monster, assured its empire by imprisoning every year four hundred thousand persons, by hanging fifteen thousand, by breaking three thousand on the wheel—and the Republic still hesitates to sacrifice a few hundred heads for its security and domination! Let us drown in blood and save the fatherland. . . ."

He was buried in these thoughts when Élodie hurried up to him, pale-faced and distraught:

"Évariste, what have you to say to me? Why not come to the *Amour peintre* to the blue chamber? Why have you made me come here?"

"To bid you an eternal farewell."

He had lost his wits, she faltered, she could not understand. . . .

He stopped her with a very slight movement of the hand.

"Élodie, I cannot any more accept your love."

"Be quiet, Évariste, be quiet!"

She begged him to walk on further; people could see them, overhear them, where they were.

He moved on a score of yards, and resumed, very quietly:

"I have made sacrifice to my country of my life and my honour. I shall die infamous; I shall have naught to leave you, unhappy girl, save an execrated memory. . . . We, love? Can anyone love me still? . . . Can I love?"

She told him he was mad; that she loved him, that she would always love him. She was ardent, sincere; but she felt as well as he, she felt better than he, that he was right. But she fought against the evidence of her senses.

He went on:

"I blame myself for nothing. What I have done, I would do again. I have made myself anathema for my country's sake. I am accursed. I have put myself outside humanity; I shall never re-enter its pale. No, the great task is not finished. O clemency, forgiveness!—Do the traitors forgive? Are the conspirators clement? Scoundrels, parricides multiply unceasingly; they spring up from underground, they swarm in from all our frontiers,—young men, who would have done better to perish with our armies, old men, children, women, with every mark of innocence, purity, and grace. They are offered up a sacrifice,—and more victims are ready for the knife! . . . You can see, Élodie, I must needs renounce love, renounce all joy, all sweetness of life, renounce life itself."

He fell silent. Born to taste tranquil joys, Élodie not for the first time was appalled to find, under the tragic kisses of a lover like Évariste, her voluptuous transports blended with images of horror and bloodshed; she offered no reply. To Évariste the girl's silence was as a draught of a bitter chalice.

"Yes, you can see, Élodie, we are on a precipice; our deeds devour us. Our days, our hours are years. I shall soon have lived a century. Look at this brow! Is it a lover's? Love! . . . "

"Évariste, you are mine, I will not let you go; I will not give you back your freedom."

She was speaking in the language of sacrifice. He felt it; she felt it herself.

"Will you be able, Élodie, one day to bear witness that I lived faithful to my duty, that my heart was upright and my soul unsullied, that I knew no passion but the public good; that I was born to feel and love? Will you say: 'He did his duty'? But no! You will not say it, and I do not ask you to say it. Perish my memory! My glory is in my own heart; shame beleaguers me about. If you loved me, never speak my name; eternal silence is best."

A child of eight or nine, trundling its hoop, ran just then between Gamelin's legs.

He lifted the boy suddenly in his arms:

"Child, you will grow up free, happy, and you will owe it to the infamous Gamelin. I am ferocious, that you may be happy. I am cruel, that you may be kind; I am pitiless, that to-morrow all Frenchmen may embrace with tears of joy."

He pressed the child to his breast.

"Little one, when you are a man, you will owe your happiness, your innocence to me; and, if ever you hear my name uttered, you will execrate it."

Then he put down the child, which ran away in terror to cling to its mother's skirts, who had hurried up to the rescue. The young mother, who was pretty and charming in her aristocratic grace, with her gown of white lawn, carried off the boy with a haughty look.

Gamelin turned his eyes on Élodie:

"I have held the child in my arms; perhaps I shall send the mother to the guillotine,"—and he walked away with long strides under the ordered trees.

Élodie stood a moment motionless, her eyes fixed on the ground. Then, suddenly, she darted after her lover, and frenzied, dishevelled, like a Mænad, she gripped him as if to tear him in pieces and cried in a voice choked with blood and tears:

"Well, then! me too, my beloved, send me to the guillotine; me too, lay me under the knife!"

And, at the thought of the knife at her neck, all her flesh melted in an ecstasy of horror and voluptuous transport.

Chapter 26

THE SUN of Thermidor was setting in a blood-red sky, while Évariste wandered, gloomy and careworn, in the Marbeuf gardens, now a National park frequented by the Parisian idlers. There were stalls for the sale of lemonade and ices; wooden horses and shooting-galleries were provided for the younger patriots. Under a tree, a little Savoyard in rags, with a black cap on his head, was making a marmot dance to the shrill notes of his hurdy-gurdy. A man, still young, slim-waisted, wearing a blue coat and his hair powdered, with a big dog at his heels, stopped to listen to the rustic music. Évariste recognized Robespierre. He found him paler, thinner, his face harder and drawn in folds of suffering. He thought to himself:

"What fatigues, how many griefs have left their imprint on his brow! How grievous a thing it is to work for the happiness of mankind! What are his thoughts at this moment? Does the sound of this mountain music perhaps distract him from the cares of government? Is he thinking that he has made a pact with Death and that the hour of reckoning is coming close? Is he dreaming of a triumphant return to the Committee of Public Safety, from which he withdrew, weary of being held in check, with Couthon and Saint-Just, by a seditious majority? Behind that impenetrable countenance what hopes are seething, or what fears?"

But Maximilien smiled at the lad, in a gentle, kind voice asked him several questions about his native valley, the humble home and parents the poor child had left behind, tossed him a small piece of silver and resumed his stroll. After taking a few steps, he turned round again to call his dog; sniffing at the marmot, it was showing its teeth at the little creature that bristled up in defiance.

"To heel, Brount!" he called, "to heel!"—and he plunged among the dark trees.

Gamelin, out of respect, did not interrupt his lonely walk; but, as he gazed after the slender form disappearing in the darkness, he mentally addressed his hero in these impassioned words:

"I have seen thy sadness, Maximilien; I have understood thy thought. Thy melancholy, thy fatigue, even the look of fear that stamps thy face, everything says: 'Let the reign of terror end and that of fraternity begin! Frenchmen, be united, be virtuous, be good and kind. Love ye one another. . . . ' Well then, I will second your designs; that you, in your wisdom and goodness, may be able to put an end to our civil discord, to our fratricidal hate, turn the headsman into a gardener who will henceforth cut off only the heads of cabbages and lettuces, I will pave the way with my colleagues of the Tribunal that must lead to clemency by exterminating conspirators and traitors. We will redouble our vigilance and our severity. No culprit shall escape us. And when the head of the last enemy of the Republic shall have fallen under the knife, then it will be given thee to be merciful without committing a crime, then thou canst inaugurate the reign of innocence and virtue in all the land, O father of thy country!"

The Incorruptible was already almost out of sight. Two men in round hats and nankeen breeches, one of whom, a tall, lean man of a wild, unkempt aspect, had a blur on one eye and resembled Tallien, met him at the corner of an avenue, looked at him askance and passed on, pretending not to recognize him. When they had gone far enough to be out of hearing, they muttered under their breath:

"So there he goes, the King, the Pope, the God. For he is God; and Catherine Théot is his prophetess."

"Dictator, traitor, tyrant! the race of Brutus is not extinct."

"Tremble, malefactor! the Tarpeian rock is near the Capitol!"

The dog Brount ran towards the pair. They said no more and quickened their pace.

Chapter 27

ROBESPIERRE, awake! The hour is come, time presses, . . . soon it will be too late. . . .

At last, on the 8 Thermidor, in the Convention, the Incorruptible rises, he is going to speak. Sun of the 31st May, is this to be a second day-spring? Gamelin waits and hopes. His mind is made up then! Robespierre is to drag from the benches they dishonour these legislators more guilty than the Federalists, more dangerous than Danton. . . . No! not yet. "I cannot," he says, "resolve to clear away entirely the veil that hides this mystery of iniquity."

It is mere summer lightning that flashes harmlessly, and without striking any one of the conspirators, terrifies all. Sixty of them at least for a fortnight had not dared sleep in their beds. Marat's way was to denounce traitors by their name, to point the finger of accusation at conspirators. The Incorruptible hesitates, and from that moment he himself is the accused. . . .

That evening at the Jacobins, the hall is filled to suffocation, the corridors, the courtyard are crowded.

They are all there, loud-voiced friends and silent enemies. Robespierre reads them the speech the Convention had heard in affrighted silence, and the Jacobins greet it with excited applause.

"It is my dying testament," declares the orator. "You will see me drain the hemlock undismayed."

"I will drink it with you," answers David.

"All, we all will!" shout the Jacobins, and separate without deciding anything.

Évariste, while the death of *The Just* was preparing, slept the sleep of the Disciples in the garden of Gethsemane. Next day, he attended the Tribunal where two Sections were sitting. That on which he served was trying twenty-one persons implicated in the conspiracy of the Lazare prison. The case was still proceeding when the tidings arrived:

"The Convention, after a six-hours' session, has decreed Maximilien Robespierre accused,—with him Couthon and Saint-Just; add Augustin Robespierre, and Lebas, who have demanded to share the lot of the accused. The five outlaws stand at the bar of the house."

News is brought that the President of the Section sitting in the next court, the *citoyen* Dumas, has been arrested on the bench, but that the sitting goes on. Drums can be heard beating the alarm, and the tocsin peals from the churches.

Évariste is still in his place when he is handed an order from the Commune to proceed to the Hôtel de Ville to sit in the General Council. To the sound of the rolling drums and clanging church-bells, he and his colleagues record their verdict; then he hurries home to embrace his mother and snatch up his scarf of office. The Place de Thionville is deserted. The Section is afraid to declare either for or against the Convention. Wayfarers creep along under the walls, slip down side-streets, sneak indoors. The call of the tocsin and alarm-drums is answered by the noise of barring shutters and bolting doors. The *citoyen* Dupont senior has secreted himself in his shop; Remacle the porter is barricaded in his lodge. Little Joséphine holds Mouton tremblingly in her arms. The widow Gamelin bemoans the dearness of victuals, cause of all the trouble. At the foot of the stairs Évariste encounters Élodie; she is panting for breath and her black locks are plastered on her hot cheek.

"I have been to look for you at the Tribunal; but you had just left. Where are you going?"

"To the Hôtel de Ville."

"Don't go there! It would be your ruin; Hanriot is arrested . . . the Sections will not stir. The *Section des Piques*, Robespierre's Section, will do nothing, I know it for a fact; my father belongs to it. If you go to the Hôtel de Ville, you are throwing away your life for nothing."

"You wish me to be a coward?"

"No! the brave thing is to be faithful to the Convention and to obey the Law."

"The law is dead when malefactors triumph."

"Évariste, hear me; hear your Élodie; hear your sister. Come and sit beside her and let her soothe your angry spirit."

He looked at her; never had she seemed so desirable in his eyes;

never had her voice sounded so seductive, so persuasive in his ears.

"A couple of paces, only a couple of paces, dear Évariste!"—
and she drew him towards the raised platform on which stood the
pedestal of the overthrown statue. It was surrounded by benches
occupied by strollers of both sexes. A dealer in fancy articles was
offering his laces, a seller of cooling drinks, his portable cistern on his
back, was tinkling his bell; little girls were showing off their airs and
graces. The parapet was lined with anglers, standing, rod in hand,
very still. The weather was stormy, the sky overcast. Gamelin leant
on the low wall and looked down on the islet below, pointed like the
prow of a ship, listening to the wind whistling in the tree-tops, and
feeling his soul penetrated with an infinite longing for peace and
solitude.

Like a sweet echo of his thoughts, Élodie's voice sighed in his ear:

"Do you remember, Évariste, how, at sight of the green fields,
you wanted to be a country justice in a village? Yes, that would be
happiness."

But above the rustling of the trees and the girl's voice, he could
hear the tocsin and alarm-drums, the distant tramp of horses, and
rumbling of cannon along the streets.

Two steps from them a young man, who was talking to an elegantly attired *citoyenne*, remarked:

"Have you heard the latest? . . . The Opera is installed in the Rue
de la Loi."

Meantime the news was spreading; Robespierre's name was
spoken, but in a shuddering whisper, for men feared him still.
Women, when they heard the muttered rumour of his fall, concealed
a smile.

Évariste Gamelin seized Élodie's hand, but dropped it again
swiftly next moment:

"Farewell! I have involved you in my hideous fortunes, I have
blasted your life for ever. Farewell! I pray you may forget me!"

"Whatever you do," she warned him, "do not go back home to-
night. Come to the *Amour peintre*. Do not ring; throw a pebble at
my shutters. I will come and open the door to you myself; I will hide
you in the loft."

"You shall see me return triumphant, or you shall never see me
more. Farewell!"

On nearing the Hôtel de Ville, he caught the well-remembered roar of the old great days rising to the grey heavens. In the Place de Grève a clash of arms, the glitter of scarfs and uniforms, Hanriot's cannon drawn up. He mounts the grand stairs and, entering the Council Hall, signs the attendance book. The Council General of the Commune, by the unanimous voice of the 491 members present, declares for the outlawed patriots.

The Mayor sends for the Table of the Rights of Man, reads the clause which runs, "When the Government violates the Rights of the people, insurrection is for the people the most sacred and the most indispensable of duties," and the first magistrate of Paris announces that the Commune's answer to the Convention's act of violence is to raise the populace in insurrection.

The members of the Council General take oath to die at their posts. Two municipal officers are deputed to go out on the Place de Grève and invite the people to join with their magistrates in saving the fatherland and freedom.

There is an endless looking for friends, exchanging news, giving advice. Among these Magistrates, artisans are the exception. The Commune assembled here is such as the Jacobin purge has made it, —judges and jurors of the Revolutionary Tribunal, artists like Beauvallet and Gamelin, householders living on their means and college professors, cosy citizens, well-to-do tradesmen, powdered heads, fat paunches, and gold watch-chains, very few sabots, striped trousers, *carmagnole* smocks and red caps.

These bourgeois councillors are numerous and determined, but, when all is said, they are pretty well all Paris possesses of true Republicans. They stand on guard in the city mansion-house, as on a rock of liberty, but an ocean of indifference washes round their refuge.

However, good news arrives. All the prisons where the proscribed had been confined open their doors and disgorge their prey. Augustin Robespierre, coming from La Force, is the first to enter the Hôtel de Ville and is welcomed with acclamation.

At eight o'clock it is announced that Maximilien, after a protracted resistance, is on his way to the Commune. He is eagerly expected; he is coming; he is here; a roar of triumph shakes the vault of the old Municipal Palace.

193

He enters, supported by twenty arms. It is he, the little man there, slim, spruce, in blue coat and yellow breeches. He takes his seat; he speaks.

At his arrival the Council orders the façade of the Hôtel de Ville to be illuminated there and then. It is there the Republic resides. He speaks in a thin voice, in picked phrases. He speaks lucidly, copiously. His hearers who have staked their lives on his head, see the naked truth, see it to their horror. He is a man of words, a man of committees, a wind-bag incapable of prompt action, incompetent to lead a Revolution.

They draw him into the Hall of Deliberation. Now they are all there, these illustrious outlaws,—Lebas, Saint-Just, Couthon. Robespierre has the word. It is midnight and past, he is still speaking. Meantime Gamelin in the Council Hall, his bent brow pressed against a window, looks out with a haggard eye and sees the lamps flare and smoke in the gloom. Hanriot's cannon are parked before the Hôtel de Ville. In the black Place de Grève surges an anxious crowd, in uncertainty and suspense. At half past twelve torches are seen turning the corner of the Rue de la Vannerie, escorting a delegate of the Convention, clad in the insignia of office, who unfolds a paper and reads by the ruddy light the decree of the Convention, the outlawry of the members of the insurgent Commune, of the members of the Council General who are its abettors and of all such citizens as shall listen to its appeal.

Outlawry, death without trial! The mere thought pales the cheek of the most determined. Gamelin feels the icy sweat on his brow. He watches the crowd hurrying with all speed from the Place. Turning his head, he finds that the Hall, packed but now with Councillors, is almost empty. But they have fled in vain; their signatures attest their attendance.

It is two in the morning. The Incorruptible is in the neighbouring Hall, in deliberation with the Commune and the proscribed representatives.

Gamelin casts a despairing look over the dark Square below. By the light of the lanterns he can see the wooden candles above the grocer's shop knocking together like ninepins; the street lamps shiver and swing; a high wind has sprung up. Next moment a deluge of rain comes down; the Place empties entirely; such as the fear of the Convention and its dread decree had not put to flight scatter in terror of a wetting. Hanriot's guns are abandoned, and when the lightning reveals the troops of the Convention debouching simultaneously from the Rue Antoine and from the Quai, the approaches to the Hôtel de Ville are utterly deserted.

At last Maximilien has resolved to make appeal from the decree of the Convention to his own Section,—the *Section des Piques.*

The Council General sends for swords, pistols, muskets. But now the clash of arms, the trampling of feet and the shiver of broken glass fill the building. The troops of the Convention sweep by like an avalanche across the Hall of Deliberation, and pour into the Council Chamber. A shot rings out; Gamelin sees Robespierre fall; his jaw is broken. He himself grasps his knife, the six-sous knife that, one day of bitter scarcity, had cut bread for a starving mother, the same knife that, one summer evening at a farm at Orangis, Élodie had held in her lap, when she cried the forfeits. He opens it, tries to plunge it into his heart, but the blade strikes on a rib, closes on the handle, the catch giving way, and two fingers are badly cut. Gamelin falls, the blood pouring from the wounds. He lies quite still, but the cold is cruel, and he is trampled underfoot in the turmoil of a fearful struggle. Through the hurly-burly he can distinctly hear the voice of the young dragoon Henry, shouting:

"The tyrant is no more; his myrmidons are broken. The Revolution will resume its course, majestic and terrible."

Gamelin fainted.

At seven in the morning a surgeon sent by the Convention dressed his hurts. The Convention was full of solicitude for Robespierre's accomplices; it would fain not have one of them escape the guillotine.

The artist, ex-juror, ex-member of the Council General of the Commune, was borne on a litter to the Conciergerie.

195

Chapter 28

ON THE 10th, when Évariste, after a fevered night passed on the pallet-bed of a dungeon, awoke with a start of indescribable horror, Paris was smiling in the sunshine in all her beauty and immensity; new-born hope filled the prisoners' hearts; tradesmen were blithely opening their shops, citizens felt themselves richer, young men happier, women more beautiful, for the fall of Robespierre. Only a handful of Jacobins, a few *Constitutional* priests and a few old women trembled to see the Government pass into the hands of the evil-minded and corrupt. Delegates from the Revolutionary Tribunal, the Public Prosecutor and two judges, were on their way to the Convention to congratulate it on having put an end to the plots. By decree of the Assembly the scaffold was again to be set up in the Place de la Révolution. They wanted the wealthy, the fashionable, the pretty women to see, without putting themselves about, the execution of Robespierre, which was to take place that same day. The Dictator and his accomplices were outlawed; it only needed their identity to be verified by two municipal officers for the Tribunal to hand them over immediately to the executioner. But a difficulty arose; the verifications could not be made in legal form, the Commune as a body having been put outside the pale of law. The Assembly authorized identification by ordinary witnesses.

The triumvirs were haled to death, with their chief accomplices, amidst shouts of joy and fury, imprecations, laughter and dances.

The next day Évariste, who had recovered some strength and could almost stand on his legs, was taken from his cell, brought before the Tribunal, and placed on the platform which he had often seen filled with prisoners, where so many victims, illustrious or obscure, had sat in succession. Now it groaned under the weight of seventy individuals, the majority members of the Commune, some

196

jurors, like Gamelin, outlawed like him. Again he saw the jury-bench, the seat where he had been accustomed to loll, the place where he had terrorized unhappy prisoners, where he had affronted the scornful eyes of Jacques Maubel, Fortuné Cassagne, and Maurice Brotteaux, the appealing glances of the *citoyenne* Rochemaure, who had got him his post as juryman and whom he had recompensed with a sentence of death. Again he saw, looking down on the daïs where the judges sat in three mahogany arm-chairs, covered in red Utrecht velvet, the busts of Chalier and Marat and that bust of Brutus which he had one day apostrophized. Nothing was altered, neither the axes, the fasces, the red caps of Liberty on the wall-paper, nor the insults shouted by the *tricoteuses* in the galleries to those about to die, nor yet the soul of Fouquier-Tinville, hard-headed, painstaking, zealously turning over his murderous papers, and, in his character of perfect magistrate, sending his friends of yesterday to the scaffold.

The *citoyens* Remacle, tailor and door-keeper, and Dupont senior, joiner, of the Place de Thionville, member of the Committee of Surveillance of the Section du Pont-Neuf, identified Gamelin (Évariste), painter, ex-juror of the Revolutionary Tribunal, ex-member of the Council General of the Commune. For their services they received an assignat of a hundred *sols* from the funds of the Section; but, having been neighbours and friends of the outlaw, they found it embarrassing to meet his eye. Anyhow, it was a hot day; they were thirsty and in a hurry to be off and drink a glass of wine.

Gamelin found difficulty in mounting the tumbrel; he had lost a great deal of blood and his wounds pained him cruelly. The driver whipped up his jade and the procession got under way amid a storm of hooting.

Some women recognized Gamelin and yelled:

"Go your ways, drinker of blood! murderer at eighteen francs a day! . . . He doesn't laugh now; look how pale he is, the coward!"

They were the same women who used in other days to insult conspirators and aristocrats, extremists and moderates, all the victims sent by Gamelin and his colleagues to the guillotine.

The cart turned into the Quai des Morfondus, made slowly for the Pont-Neuf and the Rue de la Monnaie; its destination was the Place de la Révolution and Robespierre's scaffold. The horse was lame; every other minute the driver's whip whistled about its ears. The crowd of spectators, a merry, excited crowd, delayed the progress of the escort, fraternizing with the gendarmes, who pulled in their horses to a walk. At the corner of the Rue Honoré, the insults were redoubled. Parties of young men, at table in the fashionable restaurateurs' rooms on the mezzanine floor, ran to the windows, napkin in hand, and howled:

"Cannibals, man-eaters, vampires!"

The cart having plunged into a heap of refuse that had not been removed during the two days of civil disorder, the gilded youth screamed with delight:

"The waggon's mired. . . . Hurrah! The Jacobins in the jakes!"

Gamelin was thinking, and truth seemed to dawn on him.

"I die justly," he reflected. "It is just we should receive these outrages cast at the Republic, for we should have safeguarded her against them. We have been weak; we have been guilty of supineness. We have betrayed the Republic. We have earned our fate. Robespierre himself, the immaculate, the saint, has sinned from mildness, mercifulness; his faults are wiped out by his martyrdom. He was my exemplar, and I, too, have betrayed the Republic; the Republic perishes; it is just and fair that I die with her. I have been oversparing of blood; let my blood flow! Let me perish! I have deserved it. . . ."

Such were his reflections when suddenly he caught sight of the signboard of the *Amour peintre*, and a torrent of bitter-sweet emotions swept tumultuously over his heart.

The shop was shut, the sun-blinds of the three windows on the mezzanine floor were drawn right down. As the cart passed in front of the window on the left, the window of the blue chamber, a woman's hand, wearing a silver ring on the ring-finger, pushed aside the edge of the blind and threw towards Gamelin a red carnation which his bound hands prevented him from catching, but which he adored as the token and likeness of those red and fragrant lips that had refreshed his mouth. His eyes filled with bursting tears, and his whole being was still entranced with the glamour of this farewell when he saw the bloodstained knife rise into view in the Place de la Révolution.

198

Chapter 29

I T WAS Nivôse. Masses of floating ice encumbered the Seine; the basins in the Tuileries garden, the kennels, the public fountains were frozen. The north wind swept clouds of hoar frost before it in the streets. A white steam breathed from the horses' noses, and the city folk would glance in passing at the thermometer at the opticians' doors. A shop-boy was wiping the fog from the window-panes of the *Amour peintre*, while curious passers-by threw a look at the prints in vogue,—Robespierre squeezing into a cup a heart like a pumpkin, to drink the blood, and ambitious allegorical designs with such titles as the Tigrocracy of Robespierre; it was all hydras, serpents, horrid monsters let loose on France by the tyrant. Other pictures represented the Horrible Conspiracy of Robespierre, Robespierre's Arrest, The Death of Robespierre.

That day, after the midday dinner, Philippe Desmahis walked into the *Amour peintre*, his portfolio under his arm, and brought the *citoyen* Jean Blaise a plate he had just finished, a stippled engraving of the Suicide of Robespierre. The artist's picaresque burin had made Robespierre as hideous as possible. The French people were not yet satiated with all the memorials which enshrined the horror and opprobrium felt for the man who was made the scapegoat of all the crimes of the Revolution. For all that, the printseller, who knew his public, informed Desmahis that henceforward he was going to give him military subjects to engrave.

"We shall all be wanting victories and conquests,—swords, waving plumes, triumphant generals. Glory is to be the word. I feel it in me; my heart beats high to hear the exploits of our valiant armies. And when I have a feeling, it is seldom all the world doesn't have the same feeling at the same time. What we want is warriors and women, Mars and Venus."

199

"*Citoyen* Blaise, I have still two or three drawings of Gamelin's by me, which you gave me to engrave. Is it urgent?"

"Not a bit."

"By-the-bye, about Gamelin; yesterday, strolling in the Boulevard du Temple, I saw at a dealer's, who keeps a second-hand stall opposite the House of Beaumarchais, all that poor devil's canvases, amongst the rest his *Orestes and Electra*. The head of Orestes, who's like Gamelin, is really fine, I assure you. . . . The head and arm are superb. . . . The man told me he found no difficulty in getting rid of these canvases to artists who want to paint over them. . . . Poor Gamelin! He might have been a genius of the first order, perhaps, if he hadn't taken to politics."

"He had the soul of a criminal!" replied the *citoyen* Blaise. "I unmasked him, on this very spot, when his sanguinary instincts were still held in check. He never forgave me. . . . Oh! he was a choice blackguard."

"Poor fellow! he was sincere enough. It was the fanatics were his ruin."

"You don't defend him, I presume, Desmahis! . . . There's no defending him."

"No, *citoyen* Blaise, there's no defending him."

The *citoyen* Blaise tapped the gallant Desmahis' shoulder amicably, and observed:

"Times are changed. We can call you *Barbaroux* now the Convention is recalling the proscribed. . . . Now I think of it, Desmahis, engrave me a portrait of Charlotte Corday, will you?"

A woman, a tall, handsome brunette, enveloped in furs, entered the shop and bestowed on the *citoyen* Blaise a little discreet nod that implied intimacy. It was Julie Gamelin; but she no longer bore that dishonoured name, she preferred to be called the *citoyenne* widow Chassagne, and wore, under her mantle, a red tunic in honour of the red shirts of the terror. Julie had at first felt a certain repulsion towards Évariste's mistress; anything that had come near her brother was odious to her. But the *citoyenne* Blaise, after Évariste's death, had found an asylum for the unhappy mother in the attics of the *Amour peintre*. Julie had also taken refuge there; then she had got employment again at the fashionable milliner's in the Rue des Lombards. Her short hair *à la victime*, her aristocratic looks, her mourning weeds had won the sympathies of the gilded youth. Jean Blaise, whom Rose Thévenin had pretty well thrown over, offered her his homage, which she accepted. Still Julie was fond of wearing men's clothes, as in the old tragic days; she had a fine *Muscadin* costume made for her and often went, huge bâton and all complete, to sup at some tavern at Sèvres or Meudon with a girl friend, a little assistant in a fashion shop. Inconsolable for the loss of the young noble whose name she bore, this masculine-minded Julie found the only solace to her melancholy in a savage rancour; every time she encountered Jacobins, she would set the passers-by on them, crying "Death, death!" She had small leisure left to give to her mother, who alone in her room told her beads all day, too deeply shocked at her boy's tragic death to feel the grief that might have been expected. Rose was now the constant companion of Élodie, who certainly got on amicably with her step-mothers.

"Where is Élodie?" asked the *citoyenne* Chassagne.

Jean Blaise shook his head; he did not know. He never did know; he made it a point of honour not to.

Julie had come to take her friend with her to see Rose Thévenin at Monceaux, where the actress lived in a little house with an English garden.

At the Conciergerie Rose Thévenin had made the acquaintance of a big army-contractor, the *citoyen* Montfort. She had been released first, by Jean Blaise's intervention, and had then procured the *citoyen* Montfort's pardon, who was no sooner at liberty than he started his old trade of provisioning the troops, to which he added speculation in building-lots in the Pépinière quarter. The architects Ledoux, Olivier and Wailly were erecting pretty houses in that district, and in three months the land had trebled in value. Montfort, since their imprisonment together in the Luxembourg, had been Rose Thévenin's lover; he now gave her a little house in the neighbourhood of Tivoli and the Rue du Rocher, which was very expensive,—and cost him nothing, the sale of the adjacent properties having already repaid him several times over. Jean Blaise was a man of the world, so he deemed it best to put up with what he could not hinder; he gave up Mademoiselle Thévenin to Montfort without ceasing to be on friendly terms with her.

Julie had not been long at the *Amour peintre* before Élodie came down to her in the shop, looking like a fashion plate. Under her mantle, despite the rigours of the season, she wore nothing but her white frock; her face was even paler than of old, and her figure thinner; her looks were languishing, and her whole person breathed voluptuous invitation.

The two women set off for Rose Thévenin's, who was expecting them. Desmahis accompanied them; the actress was consulting him about the decoration of her new house, and he was in love with Élodie, who had by this time half made up her mind to let him sigh no more in vain. When the party came near Monceaux, where the victims of the Place de la Révolution lay buried under a layer of lime:

"It is all very well in the cold weather," remarked Julie; "but in the spring the exhalations from the ground there will poison half the town."

Rose Thévenin received her two friends in a drawing-room furnished *à l'antique*, the sofas and armchairs of which were designed by David. Roman bas-reliefs, copied in monochrome, adorned the walls above statues, busts and candelabra of imitation bronze. She wore a curled wig of a straw colour. At that date wigs were all the rage; it was quite common to include half a dozen, a dozen, a dozen and a half in a bride's trousseau. A gown *à la Cyprienne* moulded her body like a sheath. Throwing a cloak over her shoulders, she led her two friends and the engraver into the garden, which Ledoux was laying out for her, but which as yet was a chaos of leafless trees and plaster. She showed them, however, Fingal's cave, a Gothic chapel with a bell, a temple, a torrent.

"There," she said, pointing to a clump of firs, "I should like to raise a cenotaph to the memory of the unfortunate Brotteaux des Ilettes. I was not indifferent to him; he was a lovable man. The monsters slaughtered him; I bewailed his fate. Desmahis, you shall design me an urn on a column."

Then she added almost without a pause:

"It is heart-breaking. . . . I wanted to give a ball this week; but all the fiddlers are engaged three weeks in advance. There is dancing every night at the *citoyenne* Tallien's."

After dinner Mademoiselle Thévenin's carriage took the three friends and Desmahis to the Théâtre Feydeau. All that was most elegant in Paris was gathered in the house—the women with hair dressed *à l'antique* or *à la victime*, in very low dresses, purple or white and spangled with gold, the men wearing very tall black collars and the chin disappearing in enormous white cravats.

The bill announced *Phèdre* and the *Chien du Jardinier,*—The Gardener's Dog. With one voice the audience demanded the hymn dear to the *Muscadins* and the gilded youth, the *Réveil du Peuple,*—The Awakening of the People.

The curtain rose and a little man, short and fat, took the stage; it was the celebrated Lays. He sang in his fine tenor voice:

Peuple français, peuple de frères! . . .

Such storms of applause broke out as set the lustres of the chandelier jingling. Then some murmurs made themselves heard, and the voice of a citizen in a round hat answered from the pit with the hymn of the *Marseillaise:*

Allons, enfants de la patrie. . . .

The voice was drowned by howls, and shouts were raised:

"Down with the Terrorists! Death to the Jacobins!"

Lays was recalled and sang a second time—the hymn of the Thermidorians.

Peuple français, peuple de frères! . . .

In every play-house was to be seen the bust of Marat, surmounting a column or raised on a pedestal; at the Théâtre Feydeau this bust stood on a dwarf pillar on the "prompt" side, against the masonry-framing in the stage.

While the orchestra was playing the Overture of *Phèdre et Hippolyte,* a young *Muscadin,* pointing his cane at the bust, shouted:

"Down with Marat!"—and the whole house took up the cry: "Down with Marat! Down with Marat!"

Urgent voices rose above the uproar:

"It is a black shame that bust should still be there!"

"The infamous Marat lords it everywhere, to our dishonour! His busts are as many as the heads he wanted to cut off."

"Venomous toad!"

"Tiger!"

"Vile serpent!"

Suddenly an elegantly dressed spectator clambers on to the edge of his box, pushes the bust, oversets it. The plaster head falls in shivers on the musicians' heads amid the cheers of the audience, who spring to their feet and strike up the *Réveil du Peuple:*

Peuple français, peuple de frères! . . .

Among the most enthusiastic singers Élodie recognized the handsome dragoon, the little lawyer's clerk, Henry, her first love.

After the performance the gallant Desmahis called a cabriolet and escorted the *citoyenne* Blaise back to the *Amour peintre*.

In the carriage the artist took Élodie's hand between his:

"You know, Élodie, I love you?"

"I know it, because you love all women."

"I love them in you."

She smiled:

"I should be assuming a heavy task, spite of the wigs black, blonde and red, that are the rage, if I undertook to be all women, all sorts of women, for you."

"Élodie, I swear. . . ."

"What! oaths, *citoyen* Desmahis? Either you have a deal of simplicity, or you credit me with overmuch."

Desmahis had not a word to say, and she hugged herself over the triumph of having reduced her witty admirer to silence.

At the corner of the Rue de la Loi they heard singing and shouting and saw shadows flitting round a brazier of live coals. It was a band of young bloods who had just come out of the Théâtre Français and were burning a guy representing the Friend of the People.

In the Rue Honoré the coachman struck his cocked hat against a burlesque effigy of Marat swinging from the cord of a street lantern.

The fellow, heartened by the incident, turned round to his fares and told them how, only last night, the tripe-seller in the Rue Montorgueil had smeared blood over Marat's head, declaring: "That's the stuff he liked," and how some little scamps of ten had thrown the bust into the sewer, and how the spectators had hit the nail on the head, shouting:

"That's the Panthéon for him!"

Meanwhile, from every eating-house and restaurateur's voices could be heard singing:

Peuple français, peuple de frères! . . .

"Good-bye," said Élodie, jumping out of the cabriolet, as they reached the *Amour peintre*.

But Desmahis begged so hard, he was so tenderly urgent and spoke so sweetly, that she had not the heart to leave him at the door.

"It is late," she said; "you must only stay an instant."

In the blue chamber she threw off her mantle and appeared in her white gown *à l'antique*, which displayed all the warm fulness of her shape.

"You are cold, perhaps," she said, "I will light the fire; it is already laid."

She struck the flint and put a lighted match to the fire.

Philippe took her in his arms with the gentleness that bespeaks strength, and she felt a strange, delicious thrill. She was already yielding beneath his kisses when she snatched herself from his arms, crying:

"Let me be."

Slowly she uncoiled her hair before the chimney-glass; then she looked mournfully at the ring she wore on the ring-finger of her left hand, a little silver ring on which the face of Marat, all worn and battered, could no longer be made out. She looked at it till the tears confused her sight, took it off softly and tossed it into the flames.

Then, her face shining with tears and smiles, transfigured with tenderness and passion, she threw herself into Philippe's arms.

The night was far advanced when the *citoyenne* Blaise opened the outer door of the flat for her lover and whispered to him in the darkness:

"Good-bye, sweetheart! It is the hour my father will be coming home. If you hear a noise on the stairs, go up quick to the higher floor and don't come down till all danger is over of your being seen. To have the street-door opened, give three raps on the *concierge's* window. Good-bye, my life, good-bye, my soul!"

The last dying embers were glowing on the hearth when Élodie, tired and happy, dropped her head on the pillow.

THIS ENGLISH EDITION OF
THE GODS ARE A-THIRST
WAS PLANNED BY FRANCIS MEYNELL
IN LONDON, THE SPECIMEN TYPO-
GRAPHIC PAGES BEING PREPARED TO
HIS DESIGN AT THE FANFARE PRESS
IN LONDON; THE ILLUSTRATIONS WERE
MADE BY JEAN OBERLÉ IN PARIS; THE
EXECUTION OF THE EDITION HAS BEEN
DONE IN NEW YORK: THE COMPOSITION
IN MONOTYPE COCHIN BY THE NEW YORK
MONOTYPE COMPOSITION COMPANY, THE
PRINTING OF THE LETTERPRESS BY THE
QUINN & BODEN COMPANY, THE HAND-
COLORING OF THE ILLUSTRATIONS IN
THE STUDIO OF CHARLIZE BRAKELY.